## A Murder in Passing
### The Fourth Sam Blackman Mystery

"This solid whodunit offers readers a glimpse into a curious chapter of cultural history."

*—Publishers Weekly*

"This fascinating mystery, merging past and present, brings some little-known history to light and shows that laws change much faster than attitudes, as Sam and Nakayla, an interracial couple themselves, discover."

*—Booklist*

## The Sandburg Connection
### The Third Sam Blackman Mystery

"A missing folk song, a buried treasure from Civil War days, and a pregnant goat all play a part in this marvelous blend of history and mystery seasoned with information about Carl Sandburg's life."

*—Publishers Weekly,* Starred Review

"A suspicious death on top of Glassy Mountain turns two laid-back private sleuths into prime suspects."

*—Kirkus Reviews*

"Folk songs, Sandburg, and Civil War history—what a winning combination!"

*—Library Journal*

## The Fitzgerald Ruse
### The Second Sam Blackman Mystery

"An excellent regional mystery, full of local color and historical detail."
*—Library Journal*

"The warmth of Sam and Nakayla's relationship and Sam's challenged but determined heart make for a great read."
*—Kirkus Reviews*

"Readers will hope to see a lot more of the books' amiable characters."
*—Publishers Weekly*

## Blackman's Coffin
### The First Sam Blackman Mystery

"A wealth of historical detail, an exciting treasure hunt and credible characters distinguish this fresh, adventurous read."
*—Publishers Weekly,* Starred Review

"Known for his effortless storytelling, de Castrique once again delivers a compelling tale blending fact and fiction."
*—Library Journal*

"In the struggling Sam Blackman, de Castrique has created a compelling hero whose flinty first-person narrative nicely complements Henderson's earnest, measured and equally involving account."
*—Kirkus Reviews*

## Also by Mark de Castrique

# MURDER
## IN
# RAT
# ALLEY

# MURDER
## IN
# RAT
# ALLEY

### A SAM BLACKMAN MYSTERY

## MARK DE CASTRIQUE

Published by Poisoned Pen Press, an imprint of Sourcebooks
P.O. Box 4410, Naperville, Illinois 60567-4410
(630) 961-3900
sourcebooks.com

Library of Congress Cataloging-in-Publication Data
Name: De Castrique, Mark, author.
Title: Murder in Rat Alley / Mark de Castrique.
Description: Naperville, IL : Poisoned Pen Press, [2020]
Identifiers: LCCN 2019021336 (hardcover : acid-free paper)
Subjects: | GSAFD: Mystery fiction.
Classification: LCC PS3604.E124 M87 2019 | DDC 813/.6--dc23 LC record available
at https://lccn.loc.gov/2019021336

Printed and bound in the United States of America.
SB 10 9 8 7 6 5 4 3 2 1

*For my new grandson, Sawyer.*
*May you, too, always have a book close at hand.*

slew (definitions 1 and 3):
$^1(noun)$: a large number
$^3(verb)$: past tense of *slay*; killed a person or animal in a
violent way
—Webster's Third New International Dictionary

the relatively rapid motion of a computer-controlled telescope
as it moves to a new position in the sky
—Caltech Astronomical Glossary

*"The fault, dear Brutus, is not in our stars, But in ourselves."*
—William Shakespeare, *Julius Caesar*

# Chapter 1

The noonday heat smothered me. It even rose from the sidewalk like the ground underneath was molten lava. I'd taken no more than twenty steps out of our office building when I felt my damp shirt sticking to my back.

I looked at the woman walking beside me. In the ninety-six-degree temperature, my partner and lover, Nakayla Robertson, didn't sweat; she glistened with a radiance that only made her more beautiful. I, however, probably looked like I'd walked through a car wash.

"Do you think the restaurant has a shower?" I asked.

Nakayla laughed. "Don't worry, Sam. Look around. You're in good company."

The office for our Blackman and Robertson Detective Agency was on the edge of historic Pack Square, the central landmark in the mountain city of Asheville, North Carolina. It wasn't really square but rather a sizable rectangle stretching for several hundred yards and a magnet for tourists who clustered in small groups that moved slowly and randomly across the open terrain. Everyone I saw exuded the energy of a limp noodle. The largest crowd was concentrated near the far end where water fountains doused a play area designed for children. Splashville, as we Asheville locals called it. Even at a distance, I could see adults casting aside decorum and enjoying a cool soaking in their shorts and T-shirts.

"I heard it's hotter here than down in Charlotte," I complained.

"That's the inversion effect. Warmer air's trapping colder air beneath it. You climb into the mountains, and the temperature climbs as well. There's no thermal movement, which is why this smoke's stuck in the air."

"Impressive. Are you auditioning for the Weather Channel?"

She grabbed my hand. "No. Explaining things to you is more like *Sesame Street.*"

The August heat wave shared the news with forest fires plaguing the tinder-dry mountains. The acrid smell of burning wood was strong enough to sting my nostrils, and the smoke's blue-tinged haze obscured the more distant ridges. Asheville wasn't in immediate danger from the flames, but elderly residents were advised to stay indoors to avoid respiratory complications. As a popular retirement destination, Asheville attracted seniors who'd become a significant portion of the population.

Nakayla and I were headed for lunch at the CANarchy Collaboratory. The popular brewpub was only a few blocks away and closer than our parked cars. So other than summoning an Uber, we had no choice but to hoof it on foot.

For me, the walk was a little more complicated, because I wore a prosthetic device attached below my left knee. I'd lost the limb in an attack by rocket grenades in Iraq, a physical and emotional injury that landed me in Asheville's VA hospital. The one saving grace of the ordeal was meeting Nakayla as together we solved the mystery of her sister's murder.

As a black woman from the mountains and a white man from the middle of the state, Nakayla and I were an unlikely team. Yet I couldn't imagine my life without her.

"What time is Cory coming?" I asked.

"Shirley's bringing her about twelve thirty. Cory thinks it's just the two of them."

Cory DeMille was the paralegal for the law firm of Hewitt Donaldson, whose offices were next to ours. Today, August 5, was her birthday, and Shirley, the office manager, had planned a surprise lunch. At a quarter to noon, Shirley secretly dispatched the firm's one lawyer, Hewitt Donaldson himself, to use his blustery skills to hold a table for us. Nakayla and I followed about ten minutes behind. When Cory and Shirley arrived, we'd sing "Happy Birthday" off-key and resume drinking beer.

At the rate I was perspiring, I'd need a couple of pints for fluid replacement.

Reaching the restaurant, we had to step over dogs sprawled across the floor of the outside eating area. Asheville is so doggone dog-friendly, most stores set out bowls of water for canine customers. One of our favorite spots, the Battery Park Book Exchange & Champagne Bar, claimed to have had more problems with humans than dogs. Nakayla and I shared custody of a bluetick coonhound appropriately named Blue. Most days, he came to work with us and often enjoyed hanging out after hours at the book bar while Nakayla and I read and drank wine.

We knew Blue would have been welcome at Cory's party, but the dog days of August were more than just a saying, so we'd left him in the comfort of the office air-conditioning.

I spotted Hewitt Donaldson as the sole occupant at the head of a long table. He had a pint of Perrin Black Ale in front of him.

I nudged Nakayla. "Looks like Hewitt's gotten a head start."

"I'm sure you can quickly catch up." Nakayla led the way, weaving her slim body through the crowd.

Hewitt stood, gave Nakayla a hug, and shook my hand. "Glad to see you. I was starting to get some hostile looks for holding down such a large table."

I counted the chairs. Seven. "Who all's coming? I thought it was just the five of us."

Hewitt shrugged. "Shirley just said get a table for seven." He looked at Nakayla as if she might have an explanation.

"Cory's got other friends," she said.

"Fine," Hewitt said. "But you know me. I like to know the witness list in advance."

I laughed. "It's a lunch, not a trial."

Hewitt was Asheville's premier defense attorney and a personality with no equal in the local legal community. His courtroom successes had made him the bane of the district attorney's office. Hewitt, now in his late sixties, had come of age in the sixties. His penchant for Hawaiian shirts and sandals, his long, flowing gray hair, and his booming voice made him a recognizable celebrity. The looks he described as hostile were probably nothing more than curious stares at what appeared to be Asheville's oldest hippie.

He sat back down. "I know Cory has friends. But I don't want any arguments over who's paying the bill. Shirley's the organizer, and I'm the bankroller. So order up some drinks and appetizers."

We did as he asked. Nakayla went for a pale lager, and I chose the same black ale as Hewitt's. Chicken wings and nachos had just arrived when Shirley led the blushing birthday girl to the table. Hewitt immediately launched into the birthday song, which was quickly picked up by every diner in the place. A round of applause capped the performance, and Hewitt patted the seat closest to him as the signal for where Cory was to sit.

He slid her a menu. "Now that you're old enough, order whatever you want to drink."

"Yeah, right," Cory said. "We're celebrating the twelfth anniversary of my twenty-first birthday."

I hadn't thought about her age, and I realized, other than Hewitt, the rest of us were no more than a year or two apart. But we were very different in other ways. If one had to select the grown-up in Hewitt's law firm, the clear choice was Cory. She wore the corporate clothes and looked like she'd be one of the government's attorneys sitting behind senators at a congressional hearing. Hewitt's idea of corporate wardrobe was a ratty sport coat, food-stained tie, and his hair pulled back in a ponytail.

Shirley could only be described as some energy force hovering on the edge of our astral plane. Her curly, ink-black hair seemed to swallow light, not reflect it. She wore heavy white makeup and dark eye shadow that made her face look like it was floating in the void of hair. She claimed to experience going on out-of-body travels like the rest of us experience going to the grocery store. She was a wisp of a woman who looked like she could be blown away by a breeze. She was also the smartest one at the table, and even Hewitt was afraid of her.

Ten minutes later, Shirley looked at her watch and then at the two empty chairs. "Well, I think we should go ahead and order."

Hewitt frowned. "Who else were you expecting?"

Instead of answering, Shirley turned and looked toward the front door. "Oh, good." She stood and waved her hand, catching the attention of two men just entering.

"The police?" Hewitt stammered. "You invited the police?"

"Thanks, Shirley," Cory said. "I'm glad they're here."

Hewitt and the police were like oil and water, but the two men approaching our table were in a special category. As adversarial as homicide detectives and defense attorneys could be, there was grudging respect across the gulf between them. Lead detective Curt Newland and his partner, Tuck Efird, had been instrumental in working a case in which Cory had been shot and two friends murdered. The team effort had saved my life and mellowed Hewitt's antagonistic attitude toward law enforcement.

Curt Newland, or Newly as everyone called him, was a veteran detective of the Asheville Police Department. He and I shared a bond in that I'd been a chief warrant officer in the U.S. Army and conducted hundreds of investigations. I knew how tough his job was. I'd also solved the murder of his former partner and was as close to being an honorary police officer as a private investigator could be.

Hewitt forced a smile and stood to welcome them. He raised his glass and toasted the two detectives. "To Asheville's finest. Join us. My treat."

"All right," Tuck Efird said. "How many to-go boxes can I get?"

"As many as you can carry. But you have to leave right now."

Everyone laughed.

"Nah," Efird said. "We owe it to Cory to stay and add some class to this group."

Newly sat beside me. "Sorry we're late. I was on the phone with Sheriff Hickman in Transylvania County. They've come across a body in the cleanup from the forest fire."

"That's terrible," Cory said. "Someone didn't get out in time?"

"No. It's skeletal remains that were exposed when an earth mover dug up ground trying to build a firewall."

"A cold case," Hewitt said. "But that area's way out of your jurisdiction."

"Correct," Newly said. "But Hickman wants us to go through our missing person files. We could be talking forty years back."

"Assuming the skeleton's human," Efird said.

"What do you mean?" I asked.

Efird laughed. "I mean it could be some alien from outer space. The body was discovered at PARI. The UFO nutters are going to be coming out of the woodwork."

A loud crash cut off Efird's next words. We all turned to Cory. Her glass lay toppled on its side, beer spreading across the table like a tidal flood. Her face had paled as white as raw cotton. Hewitt grabbed her wrist to steady her.

"It's him," she whispered. "It has to be him."

# Chapter 2

"Pisgah Astronomical Research Institute," Newly said. "PARI for short. That's what it's known as now."

Hewitt nodded. "A NASA tracking station back in the day." He turned to Cory. "We'll learn what's going on even if I have to file a petition under the Freedom of Information Act."

We sat around Hewitt's circular conference table. Newly and Tuck Efird's news about the human remains had jolted Cory and brought an abrupt halt to the birthday lunch. Nakayla and Shirley had escorted Cory back to the law offices while Newly, Efird, and I waited for Hewitt to settle the bill.

Efird was upset that he'd somehow upset Cory, and he wanted to know what Hewitt knew. Hewitt had declined to comment at the restaurant, saying he would talk it through with all of us if Cory was up to it.

Now that we were assembled, Hewitt asked Cory, "Do you want me to tell what I know?"

She took a sip of water and licked her lips. "Yes. You probably know more than I do."

"Well, for one thing, you weren't born yet." He swept his gaze around the table. Each of us gave him our undivided attention.

"I'd finished my first year of law school. This was the summer of 1971, and I was clerking at the U.S. District Court here in Asheville. I worked out of the Federal Building at the corner of Patton and Otis. Like now, there were a bunch of federal agencies housed there, including the IRS and the FBI. One of the big events of the summer was an Apollo moon launch. *Apollo 15.* It was the first to use the lunar roving vehicle that would extend the reach of the astronauts' physical exploration. The Saturn V rocket lifted on July 26, and the lunar module touched down on July 30 shortly after six in the afternoon. I remember because just about all the federal offices stayed open late to watch the live signals."

Hewitt paused to take a sip of water and then cleared his throat. "I also noticed an influx of FBI agents coming and going from the Western North Carolina Resident Agency. When I asked about the increased presence, I was told unofficially they were traveling back and forth from the NASA tracking station located deep in Pisgah National Forest."

"Tracking what?" Efird asked.

"The astronauts. Huge radio telescopes had been constructed in the middle of the forest. It was one of nine such sites spaced around the world. As the earth rotated, NASA would jump from station to station so they'd never lose contact with the crew."

"Go slow for Tuck," Newly said. "He thinks the world's flat."

The remark drew a smile from Cory and eased the tension in the room.

"Hey, old man," Efird said. "You should remember this as well as Hewitt."

"I was five," Newly said. "But I remember watching it on TV."

"The tracking stations made that coverage possible," Hewitt continued. "The moon was showing its half phase, so the Pisgah station was active at night. The lunar landing was the focus, although signals from the orbiting *Apollo* capsule were coming in as well. During the time the station was the main communication link, everyone at Pisgah was fully engaged in operations. It was after the torch was passed to the next station that the problem surfaced." He looked at Cory and shook his head sympathetically.

"My father said he just disappeared," Cory said.

The rest of us looked at each other with confusion.

"And Frank DeMille was what relation?" Hewitt asked.

"My father's older brother. An uncle I never knew."

Hewitt nodded and picked up his story. "Frank DeMille was a software engineer on-site for writing and maintaining the codes that kept the radio telescopes under computer control. Once the station had completed its function for that rotation, the computer scientists reprogrammed for the next pass. That was when Frank DeMille was reported missing. He was never seen again."

"This was over a decade before I was born," Cory explained. "My father, Zack DeMille, came here looking for his brother. At first, he thought Frank might have gone out for a walk that evening and gotten lost. He loved the woods. Dad hiked the area for days. He eventually took a job with the city of Asheville and wound up staying here." Her eyes welled with tears. "He and Mom were killed in a car crash ten years ago. I hate to think that they died without ever knowing what happened."

The room fell silent.

Then Hewitt said, "I knew the FBI was concerned because Frank DeMille worked with classified computer information. The scientist in charge had told them how innovative Frank was. That he was a real loss to the project. His skills went beyond the space program, and he'd drawn the attention of the Department of Defense as they began to consider the computer as another potential weapon of the Cold War. I heard the theory floated that Frank had been abducted."

Hewitt looked at Efird and smiled. "Yes, that did fuel the UFO crowd when they heard the word. Not a Soviet abduction but an alien abduction. They still consider PARI to be hiding an interstellar spaceport with more saucer traffic than the jets at the Asheville airport."

"That's crazy," Shirley said. "Everybody knows PARI is a vortex of overlapping dimensions, not some interstellar hub."

Again, Cory smiled and looked at me. We both knew Shirley wasn't kidding.

Newly leaned forward in his chair. "I would think Sheriff Hickman would know this. It's got to be in the cold case records of the Transylvania Sheriff's Department."

"Not necessarily," Hewitt said. "The location was federal property, not county. If not owned by NASA, it would be national forest patrolled by rangers."

"Why's Hickman on the case now?" I asked.

"Because the land's no longer federal," Hewitt said. "I don't know the details, but there was some kind of acreage swap with the government."

"That's right," Newly agreed. "I'd forgotten. Must be twenty years ago. The case probably didn't cross into Hickman's jurisdiction with the exchange. He might not be aware of the disappearance." The homicide detective turned to Cory. "Tuck and I will offer him any help we can. First, he needs to determine if it is indeed your uncle."

"DNA," Cory said.

Newly nodded. "Your father was your biological father?"

"Yes."

"Then I suggest you let us take a saliva swab. I'm going to notify Special Agent Lindsay Boyce, since the FBI should still have an interest. That will give us access to the Quantico labs and maybe expedite the process. Is that OK?"

"Yes. Thank you."

Hewitt took a deep breath. "Do you want Cory to go with you?"

"That's not necessary," Efird said. "I'll bring the kit here. That is if we're done."

Hewitt stood. "Thank you for your assistance. I know we're not always on the same side, but you have my unqualified respect."

The rest of us rose.

Newly gave a wry smile. "My dear counselor, I hope we're always on the same side. The side of truth."

"Had you heard that story from Cory before?" I asked Nakayla the question as we sat in the conversation area of our three-room office suite.

The layout was simple and practical. You entered a room that looked more like an old English drawing room than an office. A leather sofa, two matching chairs, a Persian rug, and antique end and coffee tables were meant to relax our clients in a homey atmosphere.

Off to the left of this main room was my office, the door usually shut so that the mess didn't give the impression I was disorganized. I simply liked to keep everything within arm's reach. On the right, Nakayla's open door revealed a tidy, orderly desk and file cabinets that assured clients that important documents wouldn't fall into the trash.

Nakayla sat in a corner of the sofa, her bare feet tucked under her thighs. "No. If Cory hasn't told Shirley, she hasn't told anyone. And it happened nearly fifty years ago."

I rose from the chair opposite her and stepped over Blue, who lay sprawled at my feet. As I paced back and forth, the coonhound followed me with his eyes. "Whether it's her uncle or not, Sheriff Hickman has to be looking at a murder investigation. You don't bury yourself."

"Newly's smart to cover the FBI," Nakayla said. "Not that Hickman wouldn't have brought them in. But you know as well as I that the local authorities don't all welcome feds into their cases."

"Hickman won't have any choice if it turns out to be Frank DeMille." I glanced at my watch as if the hour since Hewitt and Cory told their stories should have yielded some results. "I guess we'll know in the next few days."

Nakayla stretched her legs and slipped on her shoes. "Probably. My guess is Newly called Hickman immediately, asking for a skeletal fragment to go with Cory's DNA swab. The sheriff has no reason not to cooperate."

A knock sounded from the hallway door. Then Cory opened it. "Can we talk a few minutes?"

Blue sat up on his haunches, and his tail thumped the floor like a metronome.

Nakayla stood. "Certainly. Would you like a cup of coffee?"

"No, thanks. I'm coffeed out." Cory closed the door behind her and crossed to the sofa.

Nakayla sat beside her as I returned to my chair. Blue rested his head on Cory's knee and was rewarded with a scratch behind his ears.

"Did Tuck get everything he needed?" I asked.

"Yes. He and Detective Newland were going to see Sheriff Hickman and then Special Agent Boyce at the FBI office. Newland thought it would be bad to run straight to the feds. Since Hickman had called Newland, it was only fair they contact him first."

I nodded in agreement. Investigations can be very territorial, and there was no benefit in alienating the Transylvania County sheriff. It was his case until it wasn't.

Cory shifted her gaze to Blue's face as if she were more comfortable talking to the dog. "If the DNA proves it was my Uncle Frank, I don't know whether to be happy or sad. Is knowing that he's dead better than living with uncertainty when uncertainty means he could be alive?"

"It's better to know," Nakayla said. "Wouldn't your parents have taken some degree of comfort, slim as it may be, that he didn't just turn his back on his family? That he didn't reject those who loved him?"

Cory kept staring at Blue. I saw a tear trickle along one cheek and fall to the back of her hand. Blue licked it and whimpered.

Cory pushed him away and leaned back against the sofa. "Yes. I guess. But what do I do now?"

"What do you mean?" Nakayla asked.

Cory's expression hardened. "I never knew my uncle. My feelings are for my parents, if that makes any sense. I cry because they're not here to. I cry because I believe my father's brother was murdered. Someone had to have buried his body."

Nakayla and I said nothing.

"And if it is Uncle Frank and he was murdered, I cry because there's nothing I can provide the police to help find his killer, whether that killer is alive or long since dead."

"Are there no relatives of your parents' generation?" I asked.

"I have an aunt. Frank and my father's sister. She was the baby of the family. She's in Roanoke. We've never talked much about Frank, and it's been several months since I've seen her." Cory sniffled. "She's closer kin than I am. Guess she'll get the official notification."

"You should give her a call," Nakayla said. "She might see a newscast and have the same reaction you did. The story will break before any DNA analysis is complete."

Cory nodded. "OK. But that's not what I came to talk about."

I leaned forward, elbows on my knees. "Go ahead."

"This Sheriff Hickman. What do you know about him?"

I looked at Nakayla. She'd grown up here and knew the players better than I did.

"He's been sheriff a long time," Nakayla said. "Fifteen years at least. I was in high school when he was elected. Before I met Sam, I was working for an insurance company in fraud investigations. Sometimes those cases were in Transylvania County, and he served some papers for us. Nothing demanding investigative skills, so I can't speak to his competency. I would think Hewitt and he would have tangled at some point."

"They did," Cory said. "Hewitt has defended six clients over the years that were arrested by Hickman and his deputies. Hewitt got all of them acquitted. Hewitt said some of the acquittals were the DA's fault for bringing a weak case to trial. But two of the cases had bungled evidence and procedural search irregularities that Hewitt exploited. He made the sheriff look bad. You know how Hewitt can be. Cut a witness on the stand to pieces and then pour salt in the wounds. In other words, if Hewitt were drowning, instead of a life preserver, Hickman would throw him an anchor."

"And you're afraid if Hickman discovers you work for Hewitt, he'll slack off on the investigation?" I asked.

Cory shrugged. "I don't know. I would think he'd want to close a murder case. It's more the competency issue. I wouldn't worry if it were Detective Newland. He's one of the best, but if it's murder, it's outside his jurisdiction."

"There's the FBI," Nakayla said.

"Yeah. The Federal Bureau of Incommunicado. Ask them what time it is, and they answer they can't comment on an ongoing investigation."

I understood where Cory was headed. "If it's murder, we'll do it."

She blushed. "I haven't asked yet."

"See. Aren't we good detectives?"

I glanced at Nakayla. She nodded, signaling she approved.

"This will be a professional relationship," Cory said. "I'll be paying whatever's your rate."

"No, you won't," I said. "We're not busy right now, so your case will keep us occupied. Idle hands and the devil's workshop."

"But if you're not busy, then you should let me pay you. You've got bills, don't you?"

"OK. Give Hewitt a dollar and have him give it to us. Then if you and your aunt ever file a wrongful death suit, our work will be part of Hewitt's case file. That's our final offer."

What Cory didn't know was that Nakayla and I had several million dollars in an offshore account that came from two earlier investigations—one involving a long-ago theft from her family and the other tied to my service and injury in Iraq. Both "treasures" went unreported to Uncle Sam and both now trickled through our detective agency and provided a comfortable income and the ability to make generous donations to worthy causes. Causes like Cory's.

Tears welled in the paralegal's eyes. "It's too much to ask. Really."

"You didn't ask," Nakayla said. "It's something we want to do. Don't deny us the opportunity."

Cory pulled a handkerchief from her purse and dabbed her tears. "I don't know how to thank you."

"We haven't done anything yet. It might not be your uncle, and it might not be murder." I said the words, but I didn't believe them.

# Chapter 3

Confirmation came four days later. On Friday morning, Special Agent Lindsay Boyce first notified Transylvania County Sheriff Hickman that the FBI had positively identified the skeletal remains as belonging to Cory's uncle, Frank DeMille. Then, since Detective Newland had alerted her to the case, Boyce called him to see if he wanted to break the news to Cory.

Newly phoned me to share developments and to say he and Tuck Efird were coming to Cory's office and they'd like to stop in and speak with Nakayla and me afterward.

A few minutes before eleven, the two detectives made a somber entrance. Each man accepted a cup of coffee without a sarcastic remark or wisecrack. A good police officer never takes delivering news of a death as routine. Newly and Efird were good officers.

We moved to the conversation area, Nakayla and I on the sofa, Newly and Efird in the chairs.

"How'd Cory take it?" Nakayla asked.

"Pretty well," Efird said. "The initial shock occurred last Monday so she's had time to prepare herself. I mean who else could it have been?"

"Did Boyce say if an ME had determined the cause of death?" I asked.

Efird looked to his partner for what to share.

Newly shook his head. "No. The road grader's blade did some damage to the bones, but there were no other indications of violence. Clothing had rotted away except for a belt buckle and a pair of glasses. Death's labeled a homicide. No one can bury himself."

"Where's it going from here?"

"Boyce is opening a federal investigation. Sheriff Hickman will be marginalized." Newly glanced at Efird. "We'll be shut out since we have no jurisdictional authority, and the FBI's cone of silence will descend upon everything. They'll interview Cory and her aunt, so we'll get some information from them, but unless they need us for something, we'll get news from the press briefings like anyone else."

"Is a press briefing scheduled?"

"Not that we've heard, but you've seen the story of the discovery's already made the papers and local TV this week. Boyce will hold that conference sooner rather than later. And she'll make an appeal for anyone who might have known DeMille."

"Good luck with that," Efird said. "We're talking nearly half a century ago."

Nakayla and I looked at each other. Even the FBI could have a problem solving a case that cold.

Newly shifted in the chair and rubbed his palms on his thighs. "Look, we know Cory is going to be anxious for a resolution. And she'll have Hewitt Donaldson championing her cause. He could have the opposite effect in that Boyce won't want a defense attorney coming anywhere near her investigation, even if he's helping a relative of the victim. That's just not in her DNA."

"Understood," I said. "You want us to try and rein him in."

Efird smiled for the first time. "That's a harder task than solving the case. No, because we know you're also going to have trouble sitting on the sidelines."

Nakayla and I exchanged glances. I knew she was thinking the same thing: had Cory told them we'd offered to become involved? Nakayla gave a barely perceptible shake of her head. I agreed. Newly and Efird were smart guys who knew us too well. They figured we'd get involved whether Cory wanted us to or not.

"So you want us to rein ourselves in?" I asked.

Newly lowered his voice. "We want you to know we'll help behind the scenes any way we can. As you know, there are protocols working with the FBI that we have to respect. You have more latitude."

"As long as we don't obstruct justice or do something else that gets our PI licenses revoked."

"And you're too smart for that," Newly said. "At least Nakayla is."

"OK. What do you think Sheriff Hickman's response will be to all this?"

"In a word, indifference. The crime didn't happen on his watch nor on county property at the time. He'll be glad of two things—getting his picture made with Special Agent Boyce and handing off the case. He might or might not answer your questions, depending upon how you approach him."

"And what do you think Cory's reaction will be?" Nakayla asked.

"In another word, relief." Newly cocked his head and eyed us skeptically. "You're telling me you haven't already discussed it?"

"She hasn't asked us." Technically, my answer was true, since we'd volunteered before she could ask.

"Well, we'll leave that up to you as to whether you want to aid her or not. We just wanted to let you know we'll do what we can to help you."

Everyone stood. The conversation was over.

As the detectives headed toward the door, Efird paused and turned. "Don't rule out the UFO nutters. There's a vocal group that thinks our government's been colluding with little green men for decades. It's paranoia of global proportions, and God only knows what they'd do to save the planet."

"Have you run into them before?"

Efird laughed. "Run into them? I was married to one."

When Nakayla and I heard the elevator in the hall taking the two detectives to the ground floor, I asked, "What do you think we should do first?"

Nakayla refilled her coffee cup and returned to the sofa. I sat opposite her.

"I think we need to stay a step ahead of the FBI," Nakayla said. "Special Agent Boyce's loyalty is to the Bureau, and she's certainly not going to share information with private investigators. She could even instruct persons interviewed not to speak about her inquiries."

"OK. I see that."

"But it will take Boyce a little while to build her momentum. Meanwhile, we can visit the crime scene if the PARI facility isn't closed, and we might get a head start on any leads Cory can provide."

"I wonder how much information about the NASA tracking station is available online?"

"Depends upon what was classified," Nakayla said. "I can start that search immediately. But you asked what should we do first. The internet is important, but it's still going to be there tomorrow or next week."

"Then we need to see Cory as soon as possible. I was letting her have some time to come to grips with the DNA confirmation."

Nakayla set her cup aside. "No. I guarantee you she's ready to move forward." She stood. "I'll call and see if she's available."

Before Nakayla reached the phone in her office, there was a knock on the door, and Cory entered. I got to my feet.

"Can we talk a minute?" She spoke just above a whisper as if we were in a crowded room and she didn't want to be overheard. Her red-rimmed eyes betrayed the brave front she'd shown Newly and Tuck Efird.

"Certainly," Nakayla said. "Would you like some coffee? Or maybe a cup of herbal tea would be better."

"No, thank you. I guess Tuck and Newly told you the DNA had come back as a positive match."

Nakayla gestured for Cory to sit. "Yes. We're very sorry."

Nakayla and Cory shared the sofa, and I returned to my chair.

Cory shrugged. "Better to finally know. And Newly said the FBI would probably take the lead from Sheriff Hickman."

"Sam and I were just talking about that. We're ready to help any way we can."

"There's a window," I said, "before the FBI gets fully engaged. We'd like to get a head start. Fill the gap between Hickman bowing out of the case and the blackout the feds will impose upon their investigation."

"That's what Newly said you would say."

"What else?" Nakayla asked.

"He said if you were going to be involved, you should begin now. Even Tuck agreed."

Nakayla and I exchanged glances. In their own way, the two police detectives had called on us to offer their endorsement without admitting they had encouraged Cory to engage us.

"Have you been contacted by the FBI?" I asked.

"Not yet. I believe I'm on a short call list, but since the murder was before my birth, I'm probably nothing more than an interested descendant. They'll probably reach out to my aunt first."

"Then call Special Agent Boyce," I said. "Say you're requesting to be kept informed of their progress. Go on record as trying to work through channels. You don't have to say anything about our involvement. We'll deal with that when the time comes."

"Do you think my job with Hewitt will be a factor one way or the other?"

"Boyce might be a little more guarded in what she tells you, which wouldn't be that much regardless of Hewitt. But knowing he's lurking in the background will be an incentive for them to give the case attention. And when we show up as working for Hewitt rather than you, it will reinforce his behind-the-scenes presence."

"I haven't clued Hewitt yet on our arrangement," she said. "I also need to alert my aunt that the FBI will be contacting her."

"What's your aunt's name?" Nakayla asked.

"Nancy. Nancy Gilmore. Her husband was killed in Vietnam shortly after Frank disappeared. She never remarried."

"You've told her about the DNA?"

"Yes." Cory wiped her nose with the back of her hand. "I was doing all right till I heard Aunt Nancy crying. She claimed she wasn't surprised. That she'd spent the last few days going through his things. She's kept them all these years."

I leaned forward. "His things? What things?"

"Books. Some clothes, though most of them went to the Salvation Army years ago. She also kept his letters."

"Letters from whom?"

"Mostly from him to my aunt. He was renting a small apartment in Asheville. That's why some of his things were with her. Her husband was on his first tour of duty in Vietnam, and Frank had stayed with her till he got the job with NASA. He wrote to her once a week." Cory looked at Nakayla. "Aunt Nancy said Frank also had a girlfriend down here, and she wrote him letters after he disappeared in care of my aunt. After a couple of months, they stopped coming."

"What did they say?" Nakayla asked.

"Aunt Nancy says they're unopened. She wouldn't read her brother's mail."

I looked at Nakayla. "We need to see those letters. Otherwise, the FBI will take them, and we might never know the contents." I turned to Cory. "Any chance your aunt will be coming here?"

"No. Not unless I bring her. She couldn't drive this far on her own. And once the forensic examinations are complete, my uncle's remains will be interred in the family section of a cemetery in Roanoke."

"Then we need to get up there," Nakayla said. "Were you planning on seeing her any time soon?"

Cory nodded. "I'm going up tomorrow. It's Saturday, although Hewitt told me to take whatever time I need."

"Would you like some company? Sam will even drive."

"Only if you let me pay for gas and your hotel room."

"Gas will be fine," I said. "But we'll chalk the hotel up as my gift to Nakayla. I'm such a romantic."

My partner laughed. "I was searching for the one word to describe you. Thanks for reminding me that's not it."

Cory left, and Nakayla went down the hall to the restroom. I was in my office on the computer checking the hours for the Pisgah Astronomical Research Institute. I was anxious to see the site where the skeleton was unearthed. I discovered PARI was open but only had guided tours on Wednesdays and Saturdays. Tomorrow was Saturday, but we'd be in Roanoke. However, a self-guided tour option was available today and would be a good way to get oriented to the place without being limited to some prescribed sequence. Besides, I doubted if the site of a skeleton had been inserted into their tour highlights.

I was clicking on the icon for directions when I heard the hall door open. Expecting Nakayla, I called out, "Let's head over to PARI. They're open this afternoon."

A gruff voice answered, "Love to, but I'm in court this afternoon."

I looked from the computer screen to Hewitt Donaldson grinning in my doorway.

"I understand you are now in my employ."

I swiveled away from my desk. "The best money can buy."

He waved a crisp dollar bill in the air. "True. If this is the amount we're discussing."

"And at your hourly rate, that would buy me what? Ten seconds?"

"Yes. But I talk fast." He handed me the dollar. "So you're going to PARI this afternoon?"

"With the FBI in the game, I don't want to delay."

He nodded his agreement. "You going to see Sheriff Hickman?"

"Not today. Hickman might tell the FBI, and we want to stay under the radar till we see what Cory's aunt has."

"Cory told me about the letters. You're smart to prioritize them."

I held up the dollar. "See the brainpower this bought you. Now run along to court."

Hewitt just stood there. We stared at each other for a dollar's worth of the high-priced lawyer's time.

"What?" I asked. "What are you waiting for now?"

"To quote Lucas Beauchamp at the end of Faulkner's *Intruder in the Dust*, 'My receipt.'"

# Chapter 4

Highway 215 made my cruise control as useful as my appendix. The incessant twists and turns kept my foot jumping between the brake and the accelerator such that I felt like I was dancing rather than driving. My Honda CR-V rarely exceeded 35 miles per hour.

As the crow flies, the Pisgah Astronomical Research Institute wasn't that far from Asheville, but the winding two-lane black-top must have doubled the mileage. More than an hour after leaving the office, we turned onto a paved road marked only by a sign set on a stone wall with a stone column at its left edge. Half of the sign was a monochromatic teal drawing of a radio telescope rising above a forest. On the righthand side, the four words PISGAH ASTRONOMICAL RESEARCH INSTITUTE were stacked and aligned so that read vertically, the first bold letter of each word spelled PARI.

The road now ran through a narrow, unpopulated valley and was the straightest stretch we'd driven in the past fifteen miles. But with each yard we traveled, the smell of charred wood intensified. I wondered if we'd spot smoldering trees before reaching the former NASA facility.

Both appeared simultaneously.

The land widened into a small bowl, and the forest gave way

to a grassy enclave. Smoke hung on a back ridge where charcoal silhouettes of skeletal trunks with crooked limbs stood stark against the hazy blue sky.

In the foreground rose a tower of white girders holding aloft a massive dish. It was the largest radio telescope I'd ever seen. To the right were several blue buildings that looked like they housed equipment. Graders and earthmovers were parked adjacent to them. About fifty feet away, the ground had been scraped and leveled for what appeared to be a pending construction site. Beyond it, smaller dishes dotted a grassy slope.

More dishes were on the left. One had a smiley face painted on its concave surface.

The largest building lay at the end of the road. It was constructed of blue brick, and the PARI logo and the words VISITORS CENTER hung over its entrance.

"I guess we'd better check in," Nakayla said. "Let's see what they mean by a self-guided tour."

On a hot August Friday afternoon, the prospect of visiting a site bordering the burnt-out remnants of a forest fire had all the appeal of a colonoscopy. Only three cars were parked in the lot, and their distance from the visitors' entrance suggested they belonged to the staff.

The gray-haired white woman behind the counter in the small lobby seemed overjoyed to greet us. "Welcome to the Pisgah Astronomical Research Institute. Have you been with us before?"

I said no and wanted to add that we hoped to book a flight to Venus on the next spaceship out. But she'd probably heard enough UFO jokes for one lifetime, and even I realized it was rude to mock someone's livelihood. Besides, the Visitors Center entry room, small though it was, looked serious enough with quality items for sale—star charts, telescopes, planetariums, and model rockets. The curious kid in me still harbored a fascination for outer space.

"We've been meaning to visit," Nakayla said. "The forest fire made us realize how much we would have regretted missing the opportunity should this wonderful facility have been destroyed."

The woman shook her head. "It's been quite a week." She lowered her voice. "Do you know they say the fire was deliberately set?"

"No. Who would do such a thing?" Nakayla asked.

"Well, I don't know if whoever started it meant to destroy PARI, but some of the locals tell the most ridiculous lies about us."

"Like what?" I asked as innocently as I could.

"That there's an underground city beneath us. That we harbor aliens whose flying saucers come and go like cars driving in and out of a parking deck."

I shook my head sympathetically. "What would give them such crazy ideas?"

She sighed. "Well, this was a secure government site until PARI took it over. Guards coming and going. Lots of black government SUVs. I've lived in the area all my life, and I admit before I worked here it was a little spooky thinking that some secret project was underway. We wondered if the Russians had a nuclear missile with our zip code. You know what I mean?"

"Had to be scary," I said. "Also had to be scary with a fire bearing down on you."

"We had to evacuate. We were so afraid that the flames would cut off the only road in and out of here. Fortunately, the fire came from the opposite direction, but then when we heard about the body, I thought one of our staff had been killed." Her eyes grew wide as she relived the horror.

I gave a slight nod to Nakayla to continue the conversation. She leaned forward better to see the woman's name badge.

"Janet, that must have been awful. Was it someone you knew?"

"No, thank God. This morning, the sheriff told us it was someone who worked here years ago. Back during the Apollo program. I've only been here ten years. That's after the government sold it."

"What do they think happened to him?" I asked.

"The sheriff said he was probably"—Janet wet her lips and then whispered—"murdered."

"How would they know?"

She looked out the door to the earthmovers. "A road grader turned up a skeleton. All the heavy-duty equipment was up at the edge of the tree line cutting a wide path of bare dirt to keep the grass from catching on fire. Doubt if it would have worked. We're just lucky the wind shifted. Anyway, since the skeleton was buried, the sheriff knew it was a homicide."

"Did anybody know him?" I asked.

She shrugged. "Almost fifty years ago? I doubt it, unless it would be one of our volunteers."

"Why's that?"

"We have several retirees who lead the guided tours. One of them actually worked here. But he won't be in until tomorrow." She gestured to the sign on the counter. "We only have the tours on Wednesdays and Saturdays. If you want to bring your own group, then we can make other arrangements."

"And if we want to look around today?" Nakayla asked.

"Admission is ten dollars a person. You can roam inside and out. We do close at four today, but that gives you over an hour."

I reached for my wallet and handed her a twenty. "We'd be interested in talking to the tour guide who actually worked here when NASA ran it. We can't come back tomorrow, but do you know if he might be scheduled to work next Wednesday?"

Janet slid a three-ring binder in front of her and flipped it open. Viewing it upside down, I could see it was a calendar for the month with names assigned to each date.

"Yes, Joseph Gordowski is leading the two o'clock tour. He worked here as well as other tracking stations."

"Sounds great."

"Would you like to make a reservation? The charge is the same, but the spaces do fill up. That way, I can match you with Joseph." She moved the binder aside and turned to her computer keyboard. "Could I have your names, please?" She entered them and then studied her screen. "Sam Blackman. That name sounds familiar." She studied me more closely.

"I'm afraid I'm a common name and a common face."

She smiled. "Well, as Abe Lincoln said, God loves the common folk. That's why he made so many of us." She handed us some brochures. "Enjoy your visit."

Although I was anxious to walk up the hillside to where I suspected the skeleton of Frank DeMille had been unearthed, Nakayla and I headed for the exhibits.

PARI proved to be a scientific center with not only displays of items from the Apollo missions but also exhibits of communication satellites, scores of meteorites, and even a tire from the space shuttle. As we passed along a return hallway, a door abruptly opened and hit my shoulder. I stepped back as an elderly white man in work coveralls stepped into the corridor. Tufts of silver hair encircled his bald pate, and he peered at me through glasses so thick, his eyes looked more owlish than human. The large eyes fixed first on me and then on Nakayla.

"So sorry. So sorry. There's even a sign on the inside of this door reminding us to open it slowly. I hope I haven't injured you."

"No, I'm fine," I said.

He shook his head. "Sometimes I get ahead of myself. When you're my age and the sands are rushing through the old hourglass, you try to make every minute count."

"Are you a volunteer?" Nakayla asked.

"No. Believe it or not, I'm still working. Got to be useful. I mean what's life if you're not living it for a purpose? I'm helping upgrade the computer data system here. PARI's moving into secure storage for all sorts of data for all sorts of clients. The common need is for security. Can't have those Russian hackers breaching this system. Not while Theo Brecht is on the scene." A twinkle flashed in the eyes behind the thick lenses. "But I didn't mean to knock you over in the process."

"Sam walks into doors all the time," Nakayla said.

"Sam Blackman." I offered my hand, and he shook it with a surprisingly strong grip. "And this is Nakayla Robertson."

"Good to meet you both. And thanks for visiting. The more people learn about this place, the broader the support. It really is a scientific treasure."

"We're impressed," Nakayla said.

"Then I'd better let you continue your tour. And I'll try to stay out of your way." He stepped aside and let us pass.

We returned to the main entrance.

Janet looked up from her computer. "Enjoy yourselves?"

"Fascinating," Nakayla said. "Is it okay if we take a close look at the radio telescopes outside?"

"That's fine." She laughed. "Just don't climb them. We'd hate to have to call the fire department to pull you out of the upturned dish."

"The one with the smiley face is more my speed," I said.

"That's his name. Smiley. I think the Department of Defense created that. A greeting to the Russian satellites that kept us under observation."

"Should we wave?" Nakayla asked.

"As far as I know, they're still spying on us. Me, I keep my head down."

We descended the exterior steps and then headed up the hill behind the building. The grass was beaten flat by the treads of the earthmovers, but the soil wasn't overturned. It wasn't until we neared the edge of the woods that we encountered the buffer of dirt for the untested firebreak.

"Last-ditch effort," I said. "Literally."

We walked on the grass bordering the exposed soil until we came to an area cordoned off with crime scene tape and temporary orange plastic fencing.

"Here's where the skeleton must have been buried," Nakayla said. "The driver of the earthmover must have noticed the bones right away. I suspect the site would be larger if they'd been scattered."

I looked down at the Visitors Center. "This is the least visible spot from the main building. If you buried someone here at night, not only the darkness but also the angle from the windows would keep you concealed."

Nakayla turned and stared at the gouged dirt. "You'd think the murderer would have buried the body deeper. This was so shallow, I'm surprised some animal didn't dig up the remains back then."

I remembered an army lecture by an archaeologist when I was a chief warrant officer. I'd never had a chance to use his information in an investigation, but his words had stuck with me.

"Frost heaves," I said. "They put pressure on objects. Over time, things like bones can be pushed upward and shifted in their orientation. This grave could have been deep enough to avoid animal detection, but frost heaves below and erosion above may have combined to bring the skeleton closer to the surface."

"Maybe this grass hasn't always been here," Nakayla suggested. "If the woods extended closer to the building in 1971, the killer could have used fallen leaves or pine needles to mask what clearly would have been a disturbed patch of sod."

I looked farther up the hill to the scorched trees on the crest of the ridge marking where the flames had been thwarted by the wind. "Without the forest fire, this patch of sod might have kept Frank DeMille a mystery forever."

"And now that fire's left us with a bigger mystery," Nakayla said. "Who killed him?"

I looked up and waved at the hazy blue sky. "I wonder if the Russians saw anything?"

# Chapter 5

Saturday morning, the four of us traveled in my Honda CR-V from Asheville to Roanoke. Yes, the four of us—Cory, Nakayla, me, and Blue. Cory would hear nothing of us leaving the coonhound behind, claiming that her aunt loved dogs and would be more excited about seeing Blue than seeing her only niece.

The drive lasted close to four hours, which meant we arrived shortly before noon. Nakayla and I suggested we stop for lunch beforehand, but Cory insisted her aunt expected us to eat with her.

"Besides, it's too hot to have Blue stay in the car," Cory argued. "Roanoke's not Asheville where he could sit at the table with us and no one would bat an eye."

So at ten till noon, we pulled behind a blue Buick sedan and parked in the driveway of a modest brick ranch on a hill above the Roanoke rail yards.

Immediately, the front door of the home opened, and a thin, gray-haired woman in a light-green dress stepped out onto the porch and began waving furiously.

"That's Aunt Nancy." Cory hopped from the back seat and ran up the sidewalk. Blue followed close on her heels.

Nakayla and I watched from the car as aunt and niece

embraced. Then Nancy knelt to hug Blue. The coonhound licked her face like it was ice cream.

Nakayla laughed. "Do you think they'd notice if we left?"

Ten minutes later, we sat around Nancy Gilmore's dining room table. I eyed a platter of home-cooked Southern fried chicken flanked by bowls of green beans, wild rice, and a plate of biscuits still steaming from the oven.

"You shouldn't have gone to all this trouble," Nakayla said.

"No trouble at all. It's the least I can do after y'all made the trip up here. But be warned. Save room for pecan pie."

I ate like I was coming off a hunger strike.

We used our lunch conversation to bring Nancy Gilmore up to date on the investigation.

Twenty minutes and two thousand calories later, we moved to Nancy Gilmore's small living room. Nakayla and I shared a tartan upholstered sofa, Cory took a matching wingback chair, and Blue flopped down on a loop rug in front of the fireplace. The grate had been replaced for the summer by an overflowing fern.

Nancy Gilmore walked to a corner of the mantel and retrieved a stack of letters and a framed photograph. I hoped what she was about to show us would prove to be useful information.

"I thought you might like to see a picture of Frank." Nancy handed the photograph to Nakayla, who held it between us. "My brother's on the right. My husband's on the left. Eddie."

A smiling woman wearing a tie-dyed T-shirt and bell-bottom jeans stood between two men. I glanced at Nancy and saw an older face but the same smile. Her husband looked like he must have topped six feet. He had his left arm around Nancy's shoulders. His right gave a mock salute. The rugged build of his body suggested the conditioning of active duty.

Frank, on the other hand, was closer in height to his sister. Probably no more than five eight. His thick glasses and pudgy frame screamed "geek" as loudly as his brother-in-law's proclaimed soldier.

The three posed at the base of a waterfall, and the camera shutter had frozen the spray and beads of mist churned up by the tumbling torrent.

"Looking Glass Falls?" I asked.

"Yes. Eddie was on leave, and we went to see Frank for a long weekend."

Looking Glass Falls was a popular spot in Pisgah National Forest near Brevard. It was right off the road and required no hiking.

Nancy reached out for the picture with one hand and handed Nakayla the letters with the other. "Eddie was killed somewhere in Vietnam. No one's ever told me where. They said it was classified." She returned the photograph to the mantel and eased into a rocker beside Cory. "That was two months later."

"And Frank disappeared the end of July?" Nakayla asked.

She nodded. "The month after our visit. Eddie was already back in Vietnam."

"Your husband was in the army?" I asked.

"Yes. He was a lieutenant."

"Did he lead a platoon?"

"If he did, he never told me. Eddie didn't talk about the war. At least not to me."

"Who else?"

"If anyone, it would have been Frank. He once teased Eddie about being an oxymoron, whatever that means."

Nakayla looked at me as if I should have the answer. I did.

"Army intelligence. It's an old joke. That would explain the vagueness of the information the army provided you. Eddie might have been on the ground with contacts whose identities and location needed protection."

"That's why it was classified?" Nancy asked.

"Yes. That's my take. Did your brother Frank ever say anything about your husband's military duties?"

"No, not really." Then a ghost of a smile appeared.

"What?" Cory prompted.

"Once during that weekend in North Carolina, my brother teased Eddie that if they told each other what they did, they'd have to kill each other."

"So Frank's work was also classified," I said.

"He told me he was stepping into another world. One being created in a space all its own."

"Cyberspace," Nakayla whispered.

She had to be right. Fifty years ago, as Neil Armstrong stepped onto the lunar surface, scientists and engineers like Frank DeMille were uncovering a virtual world that would change us more radically than that trip to the moon. I thought how the smartphone in my pocket contained more computing power than what Frank used to track the astronauts. Probably more than what calculated the massive Saturn rocket's launch and the *Apollo* capsule's reentry. But Frank had been a pioneer, and I realized his work was probably as much a guarded secret as whatever special ops his brother-in-law executed in Southeast Asia. And both men would be dead before the end of that summer.

"Should we divide up these letters?" Nakayla asked. "Then we can swap so each of us reads all of them."

"That's fine with me," Nancy said. "But I don't know how they'll help."

Nakayla spread them out on her lap. "Cory, why don't you take the unopened ones from Frank's girlfriend. Sam and I'll split the letters to Nancy."

Nakayla handed me five letters addressed to Nancy Gilmore with a return address of an apartment in Asheville.

The envelopes had been opened, and the letters inside consisted of one or two pages of minute, precise printing. The style conveyed the authorship of someone for whom clarity and detail were paramount.

The deep creases in the aged, yellowed paper showed the

letters had been reread many times. They were the unfinished conversation with a brother who never returned.

I examined the postmarks and read the oldest first. The content was mundane. Frank talked about the weather, the excitement of a new job, and its perfect fit for his computer science degree. He asked for any news from Eddie and how he wished the war would soon be over. He invited his sister to come for a visit, especially when Eddie came home on leave. He promised to take them up on the Blue Ridge Parkway for a picnic.

The fourth and fifth letters shifted to more personal reflections on his job. Although he explained he couldn't say much about his actual responsibility and she would find it incredibly boring, he believed he was making a real contribution to the space program. One paragraph in the fifth letter read, "I'm making some breakthroughs that have earned me the nickname Slew Meister. Sounds like a medieval knight, doesn't it? I'd put it on a T-shirt, but I'd have to do too much explaining that I wasn't a killer. You know me. The poster boy for nonconfrontation."

So Frank DeMille didn't sound like a person who would aggravate someone to murder him. Unless his nonconfrontation comment was ironic because Frank DeMille would take someone to the mat over the slightest disagreement. Nancy Gilmore would need to clarify his comment, but I decided to wait until we'd read all the letters before subjecting her to Q & A.

I passed the letters on to Cory, who handed hers to Nakayla. I got the remaining five letters that Frank had written to his sister. Again, I started with the oldest postmark, but now he referenced the pending visit of his sister and brother-in-law.

He encouraged them to stay at the Grove Park Inn and to take a tour of the Biltmore House. Frank hoped to take some time off and show Eddie a few of his favorite fly-fishing spots.

A later letter revealed Frank had found a girlfriend whom he was anxious for his sister to meet. He suggested that the four of them have dinner one night, Frank's treat.

Nancy must have pressed him for details about the girl, because in the next letter, Frank wrote her name was Loretta Case and she was the secretary for the tracking station's chief administrator. She was a native who'd graduated from a local secretarial school. "She's smart beyond her limited education," he'd written. "Very curious and yet very down-to-earth. I know you'll like her."

The last letter had been written after Nancy and Eddie visited Frank. Frank asked his sister if she could send him a copy of the photographs from their trip, especially the ones from Looking Glass Falls—the one of him and Loretta and the one of Nancy, Eddie, and him.

The paragraph that stood out read:

"Loretta sends her love, and I hope to bring her to Roanoke after the next Apollo mission in July. Can you believe she's never been out of Western North Carolina? Her family's not much for the outside world and outsiders. I'm afraid they're not keen on Loretta seeing me, but Loretta tells me to pay them no mind. That they're all talk. Finally, dear sister, would you send me whatever address you have for Eddie? I need to write him for advice regarding a matter at the tracking station. I meant to ask him during your visit and never got the chance. It's probably nothing, but if there's any intelligence in military intelligence, Eddie's the one to have it. (HA HA). And let me know if there's a convenient time for Loretta and me to visit in August. Love, Frank."

I looked up to see Nakayla staring at me. She was ready to pass me the letters from Loretta, but she was also eyeing me for my reaction to the letter I'd just read. She must have drawn the same conclusions: a conflict existed between Frank and Loretta's family, and something wasn't right at the tracking station.

I gave Cory the second half of Frank's letters and took the final batch from Nakayla. The first two were to Frank DeMille in care of Nancy Gilmore. They had been unopened for nearly fifty years until today. Each was brief and urgent.

The first was dated August 8, 1971. "Dearest Frank, I'm worried as I haven't heard from you. Everyone here is concerned as there has been no word from you since the night of July 30 when the lunar module touched down. I've called the apartment many times and even talked the landlord into letting me in. It looked like all your clothes were still there. Dr. Haskford has filed a police report. I hope you haven't left because of anything my brothers might have said. Or more importantly because I didn't give you an immediate answer to your proposal. I do love you, and if this letter should find you through your sister, my answer is yes. Please come home. Love, Loretta."

The second was dated a week later, August 15, 1971. "My dear Frank. Please let me know you're all right. If I have done or said something to cause a breakup, just let me know. Or if you no longer want to talk to me, then tell Nancy. She is also worried sick. We want to know you're safe. Love, Loretta."

The third letter was addressed to Nancy Gilmore and had been opened upon receipt. It was dated August 22, 1971.

"Dear Nancy, I'm at my wit's end with worry about Frank. I hope you would tell me if you know anything I might have done or said that caused him to leave. I love your brother very much and only want what's best for him. I understand that I may not fit in his world and he's realized he can do better than a plain mountain girl for a wife, as much as I'd try to please him. I just want to know he's safe. I'll not bother you anymore, but I'll continue to pray for Frank, you, and Eddie. Sincerely, Loretta."

I looked up as Cory finished reading Frank's last letter to his sister.

She had tears in her eyes. "Let Aunt Nancy read the letters Loretta wrote to Frank."

I got up and walked them over to Nancy. Then I returned to my place beside Nakayla. The three of us waited while Cory's aunt read the letters she'd kept unopened for decades.

Nancy Gilmore wiped her eyes, refolded the pages, and gently slipped them back in their envelopes.

"Mrs. Gilmore," I started.

"Nancy, please."

"Nancy, do you mind if we ask you a few questions?"

"No. Anything at all, but I don't know how much help I'll be."

I looked at Nakayla to see if she wanted to lead. She gave a nod for me to go ahead.

"When exactly was your visit to Frank?"

"The middle of June. I remember Eddie had to report back for duty on the Fourth of July."

"Your brother asked for your husband's military address. Did you give it to him, and if so, do you know if he wrote him?"

"I sent Frank the address. The last letter I received from Eddie mentioned he'd heard from Frank and was following up on his request. He told me to pass that along to him."

"You don't know what that request was?"

"No. I assumed it had to do with Frank's work."

"Do you still have that letter?"

Nancy shifted uneasily in the rocker. "Yes, but I'd rather not share it. Our letters were very personal."

"I understand. What if after we've left, you review them and copy out anything like what you just told us your husband said about your brother?"

"All right, if you think it might be important."

"I have to be honest, Nancy. Right now, we don't know what's important and what isn't. We're just gathering information, and we appreciate your willingness to help."

Tears flowed, but she made no effort to wipe them from her cheeks. "I just want to find out what happened to my brother."

I turned to Nakayla, hoping she would take over. I'm not good at questioning weeping women.

Nakayla leaned forward on the sofa, drawing closer to Nancy. "What do you think about Frank's relationship with Loretta? Did he want to break it off?"

"Nothing would surprise me more." She lifted the letters from

Loretta off her lap. "And these letters from Loretta reinforce that Frank asked her to marry him. That matches what she told me."

"She talked to you about his marriage proposal?"

"On the phone. I called her after I received that letter from her. Her comment about being a plain, mountain girl outside of Frank's world bothered me. I wanted her to know that Frank never expressed anything but the utmost respect and love for her. He told me he'd found his soul mate."

"Was that because they worked together at the tracking station?"

Nancy shrugged. "That's part of it. But Frank said he actually got to know her through music. There was a fiddlers' convention on a farm near Asheville, and Frank ran into Loretta there. He knew her only to speak to at work, so that was the first time they'd hung out together. Frank was rather shy, and I doubt if he would have ever asked her out at work."

"Who was Dr. Haskford?" Nakayla asked.

"The man in charge of the tracking station. Loretta worked directly for him."

I remembered the question one of his letters raised. "Nancy, what do you think was going on with Loretta's family? Was your brother one who would try to avoid a confrontation?"

"Definitely. He would work around a conflict rather than face it. Up to a point. Then when there was no other recourse, his backbone transformed into steel, and he'd go face-to-face with anyone."

"Do you think that happened with Loretta's family?"

She shook her head. "I don't believe so. According to Loretta, all the pressure was put on her to break off her relationship. Her family didn't want anything to do with Frank. They thought he was stuck up because he wouldn't talk about his work. They interpreted that as his being too good for them."

"Didn't they understand what classified information means?"

"Loretta told me it was just a convenient excuse. The real problem was they thought Loretta would leave them. Not marry a local boy and settle in the valley like the rest of them."

"Is that what she did?" I asked.

"I don't know." She looked down at the letters. "We lost touch. I assume she stayed in Western North Carolina, but I don't know if she's alive or dead. Maybe now that Frank's remains have been found, she'll resurface. She could be a grandmother who has no interest in involving her family in a painful incident from her past."

"Your other brother, Zack, Cory's father. Cory said he went to Asheville to look for Frank."

Nancy smiled. "Yes, he went to look for Frank and found his own life in the mountains. Zack was between Frank and me in age. If he'd lived, he'd be sixty-eight now. I'm sixty-six. Frank, well, Frank would be seventy-two."

"Did Zack share anything he might have learned about Frank's disappearance?" I asked.

"No. Just that Frank walked out of the tracking station and was never seen again. Like he'd been beamed up to the Starship *Enterprise*."

We sat in silence for a few minutes. Again, I reviewed the letters in my head. "Did you ever learn why your brother was called Slew Meister?"

"No. Maybe because if a problem arose, Frank was the one who slew it? Like he said, the title sounded like a medieval knight."

*Yes,* I thought. *Except in this story, the knight was slain by the dragon.*

# Chapter 6

Nakayla and I left Blue to spend the night with Cory and her aunt. The coonhound didn't give us a second look as we drove away. So much for canine loyalty.

We spent the night at the Hotel Roanoke, a magnificent Tudor-style structure built with railroad money in 1882 and predating both Asheville's Biltmore House and Grove Park Inn.

After sleeping late, we took advantage of the hotel's Sunday brunch. I ate enough to nearly put me in a food coma.

We returned to Nancy Gilmore's around one to find she'd prepared a pound cake and coffee.

"Just something to tide you over for your trip back to Asheville," she said.

I forced myself to devour a slice so as not to hurt her feelings. That's the kind of guy I am.

When I declined a second piece, Nancy slid her cup aside, got up from the table, and retrieved a sheet of white paper from the sideboard behind her.

"This morning, I read through Eddie's letters to me and copied what I told you yesterday. It was from his last letter and referenced what Frank must have asked after I gave him Eddie's address." She pushed it across the table to me.

Her cursive handwriting was so perfectly penned that it looked like professional calligraphy.

"Cory hasn't seen it," Nancy said. "You can read what Eddie wrote aloud."

I cleared my throat and began. "I received a nice letter from Frank. Please tell him I'm passing his concern up the chain of command. He might be contacted directly, or a response will come to me. I'll write him if I learn something. Meanwhile, tell him to relax and go fishing for some of those elusive brown trout instead." The excerpt ended.

I looked up. "Do you know if Frank was ever contacted?"

"I don't think he could have been. Eddie wrote this letter after Frank disappeared. And like I said, Eddie was killed soon afterward."

I knew from my experience in Iraq that getting mail in and out of a war zone wasn't like dropping a letter off at your local post office. Weeks could have gone by from the time Frank wrote his letter and Eddie received it.

"What should my aunt do now?" Cory asked.

Nakayla looked at me. "FBI?"

I nodded. "Nakayla's right. Nancy, you should contact Special Agent Lindsay Boyce in Asheville. We can give you that information. Ask her if she'd like to see the letters your brother wrote shortly before he was killed. That way, you'll be on record as trying to be helpful."

"Yes," Nakayla agreed. "Don't underestimate the power of a family pressing for answers."

"That's what I'm doing," Cory added.

"Then why don't you take them?" Nancy asked her niece. "You can hand deliver, and I won't run the risk of losing them in the mail."

"All right," Cory said. "But you should still talk to Special Agent Boyce directly. The letters are your property, and you're the one authorizing their release. I'll make sure the FBI returns them."

We left with the correspondence and a disappointed coonhound who no longer enjoyed Nancy Gilmore's pampering.

Monday morning, Nakayla and I began implementing the strategy we'd devised on the drive home from Roanoke. With Cory standing by to liaise with the FBI, we split up the key aspects of the investigation that surfaced from the conversation with Nancy Gilmore—Frank's involvement with Loretta Case and the unknown concern that fueled his letter to Eddie. The fact that his brother-in-law served in army intelligence must have been a reason for Frank's request for help.

Nakayla outshone me on the computer, so she focused on tracking whatever online records existed for Loretta Case. However, where she excelled in navigating through cyberspace, I could chart a course through equally perplexing terrain—the U.S. Army.

I placed a call to the cell phone of one of my fellow warrant officers with whom I'd served in Iraq. Actually, he'd served under me before his own promotion to chief warrant officer. My reviews of his stellar performance had propelled him on the fast track, and he proved eager to stay in touch after my career-ending wound and discharge.

"You got me." The phrase was his stock answer for not giving his name until he learned the caller.

"Now that I've got you, what the hell do I do with you?"

"Sam, my man, how'd you get through? Don't you know I'm on the do-not-call list? You're supposed to be blocked."

"Don't give me that. You know I'm on your speed dial for when you're stuck on a case."

He let out a deep-throated laugh. "And who's calling whom?"

"I don't want your pride keeping you from getting my help. Surely, there's something I can assist you with, Chief Warrant Officer DeShaun Clark."

He laughed again. "Well, there is a certain major I'd like to be rid of."

"You're on your own with the brass. I solve crimes. I don't commit them."

"Ah, so now you're following a rule book?"

"No. And that's why I'm calling you. Are you still at Bragg?"

"Oh, yeah. I've been tied at the hip with a prosecutor for a couple months. It's enough to wish I was back with you in Baghdad."

"Then you have my sympathy."

"So seriously, what can I do for you?"

"We've had a body turn up, bones actually, of a computer scientist who disappeared from a NASA tracking station in the mountains up here."

"Is the guy military?"

"No. But his brother-in-law was. Army intelligence. My dead NASA guy mailed him a letter about something that was bothering him. I have correspondence from the brother-in-law that he ran the concern up his chain of command. The computer scientist disappeared, and his brother-in-law was killed in Vietnam a short time later. We have no record that any action was taken regarding the concern."

"Hmm." Clark was silent a few seconds. "When did all this go down?"

"The summer of 1971."

"And the bones just turned up?"

"Yeah. We've had some forest fires, and a work crew cutting a firebreak unearthed him."

"If he wasn't military, then I don't know how I can help."

"It's the brother-in-law I want to know about. I spoke to his widow yesterday. She was never told exactly how or where her husband was killed."

"Well, that certainly fits an intelligence profile. So you want me to discover what he kicked up the chain of command and if it ties into your bone man?"

"That's about the size of it. Off the books would be better since I don't know what I'm stepping in. But if you need to run it through channels, we have an FBI murder inquiry underway, and the feds will be interested in the brother-in-law's correspondence. If someone in the army squelched his request, it could be embarrassing."

"Wouldn't be the first time," Clark said. "But if murder's involved, then no one wants to be blindsided. Let's start off the books and see what I can quietly turn up. Give me the particulars."

I provided Clark with names, dates, and what little information Nancy Gilmore had known about her husband's time in Vietnam.

"OK," Clark said. "I'll be back to you as soon as I can."

I thought he was going to hang up, but instead he asked, "What's your gut telling you?"

"About what?"

"About Eddie Gilmore?"

"Frank DeMille's my case," I said.

"Yeah, but the Sam Blackman I know wouldn't leave it there."

"I don't like that Eddie sent a request through army intelligence and then he and Frank both die, even though they're half a world apart."

"Eddie was in the company of over fifty thousand who died there, Sam."

"Then find the evidence that will make this feeling in my gut go away."

An hour later, Nakayla came out of her office with her iPad. "I found a Loretta Case Johnson living in Transylvania County not too far from the tracking station."

I got up from my desk and followed her into the center room. She took her favorite spot on the sofa, and I sat beside her where I could more easily view whatever she wanted to show me. Blue got up from the carpet, circled three times, and lay down in the exact same position.

"Did you go through property records?" I asked.

"Not initially. Public records of weddings and deaths. I found a 1976 wedding registration for Loretta Case and Randall Johnson. I discovered no death record for either one."

"Did you search beyond Transylvania County?"

"Bordering counties only. I felt it was more productive to drill down on this Loretta before expanding beyond our region."

I pointed to the iPad. "So what's on this?"

"An interesting website." She angled the screen toward me.

The headline read "Aliens Over Asheville" and showed a saucer-shaped UFO hovering over the skyline.

"Did Shirley put you on to this?"

"No. I called Tuck Efird and asked him about his ex-wife, the one he said was into UFOs. I thought we ought to be aware of anyone else who has an interest in PARI. He gave me this URL address."

I took the iPad and scrolled down the screen to a list of articles. "Bigfoot Roams the Appalachian Trail." "Reincarnated Atlantis Citizens Uniting Once Again." "Cloudy Night Skies Bring Hordes of Interstellar Travelers to PARI."

"So what? Bigfoot's now a suspect?"

"No. It's the article about starless nights being the favorite time for incoming and outgoing spaceships at PARI. The author interviews several past employees. One is named Loretta Johnson, who worked there from 1969 to 1981."

"Really? Then I guess I'm the one with the Bigfoot in my mouth. Stellar research, my lovely, if you'll pardon the galactic reference." I pressed my finger to open the article and read how the alleged UFO activity at the astronomical facility was accelerating. The final person quoted was identified as Loretta Johnson, who claimed not to have witnessed any alien presence during her twelve years of employment. I found that a strange interview to publish on a site dedicated to asserting aliens were among us. But then Loretta qualified her answer by saying she couldn't refute any claims made after 1981 because she had been let go soon after the Department of Defense had taken over. She stated the whole tone of the facility changed and there was constant traffic of dark SUVs with tinted windows coming and going. The fence around the perimeter was fortified and poison ivy planted along its footing as a further deterrent.

Her comments were followed by an italicized footnote provided by the editor of the UFO website: *Although Mrs. Johnson claims not to have any knowledge of UFO activity during her time at the government site, others close to her state that the interstellar conspiracy did touch her life. Her fiancé, a scientist with NASA, disappeared without a trace in 1971 in what is most likely an alien abduction. Furthermore, Mrs. Johnson's reluctance to confirm that possibility can be attributed to memory alteration at the time and her subsequent dismissal as a tactic to remove her from any circumstances that might trigger her recall of what really happened.*

"Amazing," I said. "They use her denial as proof that it occurred. But it's pretty clear this Loretta Johnson is our woman. I wonder how they'll explain the discovery of the bones."

"Easy," Nakayla said. "They'll simply say Frank DeMille died while in the custody of the aliens and they returned his skeleton to be discovered."

I laughed. "Hell, these people might even claim the aliens started the forest fire with their death rays to make sure his remains were found."

"But it doesn't sound like Loretta has extreme views," Nakayla said. "It's more plausible that the Department of Defense would shut down civilian presence if the purpose and mission changed to something far more classified than tracking an Apollo spacecraft whose launch was known to the entire world."

"I'm not saying we don't talk with her. I'm just saying being quoted on a site like this doesn't bolster your credibility."

"Which is why we need to separate her from the people quoted as being close to her."

I gave the iPad back to Nakayla. "Do you have an address for her?"

"Yes. But her phone number's unlisted."

I thought for a moment and then checked my watch. Ten forty-five. "I'd rather see her in person anyway."

Nakayla frowned. "She may not know Frank DeMille's remains have been discovered."

"Then all the more reason to break the news face-to-face. And your face will certainly be more reassuring to her than a voice on the phone."

Nakayla stood. "Let's go, Blue."

The hound got to his feet and shook himself.

"Are we bringing him?"

"No. I'm taking him to Hewitt's office. Cory and Shirley will watch him." She handed me a small piece of paper with an address. "Put this in the Garmin and be ready to leave when I return."

# Chapter 7

Although Nakayla and I each had a GPS app on our cell phones, the ridges and narrow valleys around us made cellular coverage spotty, and the more remote the destination, the less likely we'd have consistent access to a tower. One minute, you might have three bars of signal, and the next, none. So we'd purchased a Garmin handheld satellite GPS that could offer not only road maps but also topographical information for hiking. The fact that Nakayla instructed me to prep the Garmin told me Loretta Case Johnson didn't live in an easy-to-reach gated community.

With Blue comfortably sleeping in the law firm, we left Asheville and headed for 8560 Dusty Hollar Road, an address that found us returning along the familiar route to the Pisgah Astronomical Research Institute. When we passed the entrance to PARI, Nakayla said, "It looks like Dusty Hollar will be a left turn in about a mile."

"She lived close to work," I said.

"Assuming that's where she's lived the past fifty years. But you're probably right. Family property kept her tied to the area. I'll bet her husband's a local. Frank DeMille would have been her one chance to get out of this valley and explore the world."

Dusty Hollar Road proved to be a narrow, potholed blacktop that tested the description "two-lane." It was more a one-and-a-halfer.

Mailboxes got sparser the farther we penetrated the narrow valley. Then the patched asphalt ended, and the surface became packed dirt mixed with bluestone gravel. The houses visible through the trees looked like they'd last seen a coat of paint when the Russians launched Sputnik.

"A hundred yards ahead," Nakayla said. "Should be right around the bend."

"Glad we're in the CR-V rather than your car. I hope we don't need four-wheel drive."

We didn't. Rounding the bend, we saw a modern log home with a red tin roof, spacious wraparound covered porch, and flowers in dark-green window boxes. A small satellite dish was mounted next to a stone chimney. No cable TV in this neck of the woods.

A freshly graveled driveway looped off the dirt road, passed in front of the house, and ended in a parking lot adjacent to an open pavilion about forty yards away. A green Jeep Cherokee was parked at the closest point to the house.

"This isn't what I expected," Nakayla said.

"That shelter looks like it could hold all of Dusty Hollar."

I swung into the driveway, tires crunching the thick gravel. A thin woman in black jeans and a pink, short-sleeved shirt stepped out as I stopped in front of the porch steps.

She held a fiddle in one hand and a bow in the other. The gray hair and lined tan face fit a woman of Loretta's age. She stood at the top of the steps, her dark eyes looking down on us with suspicion.

I lowered my window.

"You lost?" she asked before I could utter a word.

"No. Not unless Loretta Case Johnson doesn't live here."

Her eyes narrowed. "Who wants her?"

I decided not to dance around the subject with this fiddle-toting woman. "The family of Frank DeMille."

The bow dropped from her hand and tumbled down the steps. She leaned against a post and took a deep breath. "You Frank's kin?"

"Good friends. His sister's up in Roanoke, and his niece lives in Asheville. They're hoping you can share what you know in light of the discovery."

She gripped the fiddle neck with both hands. Either she was afraid of dropping it or she wanted to be ready to swing it as a weapon.

"What discovery?" she asked.

I realized we weren't showing up with questions, we were harbingers of bad news. Back here in this hollar, she'd been isolated from the press reports. I looked at Nakayla.

My partner opened the passenger's door and walked around the front hood, stopping between the headlights. "Mrs. Johnson, last week, Frank's remains were uncovered at the site of the tracking station. The evidence points to murder."

Although Nakayla spoke as gently as she could, her words hit the woman like a tidal wave. Again, she leaned back against the post, but her knees buckled, and she slid to the plank flooring. She pushed the fiddle aside and wrapped her arms around her shins, tucking herself into a ball. She made no sound. Only the shaking of her shoulders betrayed her sobs.

Nakayla picked up the bow and sat on the step below her. I felt useless behind the wheel, engine running and no idea what to do next. Nakayla jerked her head to the wider parking area, signaling me to leave her alone with the woman. I nodded, took my foot off the brake, and let the CR-V ease away.

The gravel lot was rimmed with felled tree trunks. I parked near the pavilion and got out. Nakayla and the woman hadn't moved from their positions. I stepped under the shelter of the pavilion's roof. The cement floor was swept clean and must have been approximately fifty by seventy-five feet. Several stone firepits bordered the pavilion, and their blackened grates conjured up the image of hot dogs and hamburgers on the outdoor grills. Beyond, picnic tables awaited families and friends. The layout was far more than a backyard patio with a Weber.

At the far end, a riser covered in green Astroturf served as a small stage. I saw no electronic equipment, but three microphone stands were tucked in one back corner, and a dull metal cabinet rose behind them. It looked weatherproof, and I assumed it housed speakers and a simple PA system. Nancy Gilmore told us Frank and Loretta had gotten to know each other through a fiddlers' convention. Crack detective that I am, I deduced Loretta provided a small private venue for musicians to jam or perform.

"Sam!"

I turned to find Nakayla standing in the parking lot.

"She's our Loretta. She's gone inside, but she's willing to talk with us."

"Is her husband here?"

"No. She told me they're not together anymore. She lives alone."

I followed Nakayla into the log home. The front room ran the whole width of the house. The floor consisted of wide planks and scattered rugs of the handmade hook style that Loretta could have created herself. In the center of the ceiling hung a wagon wheel chandelier. To my left was a stone fireplace with an air-tight wood-burning stove and a sofa and three chairs built for sturdiness over style. A flat-screen television sat on a sideboard beside the fireplace.

To my right was a rectangular farm table with six dining chairs and a dried flower arrangement for a centerpiece. A sideboard held a CD player flanked with speakers. Loretta had set her fiddle and bow next to them.

The three exterior log walls had sizable thermal windows that provided plenty of light. The air felt cool, and I noticed floor grates for a central HVAC system. The rustic decor of the back-woods combined with the comforts of the twenty-first century.

The interior wall of the room ran only half its width. Then a hallway was next to an open counter dividing the kitchen from the front dining area. Nakayla led me into the kitchen where Loretta sat at a table in a small breakfast nook. A teapot and three cups with saucers were in front of her. She gestured for us to take the two remaining chairs, one on either side of her.

"I'd just brewed some herbal tea," she said. "Would you like some?"

Before I could decline, Nakayla said, "That would be lovely, Mrs. Johnson. Maybe just a cup. We won't take up much of your time, but it was important to Frank's sister, Nancy, that we find you. She wanted to make sure you knew what happened."

Loretta poured the tea and then nervously tapped her fingernail on her saucer. "She wanted me to know that Frank didn't run out on me, right?"

Nakayla said, "Frank didn't run out on you or his family."

Loretta's eyes teared. She lifted her cup and took a sip. I sampled a taste of what I can only describe as dried grass.

Nakayla and I said nothing. We'd agreed not to mention the letters. Two people showing up announcing the death of her former fiancé and admitting to reading her personal love letters didn't seem like a smart move.

So we sat, the only sounds being the tick of a kitchen clock and the tapping of Loretta's fingernail on her saucer. Consciously or unconsciously, Loretta synchronized to the passing time.

Finally, she took a deep breath. "I'm glad to know Nancy's still alive. I let our friendship drift apart."

"I understand," Nakayla said.

"I liked Nancy. And her husband, Eddie. That was our last phone conversation. When she told me Eddie had been killed in Vietnam. After that, all we had in common was the loss of our loved ones. It was just too painful."

Nakayla gave me a look signaling to take the lead.

"Nancy Gilmore said her brother and her husband were close," I said. "Would you agree?"

"Yes. Frank really respected Eddie. He thought Eddie was

brave and smart. He said Eddie could learn to do what Frank did far better than he could do Eddie's work."

"Did he tell you what Eddie did?"

"No. Just that it was important to the war and it was very dangerous."

"After Nancy and Eddie came to visit, did you notice anything different in Frank's relationship with Eddie?"

Loretta gave me a hard stare. "Different how?"

"Oh, I don't know. Closer. Stronger. Nancy Gilmore said Frank asked her for Eddie's military address because he wanted to write him."

The older woman looked away as she mentally shed the years to return to that summer of 1971. "He said he thought something wasn't right at work and Eddie might have some ideas on how to fix it."

"Eddie could help him with a computer program?"

"No. It wouldn't have been the programming. Frank was a genius in that area. Everyone recognized his talent. It could have been he felt some of his colleagues weren't pulling their full share of the work. He wouldn't tell me. He said it might be nothing, and he didn't want me caught in the middle."

I took another swallow of the dreadful tea and tried to appear nonchalant. "In the middle between what?"

"I was secretary to Dr. Haskford, the tracking station's chief administrator. We knew dating in the workplace was frowned upon, and I guess Frank wanted to keep me clear of any internal clash that might be created. He knew Eddie had to deal with all sorts of people and problems in the army."

I decided to switch to a line of questioning I'd neglected to thoroughly pursue with Nancy Gilmore. "Did Frank ever talk about his brother Zack?"

"A little. He worried about him. Zack had just graduated from college that spring and didn't have a job yet."

"Did you meet him?"

"No. Not then. Zack did look me up after Frank's disappearance. When he came searching for him."

"Did he have any theories?"

"Not really. Only that he thought Frank might have gone out on one of his thinking walks. Frank did that when he was working out some problem. He could sometimes walk for hours, not really aware of his surroundings. That's why Zack kept hiking the area around the station. He thought Frank could have been lost or fallen into a ravine." She paused. "But you say he was found on the tracking station land?"

"Yes. A skeleton was uncovered during the attempt to create a firebreak to protect PARI. We have a DNA match with his niece. All these years, he's been up on the ridge behind the complex."

Loretta shook her head in disbelief. "So someone killed him that night? One of his colleagues?"

"That's a possibility. Or he came across someone on the property that night who wasn't supposed to be there. Or he was taken and killed later, then buried on the ridge to make it appear as if he'd been killed there."

She sighed. "Well, security wasn't particularly tight. Not like after the facilities were turned over to the Department of Defense. We had a gate near the highway, but coming in on foot wouldn't have been a problem. Even high school kids used to sneak in to see the big telescopes."

"Did Frank ever say anything to indicate he was in danger?"

"No, but he tended to keep things to himself."

Now that we were moving into her personal life, I looked to Nakayla to pick up the questioning.

"Mrs. Johnson, Frank's sister said he was very fond of you. How would you describe your relationship?"

She stared down into her teacup. "Frank asked me to marry him. I didn't tell him no, but I didn't tell him yes."

"What did you say?"

"That I needed to think about it. I told him it wasn't because he wasn't a wonderful man. He was. But it was whether I was ready."

"How did he react?" Nakayla asked.

"I think he was hurt. He tried not to show it. He said he understood."

"When did this happen in relation to his disappearance?"

"The week before. If he went out on one of his thinking walks, it might have been because I left his proposal up in the air." Her voice caught, and she stifled a sob. "If he did come across someone on the tracking station grounds, I fear it was because of me."

I found her self-blame unjustified, but I understood how guilt defied logic.

Nakayla leaned in a little closer. "What did your family think of Frank? Did you tell them he proposed?"

Her dark eyes flashed, and the tears evaporated. "My family put Frank out of their world a long time ago. This has nothing to do with them."

Nakayla refused to be put off. "You're saying they didn't have an opinion one way or the other?"

"I'm saying they have nothing to do with Frank's disappearance."

I jumped in, my voice firm. "Mrs. Johnson, we're no longer talking about a disappearance. We're talking about murder, and that fact is facing all of us."

She said nothing.

I softened my tone. "Please, Mrs. Johnson. We're just trying to find out what happened to Frank. We want justice for him, for his sister, and I hope you want to be a part of that effort, even though you've led a full and happy life since then."

"I have," she whispered. "For the most part. I'll help if I can."

"I understand you and Frank met at a fiddlers' convention."

She looked at me and managed a smile. "Yes. He was surprised to see me on stage."

"You're a performer?" Nakayla asked.

"Not solo. Back then, we were just an amateur family band.

Me, my two brothers, and my father. We called ourselves A Case of Tunes, you know, playing off our last name. My mother was usually our only audience."

"From the size of your pavilion, it looks like your family has grown," I said.

"That was Randall's idea. We started playing to wider audiences in the 1980s, and he thought we could have a series of mini-festivals on the property. It took a while to save up the money."

"Randall's your husband?" I asked, not wanting her to know how much we'd already checked her background.

"Ex-husband."

"How did you meet?"

"Randall worked in general maintenance at the tracking station. He wasn't a scientist or engineer, but he could construct or fix anything. After Frank disappeared, he'd speak to me every morning. I learned that a lot of people knew Frank and I were dating. And they could tell I was hurting. Randall was very kind, and we just fell into comfortable conversation. He was four years older. It was easier to stay put than move elsewhere. Five years later, he proposed. And Randall was a talented flat picker. He not only played guitar, but he taught one of my nephews."

"So you still have the band?" Nakayla asked.

"It's not called A Case of Tunes any more. My parents have passed over, and my brothers and I play occasionally, but my four nephews are the core of the band now, two from each of my brothers. Randall and I never had children."

"And the new name?" I prompted.

"Case Dismissed." Loretta Case Johnson shook her head. "At first, I thought it was disrespectful of the old band and our music. But I was told it's what every defendant likes to hear from the judge. And the younger generation likes an edgier name and music."

"You could take it to mean they had a run-in with the law," I said.

"Yeah. You could." She lifted the teapot and poured herself another cup. I winced as she topped mine off.

"Did your family know that Frank had proposed to you?" Nakayla asked.

"No. They knew we were dating, and they'd met him a few times." She paused and lifted her cup. "But like I said, they had no opinion."

While she drank, Nakayla gave me a quick glance. We knew from the letters that wasn't true. Was Loretta simply trying to keep her family from looking bad, or was there more to it?

I pressed on. "If you'd married Frank, odds were at some point you'd move away."

"Maybe," she conceded. "Or maybe Frank would have stayed when the Department of Defense took over. I heard Dr. Haskford once tell someone that Frank was a rising star and already on the Defense Department's radar."

"They had to be upset when he went missing," I said.

"They were. I was interviewed twice, the second time by the FBI." She set down her cup and eyed me closely. "A lot of the same questions you're asking me now. You say you're Nancy's friends, but you talk like police."

"We are her friends, and I was an investigator in the army. Nakayla and I are private detectives, but our goal is just what we said, learn the truth about what happened."

"Well, I've told you all I know from back then." She slid her chair away from the table.

"We read your interview," I said.

She'd started to rise, but my statement stopped her.

"What interview?"

"The one that's posted online. 'Aliens Over Asheville.'"

She laughed. "What a bunch of nonsense. I worked there for twelve years, and the only little green man I saw was the Jolly Green Giant on a can of peas in the kitchen."

"And the secret things that went on after you left?"

"Gossip. If you ask me, it was pretty clear what they were doing with all those radio telescopes. Listening to the Russians."

"You didn't say that in the interview."

"Out of respect for Randall. He stayed on in maintenance after I was let go. He's the one told me it was all about eavesdropping. I don't want anyone in the government thinking Randall shared classified information."

"Why'd you agree to the interview?"

"One of my nephews told me we were going to be discussing music. All the woman wanted to talk about was spaceships and alien technology. I should have shut up and walked out."

"Did people believe that during the Apollo days?"

"A few. But the Apollo program was public knowledge. It was mainly the rocket and communications technology that was secret." She stood from the table. "Now if you'll excuse me, I have things to do."

She walked us to the door. On the interior wall beside it hung a photograph of a group of people standing in front of a farmhouse. It wasn't Loretta's, although she was in the picture beside a young girl who was seated in a tire swing. Other children and what appeared to be at least two generations of adults also posed for the camera.

I pointed to it. "Family photograph?"

"Yes. Last Thanksgiving. I celebrated it with my brothers and their families. They gave me this for Christmas." As we stepped off the porch, she asked, "Is Nancy Gilmore still at the same address?"

"Yes," Nakayla said.

Loretta nodded and closed the door.

When we were back on Dusty Hollar Road, I asked, "What do you think?"

"What do I think?" Nakayla said softly. "I think Frank DeMille was the love of her life. Her grief is still raw after all these years. And I think she's hiding something about her family."

"Case Dismissed."

"Not if it's murder," Nakayla said.

I glanced in the rearview mirror as we started around the bend. Loretta's jeep pulled out of her driveway and headed in the opposite direction.

# Chapter 8

I expected the next day would be one of waiting—waiting on Chief Warrant Officer DeShaun Clark to call with information on Eddie Gilmore and waiting for Cory to report on any news from Special Agent Lindsay Boyce.

We got to the office at nine, and Nakayla began exploring what she could find on Loretta Case Johnson and her family. Logging onto the internet, she quickly discovered the band Case Dismissed was listed in a variety of bluegrass festivals and pub appearances.

"Sam, come look at this. They're at Jack of the Wood tonight. I think we should go."

"I'm always up for Jack of the Wood," I said. "Is Loretta playing?"

I looked over her shoulder at the computer screen. There was only the name Case Dismissed on the pub's events calendar.

Jack of the Wood was one of Asheville's most popular Irish pubs and a venue for smaller bands and open jam sessions. Located on Patton Avenue, the pub was the bottom story of a building that housed a vegetarian restaurant above it. Because Asheville was so hilly, the upper eatery, the Laughing Seed Café, had its own entrance on Wall Street, a short, narrow lane that ran atop the steep ridge directly above Patton. I wondered how the rising, wafting aromas of burgers and Irish stew tested the sensibilities of the second-story vegetarians.

"Their website doesn't specify band members," Nakayla said. "But from other appearances, I gather the older generation is involved if a play date is local. The boys do the more extended travel gigs on their own."

"It's Loretta's two brothers I'm interested in. They were the ones who seemed to be against Loretta's relationship with Frank."

"And I'm sure they're aware of us," Nakayla said. "I found her brothers' addresses. Danny and Bobby Case. They both live farther out Dusty Hollar Road."

"Where Loretta was headed after we left."

Nakayla threw her hands up in mock surprise. "Sometimes your deductive powers amaze me."

"Sometimes I amaze myself. What can I say?"

"How about nothing. Quit while you're ahead. Now let me get back to work." She swiveled her chair to her keyboard.

I'd just sat at my desk when the door from the hallway opened and a tall, thin white man entered. He appeared to be in his fifties, mainly because of his close-cropped steely gray hair. His most distinctive feature was his blue uniform and the sheriff's badge above his left chest pocket.

Nakayla and I both rose from our chairs.

"Can we help you?" she asked.

His brown eyes darted back and forth between us for a few seconds. "You Blackman and Robertson?"

Nakayla eyed the brass nameplate on his right chest pocket. "I'm Nakayla Robertson, Sheriff Hickman. This is my partner, Sam Blackman."

"Heard a lot about you. Both of you." He spoke without any emotion, leaving us to guess whether he'd heard good things or bad.

"Then what can we do for you?" I asked.

He looked beyond us to the sofa and chairs. "Got time to talk a few minutes?"

"Certainly," Nakayla said. "Would you like some coffee?"

"No, thanks. I won't be here that long." He brushed by us and went to the sofa.

Nakayla looked at me and shrugged. We took the chairs.

"I won't beat around the bush. You called on Loretta Johnson yesterday."

"We did," Nakayla said.

"Care to tell me why?"

"To make sure she heard that the remains of Frank DeMille had been discovered. We were doing so at the request of Frank's sister. I assume you knew Frank and Loretta were close."

"I did not. I had to learn about it yesterday afternoon from Lindsay Boyce at the FBI. I assume you know the feds are sticking their noses into my case."

"We're not surprised," I said. "It sounds like the jurisdictional history of when and where the crime happened could create a tangled mess of local, FBI, and even national park ranger involvement."

Hickman nodded. "What about private detectives?"

"If you're referring to Nakayla and me, our interest is in seeing justice done. If you can make that happen, then more power to you."

"I understand some letters are involved. Letters that came to the FBI."

"They didn't come from us," I said.

"But you know the contents."

I didn't want to stonewall the sheriff, especially if he was making a good faith effort to solve the crime. But I wasn't ready to share the speculations Nakayla and I were following.

"Frank had asked Loretta to marry him," I said. "He disappeared before she gave him an answer. We learned that from Frank's sister."

"Do you know if there was another boyfriend?"

"No, but it's my understanding her family wasn't thrilled that she was dating someone from the NASA tracking station." I leaned forward in my chair, locking eyes with Hickman's and hoping I looked the part of a tough-guy detective. "We've been straight with you, Sheriff. Why don't you be straight with us? You didn't learn about our visit to Loretta from the FBI. We haven't told anyone. Maybe Agent Boyce has come into possession of letters and she's ahead of you in some areas. That's not our fault. If you want our continued cooperation, then we expect you to be straight with us. When did you speak to Loretta?"

His cheeks reddened, and for a second, I thought he was going to get up and storm out. But he took a deep breath and reclined back into the sofa's leather cushion. "Yesterday afternoon, she came speeding up Dusty Hollar Road like the devil himself was on her tail. I had my patrol car parked in Bobby Case's yard and was talking to him and his brother Danny. She had to brake real hard to keep from rear-ending me."

"What did she tell you?" Nakayla asked.

"She said you two had told her Frank DeMille's bones had been found and you were talking to her like it was her fault. I had no reason to doubt what she said. It was clear she was upset and had been crying."

"Let me assure you we made no such accusation," Nakayla said.

He nodded. "Well, I got the feeling she'd raced up to talk to her brothers and I happened to be an unexpected visitor."

"Possibly she was angry at them but then redirected it at us," I said. "Avoid an ugly scene in front of the law. Were you there because of DeMille's murder?"

"No. At that point, I didn't realize there was a connection between Loretta Johnson and Frank DeMille."

"Now you do."

"Now I do. And now I'll follow up on it."

He emphasized *I'll* to make us understand we sure as hell weren't going to mess any further with his investigation.

"I told you the truth about speaking to Lindsay Boyce," he said. "She told me about the letters. She also said the more thorough FBI forensic exam of DeMille's skull revealed bone damage that occurred earlier than that caused by the road scraper's blade. Could have been anything from a blackjack to a shovel. I'm betting on a shovel, the one that probably then dug his grave."

"So death was caused by a blunt object," I said.

"Unless he was knocked out and buried alive."

"Would either of Loretta's brothers be capable of something like that?"

He shrugged. "Singly? Probably not. But Danny and Bobby Case are identical twins. Put them together and they can be mean as two snakes. They've got to be seventy-five by now, and I tell you, they haven't mellowed with age."

"I suspect they'll alibi each other regardless of whether it's true or not," I said.

Hickman pointed a finger at me. "You got the picture. They'll swear to have been together the night Frank DeMille disappeared whether they're guilty or not."

I thought about what the sheriff had and had not said. "Then why were you there?"

Hickman stood. "Thanks for your time. If you're really interested in justice, you'll let me know if something else comes to light." And he was out the door.

# Chapter 9

I called Jack of the Wood to confirm that Case Dismissed was playing that night and learned that although their start time was scheduled for eight, they often took the small stage anywhere from thirty minutes to an hour early.

"Why's that?" I asked the man on the phone.

"You know the difference between a bluegrass band and a rock band?"

"You mean other than the music?"

He laughed. "Yeah. A bluegrass band will tune all night without playing, and a rock band will play all night without tuning. Case Dismissed is one of those groups that can spend half an hour preparing to play."

"I know sometimes there are four band members and at other times seven."

"We're set up for seven. They're here a lot. The three old-timers play a couple of the classics, take a break, and then join for a few more tunes toward the end. The whole show will be over by nine, and then we open up the stage for a jam session. So come early and stay late."

Nakayla and I decided to shoot for around six thirty when we felt pretty sure we could get a table close to the stage and easily stretch our drinks, appetizers, dinner, and dessert for a couple of hours. Our outing expanded when we brought Cory up to date and she asked to come. She wanted to see the woman who nearly became her aunt. Hewitt Donaldson then invited himself, claiming the evening would make up for the interrupted birthday lunch. Only Shirley begged off, saying a night of bluegrass would set back her meditation progress. Something about banjos disturbing her harmonic balance. She offered to take Blue to her house for a sleepover.

The temperature had dropped into the midseventies when we left the office. The pleasant walk to the pub took about ten minutes.

Stepping into Jack of the Wood was like stepping into any good Irish pub. It made no difference whether you were in Dublin, Boston, or Asheville. Rich, dark wood; a full bar heavy on the Irish whiskies; Harp, Guinness, and Smithwick's on tap. The geographical distinction played out in the local beer offerings, and Asheville, a multiyear winner of the Beer City, USA, designation, had the full run of excellent brews from lager to stout.

We entered to find about half the tables occupied. Lively pockets of conversation rose above the clink of glasses. The stage fit snugly into one corner diagonal from the bar, and we claimed an empty table right in front. Loretta would have to close her eyes the entire set not to see us.

Hewitt intercepted a waiter and made it clear he was picking up the tab and didn't want to be rushed. We ordered drinks, fried dill pickle chips, and loaded nachos to get the evening started.

With the food in the center of the table and pints of beer in hand, Hewitt gave Cory another birthday toast and then said, "So where do we stand? I know we're here to see this Loretta Johnson and her family, but what else is going on?"

I took a sip of Guinness and licked the unavoidable foam mustache from my upper lip. "I've got a call into an army buddy who might make inroads into Eddie Gilmore's service record."

"The point being?"

"I'd like to pick up any trail on what Frank DeMille wrote to his brother-in-law. With both Eddie and Frank out of the picture, the army might have dropped its pursuit of the matter, but it still might be in some dusty file box somewhere."

"Sounds like a long shot," Hewitt said. "But that's what it's going to take—a long shot."

"At least the FBI is taking an interest," Cory said. "I believe Agent Boyce will do what she can. She's trying to track down everyone from the NASA station who's still alive."

"That means she'll interview Loretta," Nakayla said. "I'd like to see if there's any discrepancy between what she told us and what she tells the FBI."

An unanswered question sprang to my mind. Unanswered because we'd neglected to ask it. "Damn."

Hewitt stared at me. "What?"

"We never asked Loretta where she was the night Frank disappeared. Rule number one's always look at the people closest to the victim. On a night when the *Apollo 15* mission was in full execution, all hands could have been on deck, including Loretta."

"Then ask her tonight," Cory said. "She's got to walk right by us to get to the stage."

Hewitt speared three fried dill pickles with his fork. "Frankly, I'm surprised Sheriff Hickman seems determined to pursue the case."

"I'm not sure he's pursuing the case as much as pursuing the Cases," I said. "He wouldn't tell us why he was talking to Bobby and Danny."

"Maybe Newly or Tuck have some police contacts in Hickman's county," Hewitt said. "Have you run a background check on the four sons? They're probably in their forties. I doubt if they make enough to live on playing bluegrass."

"I'll check in with Newly first thing in the morning," Nakayla said.

There was a commotion at the pub's front door as a group wrestled cases of musical instruments inside. From the shapes, I spotted two guitars, a banjo, two mandolins, and a stand-up bass bigger than the person carrying it. I didn't recognize any of the six men, although they could have been in Loretta's family photograph. I hadn't studied it in great detail. Only when Loretta and her fiddle case followed behind them did I know for sure that Case Dismissed had arrived.

Her brothers were easy to distinguish. Gray hair pulled back in ponytails, matching beards that brushed their chests, tall and broad shouldered, dressed in bib overalls over white T-shirts and round-toed brown boots. In short, they were seventy-five-year-old clones except that one nurtured a larger beer gut.

The sons were more diverse in appearance, at least beyond blue jeans and boots. Where the fathers had plain white T-shirts, the younger men sported colors that ranged from tie-dyed to something that looked like shiny chain mail. The smallest of the four, a narrow-faced, weaselly man with a shaved head and diamond-stud left earring, wore a star-speckled black shirt with the ghostly image of the classic yellow alien face—almond-shaped black eyes and slits for nostrils and a mouth. Beneath this cosmic visage were the blood-red words "I'm coming for you." The man stepped up on the stage carrying a banjo case. He turned and surveyed the room as if fearful one of the patrons might be abducting him to the mothership.

Nakayla leaned over and whispered, "Why are the banjo players always the weird ones?"

Loretta let her brothers and nephews arrange themselves while she waited just inside the pub door. Her outfit was more in line with what I expected of a professional performer—wheat jeans and a sky-blue, square-necked tunic with three-quarter sleeves. Her hair was pulled back by a turquoise band.

She too scanned the room that was now nearly full. Her eyes passed over me, then snapped back to fix me with a stare of recognition.

I smiled and gave her a nod. Her brow furrowed, and she raised the fiddle case to her chest. She appeared to be debating whether to stay or leave. I decided to make the first move.

I rose from the table and walked to her.

"What are you doing here?" she asked.

"Having dinner. And looking forward to hearing your music."

"And?"

"And I thought of a question or two since yesterday. Again, I'm just trying to get to the truth about what happened to Frank."

She sighed. "So am I."

She looked over my shoulder, and I knew she was studying the others at my table.

"Who's the white woman and the old man?"

"The woman is Cory DeMille. Frank's niece he never knew. The man is Hewitt Donaldson, an Asheville defense attorney."

Her eyes narrowed. "Defense attorney? Is he planning to defend Frank's killer?"

"No. Cory's his paralegal. He's helping us investigate Frank's death."

"Death? I thought you said it was murder?"

"Yes. We now know he was struck in the head with a blunt instrument. Possibly the shovel used to bury him."

Her face paled. "Shovel," she whispered.

"Yes. You might be able to help us with some more information. Were you at the tracking station that night?"

"Aunt Loretta, we need to tune up."

I turned to see the alien T-shirt guy lifting his banjo in his right hand like Moses parting the Red Sea. With his left, he urged her to the stage.

She scooted around me. "We'll talk afterward."

I watched her step up on the stage and immediately become engulfed by the six men. It was clear they were grilling her about me, as at various points, each of them gave me a hostile glare.

I returned to the table. Hewitt was draining the last of his first porter.

He set the empty glass down with a thud. "Well, what did you learn?"

"We're going to talk when they finish playing. I think she has something to share."

"Good," Hewitt said. "My advice is that you talk to her one-on-one. Otherwise, it might look like we're ganging up on her."

Cory laughed. "You're going easy on a witness?"

"Of course. What else would you expect from someone who has the milk of human kindness flowing through his veins?"

"Not the title of attorney at law after his name."

Hewitt waved at our waiter and pointed to his empty glass. "I'm mellowing," he told Cory. "Like a fine wine."

His paralegal flashed a devilish grin. "Then put a cork in it."

Even Hewitt had to laugh. I was glad to see Cory in such good spirits, the happiest she'd been since the discovery of her uncle's remains.

Case Dismissed took about twenty minutes with what seemed an unending process of tuning and retuning. My mental calculation of two guitars, two mandolins, one banjo, one bass, and one fiddle totaled forty-one strings. On average, thirty seconds for each one. I was grateful they didn't bring a piano.

The band finally moved from tuning to playing. The transition was simply Danny or Bobby (I had no idea which twin was which) coming to the microphone and announcing, "We're Case Dismissed, and we're going to play for y'all."

Loretta kicked off a fiddle intro to "Darlin' Cory."

"Just for you," Hewitt said, teasing Cory.

Loretta didn't hold the instrument under her chin but tucked it into her collarbone so that she could sing and play at the same time. The band put out a wall of sound, even though only the vocal microphone was amplified. Players moved in and out for solos and harmonies. The fast instrumentation was tight, like you'd expect from a family who had been playing together all their lives. They ran through a medley of old mountain and bluegrass standards: "Cripple Creek," "Rocky Top," "Salty Dog Blues," and "Alabama Jubilee."

One of the twins announced the next series of songs would be performed by the four boys. He said boys although they were clearly in their late thirties and forties. He and his brother set down their instruments, but Loretta stepped to the microphone.

"I've got one more to play before we take our break."

The others looked surprised.

"Just me and the fiddle," she said. "I haven't sung it like this before."

Her brothers and nephews stepped back. She started a slow tap of one foot and then drew the bow across the strings. The plaintive melody soon became recognizable as the old mountain ballad, "Come All You Fair and Tender Ladies." She played the tune through once, dropped the fiddle and bow to her sides, and sang a cappella:

> *Come all you fair and tender ladies,*
> *Be careful how you court your man,*
> *He's like a star in a summer's morning,*
> *First appears and then he's gone.*
>
> *He'll tell to you some lovely story,*
> *He'll steal your heart, he'll make you cry,*
> *And then he'll leave like dew arising,*
> *No way to know his truth from lies.*
>
> *But when you learn his soul was faithful,*
> *And that his life had been struck down,*
> *You find your love can be rekindled,*
> *For one once slain and sent to ground.*

*Come all you fair and tender ladies,*
*And praise who slew the stars of night,*
*But one with spade and knees earth-covered,*
*Has killed my love, my heart's delight.*

*So all you fair and tender ladies,*
*Take warning for the man you love,*
*His breath is frail, and time is fleeting,*
*When death lies veiled in stars above.*

Tears glistened in her eyes. The noisy bar had grown quiet, and her last word rang clear and pure until it faded into silence. A beat and then thunderous applause. Loretta didn't acknowledge the unbridled response. She only looked at me. Then she set down the fiddle and bow, stepped from the stage, and skirted around us to head toward the restrooms in the rear.

"Wow," Nakayla said. "That was a surprise."

"Especially to the band," Hewitt said.

Loretta's brothers and nephews appeared stunned, obviously taken aback by the unplanned performance.

"Those weren't the real words, were they?" Cory asked.

"The first verse was the old song," Nakayla said. "Then she improvised the rest." She turned to me. "How did she know about the shovel?"

"I told her it was a possible murder weapon. She wove it into the lyrics."

"Are you going to talk to her now?" Hewitt asked.

Loretta's nephews had started playing more contemporary bluegrass songs. I noticed Danny and Bobby at the far end of the bar.

"She said after they finished playing. I assume that means when they quit for the night."

Nakayla stood. "I don't think it's a good idea to let her out of our sight. Not if she has information that could break open the case. I'm going to visit the restroom." She made her way through the crowded tables and disappeared around the bar.

For the next ten minutes, I kept glancing toward the rear of the pub. Loretta reappeared and joined her brothers at the bar. One of them said something to her, but she only shook her head.

Nakayla slid into her chair beside me.

I leaned close to her so as not to have to shout over the music. "Did you speak to her?"

"It was more like she spoke to me. She told me to stay away from her. She wasn't ready to talk, and I would only screw things up."

"What do you think that meant?" Hewitt asked.

"I don't know. We were the only ones in the women's restroom. When I entered, Loretta was texting on her phone. She immediately stopped. I told her I liked her version of the song. That's when she got defensive and said she wasn't ready to talk about it."

I looked back at the bar. Loretta was still standing by her brothers. They had beers; she had what appeared to be ice water. The brothers watched the performance; she watched our table. I looked away, not wanting to aggravate what I hoped would be a spirit of cooperation.

It soon became apparent that Case Dismissed shared the spotlight. Different band members would be featured for solo songs, and the others would leave the stage for the bar or restroom. It gave everyone a chance to shine. Loretta was the only one who didn't make a repeat appearance.

We'd just listened to a couple of lightning-fast bluegrass tunes by the banjo player when I noticed Loretta was gone from the bar. Her brothers were headed toward the stage, but she had vanished.

"Did anyone see where Loretta went?" I asked.

"No," Nakayla said.

"Maybe she went back to the restroom," Hewitt said.

Cory slid back her chair. "Do you want me to check this time?"

"Yes," Nakayla said. "I don't want her to think I'm stalking her."

Cory left. Five minutes later, she returned. "Loretta's not in the restroom. I didn't see her anywhere."

Nakayla's brow furrowed. "Sam, let's find her."

We circled to the rear of the pub, searching the tables along the way.

"I'll check the restroom again," Nakayla said. "Loretta might have gone in after Cory left."

Nakayla returned a few seconds later. "She's not in there."

I stopped a waiter coming out of the men's room. "Excuse me. Have you seen the woman who's in the band?"

The man shook his head. "No. You tried the restroom?"

"Yes," Nakayla said.

"Maybe she ducked out for a smoke." He gestured to a door on the back wall. "That goes to Rat Alley. She might be out there."

I opened the door and stepped into a sauna of trapped August heat. The alley was actually a tunnel with only one far entrance. I realized we were underneath Wall Street, the road that fronted the second stories of the buildings built on Patton Avenue. The alley was the only access for back doors on the lower level.

"It stinks out here," Nakayla complained.

"Well, with a name like Rat Alley, it's not going to be prime real estate."

The tunnel looked like it was about forty yards long. Other restaurants and shops had back doors with trash cans, empty beer kegs, and HVAC units lining their walls. Bright, single-bulb lamps hung high on the concrete-block wall opposite the doors.

"If Loretta wanted to leave without her family knowing, all she had to do was walk out the tunnel entrance," Nakayla said.

"Maybe. But do you think she would have left her fiddle?"

I turned away from the tunnel entrance and walked to the closer dark end. A rear bicycle wheel protruded from behind a stack of metal kegs. Someone had knocked it over. I stepped around the kegs into the niche between them and the wall.

The bike was an old Schwinn for girls, the kind with a spring saddle seat and balloon tires.

There were pink tassels on the handlebar grips, tassels that draped across the open, sightless eyes of Loretta Case Johnson.

# Chapter 10

Detective Newland had quarantined Nakayla and me at a table in the rear of Jack of the Wood just inside the alley door. In addition to being detained as material witnesses, we'd been instructed to stop anyone from exiting into Rat Alley. That freed up a uniformed officer to gather contact information from the patrons for a more extensive follow-up later. At the moment, the police were only saying there had been an incident in the alley. The word *murder* and the name *Loretta* weren't mentioned.

I'd called the police as soon as I'd discovered Loretta's body, and the first patrol car had arrived within five minutes. Backup came within another five, and officers stationed themselves at the rear doors of all the businesses with exits into Rat Alley. I'd also phoned Detective Newland's private cell phone and given him the news. He'd said that he and Tuck Efird were still at the police station and would be at the scene inside of ten minutes.

Nakayla had quietly briefed the on-duty manager of Jack of the Wood and asked that the processing of any payments by patrons wanting to leave be delayed until the police arrived. I'd stayed with the body and watched the alley until a uniformed officer instructed me to return to the pub. I'd requested he tell Detective Newland to see me as soon as possible.

Newly and Tuck Efird arrived together, listened to our brief account, and then moved to the alley to oversee the crime scene investigation. All Nakayla and I could do was wait for their return.

We were joined at the table by Cory and Hewitt. I brought them up to date.

"Can you tell how she might have been killed?" Hewitt asked me.

"I didn't touch her or the bicycle, but I could see a thin red mark where something had severely pressed into the skin of her neck. My guess is that she was garroted. If someone knew what he was doing, she wouldn't have been able to cry out and would have lost consciousness quickly."

Cory's eyes widened. "Do you think it could have happened in here? Someone slipped a wire over her head and dragged her through the door into the alley?"

"Highly unlikely," I said. "Even though attention would have been focused on the stage, the restrooms would have meant patrons coming at unpredictable times."

"We should find out if she was a smoker," Nakayla suggested. "She could have stepped outside for a quick cigarette."

"Good point," I said. "Mention it to Newly. If so, there should be either a pack or single cigarette near the body."

Hewitt tapped his finger on the table. "You know who the police will zero in on."

"The family," Nakayla said.

He pointed the finger at her. "Right as rain. And the way the band juggled between solos and duets, each one of them was offstage for a brief period." He turned to me. "How long would it take for Loretta to die?"

"Properly done, in as little as a few minutes. We're talking irreversible brain damage even if the garroting was halted before death. The perpetrator took a hell of a chance, but in the alley and quickly overpowering her, he could have pulled her down behind the empty beer kegs and gone unnoticed. The bicycle was probably used to further hide the body."

Cory shook her head. "But if it was family, why here? Why now? There would have been plenty of opportunities later in more isolated settings."

I thought back to my brief conversation with Loretta. "She told me she'd speak with me after the music. I didn't get the sense that it was what I was going to ask her but rather what she was going to tell me. And the possibility of that later conversation could have created the urgency that prompted the killer. He was forced to strike when he did."

"And her song," Nakayla added. "You could tell it caught her family off guard."

"How'd they react when the police arrived?" I asked.

"They were startled," Hewitt said. "Hell, we all were. Everyone was onstage but Loretta. They stopped playing when it was clear the officers weren't here to listen to the music. The police told them to stay onstage."

"But I heard the banjo player arguing with one of the patrolmen," Cory said. "He was complaining that he needed to find his aunt. The officer said he'd be taken into custody if he didn't comply. One of the twins, I guess it was his father, told him to calm down. They'd find Loretta later."

"Here they come," Hewitt said.

I looked over my shoulder and saw double. Double double. Bobby and Danny Case were walking side by side toward us, identical scowls on their identical faces. Beside each of them walked a uniformed policeman, doppelgängers themselves. Al and Ted Newland, Detective Newland's twin nephews. Each of them had a Case brother by the arm and was unsuccessfully ordering him to halt.

I rose from my chair, suspecting I was the destination.

"Where's our sister?" shouted one of the Cases.

"We know you talked to her," his brother accused.

I glanced down and read the name bar of the nearer officer. "Al, what's going on?"

"We told them to remain on the stage. Those were the instructions Uncle Newly gave us."

The fact that he said "Uncle Newly" told me the nephews were upset. Otherwise, they would have called him Detective Newland.

The Case brother beside Al shook his arm free. "We keep asking but no one will tell us what the hell's going on. You talked to Loretta. Where is she?"

The Newland twins looked away. Hewitt got up from his chair. "Why don't Cory and I return to our table. You gentlemen can sit here."

"We ain't sitting till we get some answers," said the other brother.

Both men folded their arms across their bib overalls, signaling they weren't about to budge.

I stepped to the side, putting myself between them and the alley door. "I'm very sorry to say that Loretta's been killed. Her body was discovered behind the pub."

Ted Newland and Hewitt moved to my side.

The color drained from the brothers' faces.

"That's not possible."

"It's some mistake." The brothers' words came out as desperate whispers.

"I wish it were so," I said.

A moment of stillness, and then both men lunged forward. Al tried to intercept the nearer man but not before he'd crashed into me, knocking me backward against the door. Hewitt grabbed the other twin in a bear hug, but the older man flung him aside. The delay enabled Ted to yank that Case brother by the back of his overalls and shove him into a chair. I slid to the floor, pulling the second twin with me.

He screamed in my face, "You killed her! You killed her!"

Nakayla grabbed a handful of beard and pulled sideways,

turning his head like a bridled horse. He let out a yelp of pain and tried to punch her. Al grabbed his wrist in midswing and snapped a handcuff on it. Then he wrestled the other arm behind the man's back and cuffed it as well.

I crawled free just as the door opened behind me.

"What's going on?" Newly stepped inside and quickly closed the door behind him.

"They wouldn't stay on the stage," Al said. "Ted and I tried to stop them, but they forced their way past us."

"We want to see our sister!" the brother in the chair yelled. "You can't keep us from our sister." He too had been cuffed with his hands behind his back.

The four sons rushed up, angry but unsure what to do.

"This is police brutality," shouted the banjo player in the alien shirt. He pointed at me. "He's the one who should be in handcuffs."

"This isn't police brutality," Newly said. "It's a homicide investigation, and you can't interfere with it."

"Homicide?" Alien shirt looked at the older men for confirmation.

"Loretta's dead," the Case brother in the chair said. "Somebody killed her in the alley."

"Then he really should be in handcuffs." The banjo player took a menacing step toward me. "He's the one talked to her. He's the one she came to meet."

Newly ignored him and spoke to his nephews. "Get transportation to take all six to the station for proper questioning. I'll be there as soon as I can."

When the Case family had been taken back to the front of the pub, Newly handed me a pair of shoe coverings. "These are probably useless now since you were already at the scene, but slip them on and retrace your steps in the alley."

Night had fallen, but Rat Alley was ablaze with the halogen lights the Asheville Police Department set up to illuminate the crime scene. The press and onlookers stood behind a barricade that had been erected at the tunnel's entrance. A forensic team in protective suits searched through every garbage bin and collected each discarded bottle or can that might hold a clue.

Newly's partner, Tuck Efird was bent over Loretta's body. The bicycle had been leaned against the far wall and the empty kegs had been moved to give the forensics team more room as well as create a barricade against the long-lens cameras of the television and newspaper photographers.

"Give it to me again," Newly prompted. "So you came out here looking for the victim."

"Nakayla and I. She went toward the head of the alley. I looked around here and in the rear. I noticed the bicycle wheel, walked over, and saw Loretta. I bent over like Tuck's doing, but I didn't touch her. The open eyes told me she was dead. I also saw the bruising around her neck."

"And then Nakayla went inside to alert the manager while you phoned it in."

"Yes. I didn't want anyone getting away. Not that one of them was the perp, but they could be potential witnesses."

"Quick thinking," Newly said. "Did you see her with anyone other than her family?"

"No. She and I were supposed to talk after their set. Evidently, she had something to tell me. Then her brothers and her nephews got up in her face after she spoke to me."

"You hadn't come tonight for a prearranged meeting?"

"No. I'd thought of a few questions I hadn't asked when we were at her house. I caught her right after she came in, and she agreed to talk with me. Later, Nakayla saw her in the restroom texting someone. Loretta warned her to keep away. She would speak to us when she was ready."

"How long do you think she could have been gone before you noticed?"

"Fifteen or twenty minutes. She seemed settled at the bar with her brothers."

Newly took a deep breath and looked at his partner. "How's it going?"

"We can move the body," Efird said.

"Okay. I'll fill you in on what Sam's telling me back at the station." Newly turned to me. "Let's go inside where it's cooler. I'm sweating like a lathered horse." Newly wiped his brow with the back of his hand and gestured for me to precede him into the pub. No one was at the back table and he told me to sit. "So what did you want to ask her?"

"The first question I should have. Where was she the night Frank DeMille disappeared?"

Newly smiled. "Glad to know you're human. And she just said she'd talk later?"

"I managed to ask where she was that night, but her family called her up to the stage before she could answer. And I think I upset her?"

"With that one question?"

"No. I told her Frank could have been killed with a shovel."

Newly straightened in the chair. "Where'd you hear that?"

"Sheriff Hickman paid us a visit this morning."

"Well, thanks for sharing."

I could tell he was pissed that I hadn't immediately brought the forensics report to his attention. "Look, I just learned about it this morning. Yes, I should have called you, but it wasn't your case. You said you couldn't get involved."

"I couldn't get involved officially. But when has that ever stopped either of us?"

"And now?"

"Now? Loretta Case Johnson's killer just brought us to the dance. So anything else I should know?"

"She sang a song," I said. "One that surprised her family. One that she might have made up on the spot because she mentioned a shovel."

"A song?" Newly repeated. "You remember the words?"

"Not all of them. It was based on the old ballad, 'Come All You Fair and Tender Ladies.' The same tune with new verses." I paused. There had been a number of verses, and I wondered how she'd been able to create so many so quickly. "Maybe she'd written the verses years ago and just changed one on the spur of the moment. It was clear to me the song was about Frank DeMille."

"Maybe her brothers will know," Newly suggested.

"Maybe. But like I said, they were surprised. I don't think they'd heard it before."

I stood.

"Where are you going?" Newly asked.

"To see if the Cases left her fiddle."

I walked to the main area of the pub. Nakayla, Cory, and Hewitt sat at our original table. It looked like the only other people present were staff and a single uniformed officer at the front door.

"We ready?" Hewitt called.

"One moment." I saw all the instruments had been put away but the cases remained. "I want to check something."

"The band had a fit when they couldn't pack up before going to the station," Hewitt said. "They only calmed down when the manager said he'd stay until they returned."

I climbed on the stage and found Loretta's fiddle case behind the stand-up bass. It looked like the larger instrument's offspring. I brought it to the table where Newly joined our group.

"What are you looking for?" Newly asked.

"I'm not sure." I flipped open the latches and lifted the top. The fiddle showed wear but clearly had been well cared for. It lay cushioned in the case's plush green lining. The bow was held in place on the underside of the cover. In a strange way, I felt like I was touching a sacred object, a part of the spirit that once inhabited a body now on its way to the morgue. I gently handed the instrument to Nakayla.

A folded sheet of white paper lay flat on the bottom of the case's interior.

Newly nudged me away. "Better let me handle that." He rolled on gloves and grabbed the paper by one corner. Then he carefully unfolded it to the full size of 8½" x 11" computer paper. The sheet had been folded twice so that the fresh crease marks divided the surface into four quadrants. Words arranged as verses had been handwritten in ink. The writing was neatly penned in cursive with the printed heading, "For Frank, Who Loved Me."

"This isn't years old," Newly said. He angled the page so I could read it. Nakayla peered over my shoulder.

"These are the lyrics she sang," I said.

"Except one verse is missing," Nakayla said. "The one with the lyric:

> *"Come all you fair and tender ladies,*
> *And praise who slew the stars of night,*
> *But one with spade and knees earth-covered,*
> *Has killed my love, my heart's delight."*

The rest of us looked at her in amazement.

"How did you memorize that after only hearing it once?" Newly asked.

"Because I know the original verses, and the differences stood out. Particularly the missing verse because it contained the words *slew, spade,* and *killed.* I made it a point to reconstruct those verses in my mind while we were sitting here."

Newly nodded. "I understand spade and killed but why slew?"

"Because in one of the letters from Frank, he refers to his nickname as the Slew Meister, but he doesn't explain what it means."

Newly studied the verses in greater detail.

Hewitt edged beside him. "Detective Newland, I'd say it's not what's here that's important but the verse that isn't here. That's the one that Loretta most likely made up on the spot."

Newly carefully refolded the paper. "You're right, Counselor. And the one that most likely got her killed."

# Chapter 11

At nine the next morning, Nakayla and I met Newly and Efird at the police station. We wrote down our individual statements describing the events of the previous evening and waited in an interview room while one of the administrative staff typed them for our signatures.

Newly and Efird entered holding two cups of coffee each. I took one from Efird.

"I know it tastes like varnish," he said. "Maybe you'll have some sympathy for our plight."

I took a sip and winced. "Here I thought you were exaggerating."

"Well, it certainly wakes you up," Nakayla said diplomatically. "And I doubt if either of you got much sleep last night."

The detective team eased into the chairs on the opposite side of the table.

"Three hours," Newly said. "We didn't finish with the Case family till two. They were a handful, especially since we kept them separated to prevent them from collaborating on a story."

I took another sip of coffee. It wasn't so bad now that my taste buds had been annihilated. "Anything you can share?"

"They don't like you," Efird said. "They think you either killed her or got her so riled up that someone else killed her."

"Well, I didn't kill her." I wasn't so sure about the second of their accusations. That bothered me. Had her reaction to the news of Frank's death led to her own?

"Any evidence as to why she was in the alley?" Nakayla asked. "Was she going for a smoke?"

Newly shook his head. "Her brothers said she didn't smoke. We found no cigarettes on her body. There were a few scattered butts, but nothing looked recent. We're testing them for DNA, but I doubt that will lead anywhere."

"The Cases believe you spoke to her in the alley," Efird said. "They saw you and Nakayla get up and leave while she was off the stage. She'd told them on the road in she had to see someone."

"That wouldn't have been us, because she didn't know we were going to be there," I said. "Did you check her phone?"

"It wasn't on her body," Efird said. He turned to Nakayla. "You said you saw her texting?"

"Yes. Are you checking her carrier's records?"

"We will."

"She had to set up this alleged appointment somehow," I said. "Surely one of the numbers in the phone log will provide a lead."

Nakayla shook her head. "Not if it was texted via something like WhatsApp Messenger. Those texts are heavily encrypted, and I doubt if you'll be able to read them. There's also email as a possibility. Do you know if she had a computer? We didn't see one at her house."

"We're going out there as soon as we finish here," Newly said.

"Good," I said. "Nakayla and I happen to be free this morning."

"And you'll stay that way as far as we're concerned," Newly said.

"You encouraged us to investigate," I protested.

"Frank DeMille's death for Cory," Newly countered. "We're in an ongoing investigation of Loretta's murder, and that means you're out. If we find something that overlaps, we'll let you know. That's our official position, and with Tuck as my witness, you've now been informed."

"Your official position," I repeated.

Newly smiled. "The department's official position."

I returned the smile. "Understood." And I did understand. Newly's own words from the previous day rang in my ears. *I couldn't get involved officially. But when has that ever stopped either of us?*

We left the police station with a couple of hours free before we needed to drive to PARI for our two o'clock tour. Loretta's death meant our guide, the retired scientist Joseph Gordowski, became our main source of information about that Apollo summer nearly fifty years ago.

"We might want to get there early and maybe catch Gordowski before the tour." I made the suggestion as we walked up the sidewalk toward our office. Already I could tell we were in for another record-breaking scorcher of a day.

"How early?"

"Maybe one. We could always putter around the exhibits in the air-conditioning if Gordowski's not there yet."

"What about lunch?"

I had a ready answer. Actually, it was the real reason I'd suggested leaving early for PARI. "Let's ditch lunch for brunch. While we're out and sweating, we might as well go to the Over Easy Cafe. The breakfast crowd has passed."

The Over Easy Cafe was a great eatery only a few blocks away. Their food was primarily prepared using ingredients from area farms.

"Then we can swing by the office afterward," I said. "In the meantime, Blue's there to man the phones."

Nakayla eyed me suspiciously. "Which idea came first? The early meal or early interview?"

"It's a chicken and egg thing. Hard to separate which came first."

"Right. I'm guessing your egg will be a full-blown omelet and more biscuits than your waistline should encounter in one meal."

"You know, having a girlfriend who's a detective can be a real pain sometimes."

Nakayla laughed and quickened her stride. "Race you."

Forty-five minutes later, we returned to the office with about half an hour to spare. Nakayla decided to go online and see if she could find any background on the Cases, not only the brothers but the sons as well. I used the time to make some notes on what I wanted to ask Gordowski. I'd jotted down a few questions when my cell phone rang, flashing the ID for Chief Warrant Officer DeShaun Clark.

"DeShaun. Glad you're still alive. I've started searching milk cartons for your face."

"Hey, man. I got back to you as quick as I could. You don't ask for simple favors."

"If it was simple, I could do it myself."

He laughed. "Yeah, I forgot. Simple is your specialty."

"So what's so complicated about Eddie Gilmore?"

"I worked the unofficial route first. You know, called a few friends who could have access to records. All of them hit trip wires when they inquired about your man."

"Trip wires? What kind of trip wires?"

"The callbacks with 'who wants to know' attached. Evidently, Eddie Gilmore's history is still sensitive and remains classified, probably because no one's ever officially asked for it before."

"That's because his widow just accepted what the army told her. She's never pressed for more."

"That's what I figured," DeShaun said. "So I used your name."

"You what?" I felt a knot in my stomach. I'd gone to DeShaun to keep my name out of the inquiry. During my recovery in the VA hospital system, particularly at Walter Reed, I'd made waves testifying to Congress regarding what I considered insufficient care. The more politically oriented army brass (translation asskissers) didn't appreciate my outspokenness.

"Hey, man. Give me credit. Just to Nicky Diamond."

"Who's he?"

"A young lieutenant in army intelligence. His dad was Major Art Diamond."

I remembered the major. He'd been tough but fair-minded. DeShaun and I had run an investigation for him into some corruption he suspected in a supply chain. Materials were being pilfered and sold on the black market. Major Diamond had sent me a letter of encouragement after I'd lost my left leg.

"Lieutenant Diamond had heard his father speak highly of you."

"So you got the information?"

"Not exactly. I'd positioned my request as a way to get what you needed without other parties petitioning the Department of the Army Freedom of Information Act Program and enlisting some headline-seeking congressman in the process. I said you were trying to avoid an avalanche of paperwork for everyone."

"He didn't buy it?"

"Oh, he bought it and was sympathetic. But Gilmore's file is tagged for a review before being released. The knee-jerk reaction is to keep such information classified as long as possible."

"For over four decades?"

"I'm sorry," DeShaun said. "What army were you in? Mine never met a time-consuming protocol it didn't like. I made the assumption you wanted the information before another four decades elapsed."

I backed off. "You're right. Did Lieutenant Diamond propose a workaround?"

"Better than that. We didn't hear it from him, but Chuck McNulty lives in Charlotte."

"Who's Chuck McNulty?"

"The man who may have been with Eddie Gilmore when he died."

"How'd you find that?"

"Diamond discovered the files were linked and both classified."

"DeShaun, you are the man."

"What did you expect, brother? I learned from the best." He laughed that deep, throaty laugh. "And I also picked up a tip or two from you."

DeShaun gave me enough data on McNulty that I'd have no trouble contacting him in Charlotte. I thanked him and promised to let him know how things turned out.

We were too close to when we had to leave for PARI for me to begin a conversation with our new lead. And as any good investigator knows, there's no substitute for a person-to-person interview. Body language can speak as loudly as words. A trip to Charlotte needed to occur sooner rather than later.

It was too hot to take Blue to PARI where he'd have to stay in the car, so we left him in the office, perfectly content to sleep on the rug with a big bowl of water nearby. As we headed out of town, I briefed Nakayla on DeShaun's discovery.

"Will you try and reach McNulty when we return?" she asked.

"Yes. But I want that conversation as brief as possible. The only goal is to set up an in-person meeting, with luck either tomorrow or Friday."

"Do you think you should go to Charlotte alone? Keep it army to army?"

"I assumed you'd accompany me, but you raise a good point. McNulty might be more open if it's just me. We don't know what he and Eddie Gilmore experienced or what makes Eddie's service record classified. Maybe I should take this solo. And you might be more productive back here, especially if Joseph Gordowski proves helpful. And my trip could be a wild goose chase. Odds are Eddie's death has no connection to this case."

I took my eyes off the road to see Nakayla shaking her head.

"You're wrong there, Sam. Whatever you learn, connected or not, has an impact on Nancy Gilmore and Cory. Nancy lost a brother and a husband. Cory lost two uncles she never knew. They deserve any information we can give them."

I didn't say anything. Nakayla was right. I wasn't doing this to satisfy my own curiosity about the dead but to find answers that might bring a degree of comfort to the living.

Nakayla knew she'd made her point and graciously changed the subject. "I had a breakthrough with the Case family. I narrowed the suspects to Danny and Bobby."

"But they were the only ones alive in 1971," I argued. "Their sons hadn't been born."

"I'm including Loretta's death. If she was killed by a family member, it had to be Danny or Bobby."

Something about the way she phrased the assertion told me there was more to the story. Murder with a punchline.

"OK. I'll bite. How do you know it's Danny or Bobby?"

She laughed. "Because they're all named Danny or Bobby."

"What?"

"It's true. Each twin named his first son after himself. Bobby Lee Case Junior and Danny Ray Case Junior. Then when the second sons came, each twin named the boy after the brother. So one family is Bobby Case Senior, Bobby Case Junior, and Danny Case. The other family is Danny Case Senior, Danny Case Junior, and Bobby Case."

"Three Dannys and three Bobbys?"

"Yes. It must have been confusing unless they created nicknames like DJ or Bubba Bobby."

"That's almost as bad as George Foreman," I said.

"The boxer?"

"Yes. And father of George Junior, George II, George III, George IV, and George V. George Senior said he wanted them always to have something in common."

"Matching watches would have been nice and far simpler."

I laughed. "Maybe you should mention that to the Cases."

"The Cases," Nakayla mused. "How appropriate. Of all our cases, Sam, this is shaping up to be a strange one."

"I'm getting that feeling too." The scope was widening, not

narrowing. From outer space to Vietnam to Rat Alley and over a span of nearly half a century. Strange was hardly the word.

# Chapter 12

"I knew I recognized your name." Janet stood up from behind her computer at the counter of the Visitors Center. "Sam Blackman. I've read your name in the newspaper. The famous Asheville detective."

The enthusiastic heralding of my arrival by the PARI staffer drew the attention of a family browsing through a selection of model rockets. The boy and girl, who looked to be ten and eight, stared at me like I should start to fly at any second. Their parents appeared underwhelmed. I hurried to Janet, Nakayla trailing behind.

"Yes," I whispered, hoping Janet would follow suit. I forced a smile. "But I don't know about the famous part."

Janet lowered her voice. "You're here investigating the discovery of that skeleton, aren't you? I told Joseph and Theo, 'Sam Blackman just doesn't happen to show up a few days after something like that occurs.' Or you're helping Sheriff Hickman catch whoever started the fire. Am I right?"

I decided there was no point in trying to be evasive, especially since Janet had announced our presence to her colleagues. "We're friends with the niece of the man the FBI has identified as the victim, Frank DeMille. That's why we hoped to speak to Joseph Gordowski. He must have known Frank."

"I understand," Janet said. "Some agents from the FBI were out here this morning and met with Joseph and Theo."

"Theo Brecht?" I asked. "We met him when we were here before."

"Yes. Theo also worked for NASA at that time."

"Is he also a tour guide like Gordowski?"

"No. But he's out here a lot. Theo's helping to set up our secure data repository. It's a big project, and nobody knows the existing layout better."

I silently kicked myself for not asking him more questions, like how far back he went with the site.

"Then Theo sounds like someone we should also speak with," Nakayla said to Janet.

"Yes. But he's not here right now. I don't know if he'll be back today. He has another full-time job. I wish I had half his energy."

"Do you know how we could get in touch with him?" I asked.

Janet gave a quick glance at the family. The kids were narrowing their purchase down to a model of the International Space Station or the Saturn rocket. Janet licked her lips nervously. "I really shouldn't, but since you're helping the police, I guess it's all right." She sat and clicked several keys on her computer. She tore off the top sheet from a stack of Post-it Notes and wrote down a number. "Here's his cell."

I tucked the paper in my shirt pocket. "Thanks. Do you know if Joseph Gordowski is here yet?"

"I don't believe he ever left after speaking with the agents. He might be in the far exhibit room. He said there was a problem with one of the AV projectors."

I reached for my wallet. "The guided tour's the same price as the self-guided, right? Ten dollars?"

She waved her hand dismissively. "No charge. You're on official business."

I dropped a twenty on her keyboard and smiled. "Thank you, but I'd prefer you consider us visitors, not inquisitors."

"Like off the record?"

"Something like that. I wouldn't want the FBI to think we were checking up on them."

Nakayla and I found Joseph Gordowski bent over a multimedia projector. He held a screwdriver in one hand and a metal panel in the other. I couldn't tell if he was taking the projector apart or putting it back together.

"Mr. Gordowski?" I called his name as we entered the room.

He stepped away from the projector and turned to face us. The man could best be described as two spheres—a small one for a head and a larger one for a body with thin, protruding arms and legs. His round, pink face was complemented by a white beard and tousled white hair. Gold-rimmed glasses perched halfway down his nose. For a man in his seventies, he appeared to be wrinkle-free, one benefit of a plump body. Despite the Polish-sounding name, he looked like an Irish elf who enjoyed his stout.

He adjusted his glasses where he could peer through them. "Yes?"

I walked forward, extending my hand. "I'm Sam Blackman. This is my partner, Nakayla Robertson."

Gordowski set down the screwdriver and panel and shook our hands. "Right. Janet told me you're signed up for the two o'clock tour. And she said you are detectives."

"Yes. We were hoping to speak to you in private first. We're working with Frank DeMille's sister to find out what happened."

Gordowski sighed. "I can't believe it. All these years and Frank was less than a hundred yards away. Well, I don't know how much help I'll be, but as soon as I get this projector back together, I can talk until the tour starts."

"Can we help?"

He turned back to his work. "No. I changed the bulb. Just have to screw the casing back on and line it up with the screen. It will only take a minute."

Nakayla and I stood to the side as he finished the task.

After a final check that the projector functioned properly, he pointed down the hall. "I share an office with some of the other volunteers, but no one's here now. We can talk in private."

The office had a desk and a couple of chairs. NASA photographs hung on the walls as well as a calendar with initials written in the days. I assumed it was the volunteers' schedules.

Gordowski pulled a chair from behind the desk, and we sat in a makeshift triangle.

The elderly scientist didn't wait for me to begin. "First let me say how shocked and saddened I am to learn about Loretta Johnson's death. What a sweet, sweet girl. At least she was a girl when I first met her."

"And was that here at the tracking station?"

"Yes. I came in the summer of 1969. She had started working for the director, Dr. James Haskford, only a few weeks before."

"Were you here before Frank DeMille?" Nakayla asked.

"Yes. Frank came the following year. He'd just finished his master's in computer science." Gordowski shook his head. "Maybe the only true genius I've ever worked with. He not only mastered computer programming but he could see where it was going, possibilities that eluded the rest of us."

"Let me cut straight to the chase," I said. "Do you know anyone who would want to harm him?"

"No one here."

His answer certainly didn't rule out someone elsewhere.

"No one here," I repeated. "Are you saying that because you're not sure what was going on outside here?"

Gordowski scratched at his beard a moment. "Well, one of Loretta's brothers had to be escorted off the property one night."

"How did that happen?"

"This land was part of the Pisgah National Forest back then. Security was lax. I guess he just hiked in. The Case property bordered us."

"What did he want?" I asked.

"He was looking for Frank. I think he came at night knowing Loretta wouldn't be here. Frank wasn't here either. We were running some tests on the radio telescopes, you know, adjusting for sensitivity and filtering out any ambient signals."

I didn't know but nodded my head like I did.

"Anyway, he'd been drinking, probably some homemade moonshine, and when I told him Frank wasn't working that night, he tried to push past me. Believe it or not, I was stronger and more wiry in those days. I shoved him back and called for help. The night security guard who had been making his rounds at the time came as a reinforcement. We convinced the man Frank wasn't working. He said to tell Frank to stay away from his sister. That was the first time I learned Frank and Loretta were dating."

"What happened then?"

"The guard asked him how he got here. That's when he said he'd hiked in. How he did that drunk I'll never know. I told the guard to drive him home. I didn't want us responsible for him falling into a ravine."

Nakayla cut in, "Do you know which brother it was?"

"No. He just said Loretta was his sister and somebody had to look out for her. The guard wrote up a report for the files. That would have the name, but I'm sure it was shredded years ago."

"Were you here the night Frank disappeared?"

"Part of the night. We handed the communications off around two in the morning. My job was to oversee reception strength between *Apollo* and Houston. I worked closely with Frank because he would program the motion of the telescopes as the moon moved across the sky." He smiled. "Well, as the earth rotated, I should say."

"So Frank was still here when you left," I said.

"I assumed so, but then after he disappeared, we all were interviewed, and I remembered I didn't actually see him before I left. Loretta had come in looking for him, but I thought he was probably programming the next cycle of contact. He had to slew the instruments to the eastern part of the horizon where the moon would appear."

"Slew?" The word came from Nakayla and me simultaneously.

"That's right. Slew is what you call the action of moving the telescopes quickly across the sky. Frank was always spot on, both in picking up the signal and tracking it while we were primary contact."

"The Slew Meister," Nakayla said.

"Yes." Gordowski grinned and slapped his thigh with a pudgy hand. "I haven't heard that in years. Theo gave Frank that nickname. I think it pleased him. We were all kids back then on a grand adventure."

"It sounds like it," Nakayla agreed. "And other than one of Loretta's brothers, no one else comes to mind who might have had a conflict with Frank?"

"No. Frank was well liked, dedicated to his work, but not one to get in anyone else's business. You know what I mean? Pleasant but kind of in his own world."

"So he never confided in you?" I asked.

Gordowski looked genuinely puzzled. "Confided? About what?"

"Concerns about his work or the way the tracking station was being run."

Gordowski scratched his beard more vigorously. "Frank? No, he and Dr. Haskford got along really well. If there were any negative feelings at all, it might be that some of us felt a little jealous that Frank was Haskford's golden boy. But that's just the way it was. Frank outshone us all. He really was the Slew Meister."

I glanced at Nakayla to pick up the questioning.

"Have you seen where Frank's remains were uncovered?"

"Yes. I walked up there a few days ago."

"Is the terrain the same as in 1971?"

"No. The tree line was much closer then. That section would

have been in a stand of white pines. No one had any reason to go up there. The trees were cut back when the Department of Defense took over the facility."

"In other words, Frank's body would have been buried in woods, not pasture grass," Nakayla said.

"Yes. That's what I told the FBI. I imagine overturned earth could easily have been hidden beneath a layer of pine needles. The underbrush wasn't very thick, and like I said, there was no reason for any of us to go up there. And I remember we had three days of rain after Frank's disappearance."

"So whoever killed Frank must have used a shovel to bury him," Nakayla said. "Do you know where one might have been kept and who had access?"

Gordowski thought a moment. "The maintenance people would have kept those kinds of tools. They had a couple of metal sheds on the property. I'd be surprised if a shovel wasn't in one of them. Randall Johnson would be the man to ask."

"Loretta's ex-husband?" I interjected.

"Yes. He headed general maintenance. As far as I know, he's still in the area."

"Do you know why he and Loretta divorced?"

"No. We didn't keep in touch. Loretta was let go when the tracking station was ceded to the Department of Defense. Randall stayed on, but we never spoke much."

"How did you know they were divorced?"

"Loretta and I ran into each other in Asheville." He shook his head at the memory. "Jack of the Wood, if you can believe it. I went in for a drink and was surprised to see her with the band. We spoke afterward. This was a few years ago. She mentioned that she and Randall had split up. I didn't ask why, and she didn't volunteer any additional information."

"Was Randall there the night Frank disappeared?" I asked.

"I don't specifically remember seeing him, but I'm sure he would have been there. During the Apollo flights, we had all hands on deck while we were the primary communications site. Randall would be ready in case we had a generator problem or a breaker trip or an air-conditioning unit go down."

"And Loretta would have been there supporting Dr. Haskford?"

"Yes. Remember I said she came looking for Frank. That was right as I was leaving."

"What about Frank's car? Didn't anyone think it strange if it was still here but he was gone?"

Gordowski shook his head. "I believe he rode in with Dr. Haskford. Frank's car wasn't the most reliable. When Haskford couldn't find Frank, he just assumed Frank had hitched a ride with someone else."

Nakayla and I were silent for a moment, reflecting on the answers Gordowski had provided.

"Anything else?" he asked.

I swung my gaze around the office as if some inspiration could be found there. The NASA photographs on the wall—shots of the lunar surface, the enormous Saturn booster rocket, the blue marble of Earth seen from the moon—conveyed the magnitude of the scientific achievements during the glory days of the space program.

"Just a few more questions," I said. "Loretta and Randall were here because you said during the mission it was all hands on deck. Yet you said you left the facility while the others stayed."

Gordowski frowned, not appreciating what must have sounded like an accusatory statement. "Not during the whole mission but when we were the active tracking site. I made sure the communications between the astronauts and Houston mission control were maintained through various channels. Once the handoff to the next site happened, we would monitor those comm channels as long as we could but not be the primary source. My colleagues, with other tasks, would continue on but not come back as early as I would."

I nodded. "That's when Frank would program the radio telescopes for the next pass."

"Yes. And he'd run simulations to ensure everything worked perfectly. He guarded his computer programs like a mother hen protecting her chicks. Sometimes Haskford had to force him to go home and get some sleep. That's why the alarm went up so quickly when he didn't appear the next day."

"And who replaced him?"

"Theo Brecht. Fortunately, he'd come on board to work with Frank about six months earlier. He was then supposed to move on to one of the other tracking stations." Gordowski smiled ruefully. "As it turned out, he and I never left. We've both been through three incarnations."

"Three?"

"Apollo, NSA, and now PARI and its expansion."

Nakayla leaned forward in her chair. "NSA? You mean the National Security Agency?"

Gordowski's round face colored. "Well, we were supposed to always say Department of Defense, but we were the ears for the NSA. Russian satellites. Let's just leave it at that."

"And PARI's expansion?" I prompted.

"Housing secure data. The location and infrastructure are ideal. We're constructing a new building. That's why the grading equipment was here. Theo's doing most of the computer up-fitting work, but I help him as needed. It's like the old days, except my knees crack much louder when I get up from running cable underneath these floors." He shook his head. "Frank should be here with us. It's a real shame what happened to him."

Nakayla and I thanked him for his cooperation and then spent the next hour with about ten other visitors as Joseph Gordowski shared information and anecdotes throughout his guided tour.

As soon as we were on the road back to Asheville, I asked, "What do you think was the most significant thing we learned from Gordowski?"

"Two things," Nakayla answered. "Randall Johnson had access to a shovel, and Gordowski has no alibi. We have no proof that

Loretta came looking for Frank that night while Gordowski was still working. Loretta's now not around to verify or contradict his account."

"Yes," I agreed. "Frank could have disappeared later, and Gordowski would have had the rest of the night to bury him."

# Chapter 13

We returned to our office around four thirty. Nakayla took Blue out for a walk through Pack Square while I followed up on the Chuck McNulty lead provided by DeShaun Clark. I figured the Vietnam veteran had to be in his seventies and therefore retired. DeShaun said he'd been given the contact information through someone in the VA. Evidently, McNulty was receiving disability checks, but DeShaun hadn't discovered why.

The number rang seven or eight times before someone picked up.

"Hello?" A woman sounded out of breath.

"Is this the residence of Chuck McNulty?"

"Are you selling something?"

"No."

"Are you running for office?"

"No, ma'am," I said as politely as I could. "My name's Sam Blackman. I used to be a chief warrant officer in the U.S. Army, and I'm calling about a soldier who served with Chuck McNulty."

There was a pause as she digested the information. "Does he know you?"

"He doesn't. But he might be able to help a family who lost a loved one in the war."

Another pause. I held my tongue, not wanting to push her into a quick decision. It was clear McNulty was either there or the woman knew where to find him.

"I'm his daughter." The suspicion had subsided from her voice. "He's out in his rose garden. Hold on a few minutes. He doesn't have a cordless phone."

I waited, wondering if the daughter lived with the father because he could no longer take care of himself. Was he under some umbrella surrounded by a few rose bushes, hardly able to remember his own name let alone a fellow officer from close to fifty years ago?

I heard the phone receiver scrape across a hard surface.

"A chief warrant officer? What the hell? Did I steal something from the PX?" The gravelly voice held a hint of mischief.

"Is this Chuck McNulty?"

"Last time I checked my wallet."

"I'm Sam Blackman, Mr. McNulty. I was a chief warrant officer, and now I'm a private detective in Asheville. I'm hoping you might be able to help me. I'm helping a friend whose uncle disappeared in 1971. His remains were just uncovered last week."

"I read something about that. How does that concern me?"

"The man was Frank DeMille. His brother-in-law was Eddie Gilmore."

"Eddie?" The name came out as a whisper. "How did you get my name?"

"I still have ties inside the military. I was told you served with Eddie. I assume you were intelligence officers from the lack of information available."

"But what's Eddie have to do with any of this?"

"Eddie died shortly after Frank DeMille disappeared. Eddie might have been trying to help his brother-in-law in some way. Eddie's widow is still alive. She lost both a brother and a husband and doesn't know how or why. I'm trying to help her. I'm also trying to help her niece who lost two uncles."

McNulty was silent except for the rhythmic sound of breathing.

"All I want is a conversation," I urged. "Nothing may come of it, but at least I'll have pursued every avenue."

"This Frank DeMille, you say he disappeared around the time of Eddie's death?"

"Yes. A few months before."

"And he was murdered?"

"No doubt about it."

"That's very interesting," McNulty said.

"Why's that?"

"Because Eddie Gilmore was also murdered."

That revelation solidified the need to talk in person. I told McNulty I could come tomorrow if he was available. The drive to Charlotte was a little over two hours, and I offered to pick him up for lunch. We agreed on eleven thirty, and he would choose a place he liked as long as it offered enough privacy. I gave him my cell phone number in case he needed to reach me.

Nakayla and Blue had returned while I was talking to McNulty. I walked into her office where she was reading a page from a website.

She swiveled in her chair to face me. "Sounds like you're set for tomorrow with McNulty."

"Yes. He told me Eddie Gilmore was murdered."

Nakayla's eyebrows arched. "Really? Did he say who or why?"

"No. I didn't ask. I wanted to save those questions for our face-to-face." I looked past her to her screen. There was a picture of a sprawling building and the text headline, "History of NOAA's National Climate Data Center." I leaned in for a closer look. "What are you working on?"

"I'm learning about the National Centers for Environmental Information or NCEI as it's known."

"Is it in Asheville?"

"Yes. It's part of NOAA, the National Oceanic and Atmospheric Administration. The government never met an acronym it didn't like. Asheville houses the largest collection of weather data in the country. Back in 1951, the federal government moved all weather records here. We're talking about archives of the U.S. Weather Bureau, Air Force, and Navy. Now it archives weather data from all over the world, and it's housed in the Federal Building."

"Along with the FBI," I added.

"Yes, but Asheville's not the heart of the FBI. However, it is the heart of this country's weather records. I imagine the whole global warming debate has made those records even more critical." She turned back to the screen. "Some quick statistics. In 2014, the NCEI's website had more than one billion hits for information. NCEI stores over 17 petabytes of information, 35 petabytes counting the backup data."

"How much is a petabyte?"

"We'll have to look it up, but they say if 17 petabytes of weather information were an HD video, it would play for 230 years before repeating."

"That would keep Netflix busy."

Nakayla elbowed me in the stomach. "I'm serious. It's a big deal that most people here don't even know about."

"And this is important to us how?"

"You remember Janet said Theo Brecht had a full-time job in addition to his project work for PARI?"

"Yes."

Nakayla tapped her computer screen. "This is it. I found a reference to Brecht as one of the chief computer scientists overseeing the NCEI computer systems. From the space age to the information age, he's had quite a career."

"Did you phone him for an appointment?"

"No. You have the number Janet gave you. Can you call and arrange a meeting? Maybe late tomorrow afternoon if you think you'll be back from Charlotte in time."

I fished the number out of my pocket. "All right. I'll see if he wants to meet for a drink after work."

The call went to voicemail. I left my name and the brief message that we were helping Frank DeMille's family try to learn what happened. I said that Joseph Gordowski suggested we speak with him.

"You ready to call it a day?" I asked Nakayla. "I don't know about you, but I'm up for a drink."

She nodded toward Blue, who lay at her feet. "Our assistant has had a long day alone. Why don't we pick up a bottle of wine and I'll make pasta at my place? I'll keep Blue tonight if you're leaving early in the morning."

"Or we might check if I have a change of clothes in your bedroom closet. Then I won't have a long night alone trying to get to sleep."

Nakayla laughed. "I've got the remedy for that."

"I was hoping you would."

"Count petabytes."

Nakayla's bungalow in West Asheville was compact—two bedrooms, a kitchen, a dining room, and a front living room. She'd converted the smaller bedroom into a home office, and while she prepared pasta and salad, I took a glass of pinot grigio to her desk.

I logged onto her laptop to search for how many bytes I'd have to count to reach a petabyte. A one followed by fifteen zeroes. Was that a quadrillion? No matter. I'd be long dead before counting to a measly trillion.

"Ten-minute warning!" Nakayla yelled the alert so that I wouldn't take Blue out for a walk or wait until the last minute to wash up.

I used the time to look for the weather data Nakayla had found at the office earlier. That information had primarily been the history of how Asheville's weather data prominence came into being. I followed links to a webpage about NOAA, the National

Oceanic and Atmospheric Administration, and learned that the original name for Asheville's data collection had been the National Climate Data Center. In recent years, it had been merged into NCEI along with the National Geophysical Data Center and the National Oceanic Data Center. As the webpage expressed it, "From the depths of the ocean to the surface of the sun and from million-year-old ice core records to near real-time satellite images, NCEI is the Nation's leading authority for environmental information."

Nakayla was right. It was a big deal. All that comprehensive information linked together in an organization headquartered in little old Asheville, North Carolina. Well, our current heat wave would be one for their record books.

I read further regarding the NCEI's mission and explored other areas of the website, discovering I could access weather data from global to local, although some fees might apply, which only made sense as a way to help offset the cost of maintaining and expanding such a trove of information.

I also saw how important the computer programs would be for providing safe, secure access to the data. It would be the kind of project where those pioneering Apollo computer scientists like Brecht and Gordowski could still make contributions.

Nakayla stuck her head through the doorway. "Wake up. Dinner's on the table."

I exited the website and stood. "I'll have you know I've been working on our investigation."

"Solved it?"

"No. But if you need an ice core reading from twelve thousand years ago, I can get it for you."

"Good to know if we ever get a really cold case."

Dinner proved to be a success as Nakayla surprised me by adding boiled shrimp to the pasta.

Seated in the living room, we finished the bottle of wine, and then I helped Nakayla clean the dishes. When the last plate and pot had been shelved, I asked the important question.

"Are you really going to make me count petabytes tonight?"

"What would you rather count?"

"I was hoping I could count on you. You know you can count on me."

"Then I can count on you to take Blue out for his final pee."

"And then?"

She stepped forward and stroked my cheek with the back of her hand. "Then come to bed and leave Blue on the other side of the door."

It didn't take Sherlock Holmes to understand her meaning. We'd decided Blue's name in Latin should be Amorous Interruptus. Nothing like having an intimate encounter destroyed by a playful, seventy-five-pound coonhound jumping in your bed. It only took once to establish our closed door policy.

I drifted off to the Land of Nod without counting a single byte.

A howl penetrated the depths of my sleep, rudely pulling me into the world of the conscious. There were more howls, frantic and punctuated with pounding on the bedroom door as Blue flung himself against it.

I sat up as Nakayla stirred beside me. "What's wrong with Blue?" she asked.

Before I could say that I didn't know, a rushing noise sounded from outside, and the bedroom window flashed yellow with flames.

"Someone's setting fire to the house," I yelled. "Grab a robe and open the door. I need my leg."

My prosthesis lay on the floor by my side of the bed.

"There's no time," Nakayla shouted. "Lean on me."

I scooped up the leg as Nakayla ran to me in her nightgown. I wrapped my left arm around her shoulder, and we hobbled out of the bedroom. Blue was running in tight circles, his howls transformed into excited barks. Smoke poured into the house, and the flames appeared to be blazing at every window.

"Drop down," I said. "There's less smoke near the floor."

Nakayla let go of me, and we crawled through the kitchen to the back door. Flames were visible through the two panes in the upper half, but I hoped if we could open it, we could rush through into the safety of the backyard. I reached for the deadbolt. The brass was hot to the touch. I threw it and then grabbed the knob. Pain flooded my palm and fingers, but I turned it and pulled the door inward. The fire came with it, licking at the exterior panels and bringing the searing heat inside. The narrow back porch burned, but the steps to the backyard were relatively clear. The thought flashed through my mind that someone had thrown gasoline against the side of the house. The nearly instantaneous eruption of flames meant it wasn't kerosene or heating oil, which burn much slower. And gasoline's faster evaporation meant I could smell it.

"Can you jump across the porch to the back steps?" I asked.

"Yes, but what about you?"

"I'll be fine. Get out, and Blue and I will be behind you." I eased away from the burning door.

Nakayla stepped back about eight feet into the kitchen and then ran like a sprinter leaping from the starting blocks. She soared over the flames and landed beyond the steps, rolling across the grass in case her nightgown had caught fire.

I was left in the burning house in my boxer shorts with Blue and my prosthesis. I tossed the artificial limb through the burning doorway. Nakayla called Blue. He whined and shied away from the flames. I would have to spring across, pushing off on one leg, but there was no guarantee Blue would follow. I didn't think I could pick him up and throw him into the yard.

The smoke thickened, and I started coughing. Nakayla now yelled my name, urging me to get out. I looked back at Blue and then beyond him into the kitchen. My eyes went to the rug stretched beneath the sink. It was an inexpensive runner meant to provide a softer surface than the hardwood floor. Crawling on hands and knees, I moved to it, grabbed a corner, and dragged it to the door. I tossed the narrow side through, holding on to the bottom edge so that the rug lay across the threshold and onto the porch. The flames beneath were smothered.

"Come on, Blue. Let's go." I grabbed his collar and yanked him behind me as I crawled across the makeshift bridge. My eyes stung from the heat and smoke. I tumbled down the steps, and Blue broke free.

"Keep moving." Nakayla clutched my upper arm and pulled me farther from the house.

Sirens screamed above the crackle of burning wood. Nakayla sat on the ground beside me and tucked my head against her neck. Her skin was hot. Her tears falling on my face were cool.

Blue licked the exposed end of my amputated leg. Then he sat on his haunches and howled, adding his mournful wail to the sirens piercing the night.

# Chapter 14

Nakayla and I stood on the sidewalk, staring at the smoldering skeleton that three hours earlier had been her home. We were joined by Hewitt, Cory, and Shirley, who had rushed to the scene when Nakayla called from a neighbor's phone.

Cory brought clothes for Nakayla, Shirley brought biscuits for Blue, and Hewitt brought me an oversized bathrobe. I looked like my head was sticking out of the top of a red tepee. Neighbors offered coffee, condolences, and their homes as refuge from our horrifying experience.

It was seven in the morning. I'd attached my prosthesis but without the cushioning sleeve that kept the device from rubbing directly against the bare skin of my stump. My leg hurt, my burned hand hurt, but both paled in comparison to my seething anger.

Fire trucks and police vehicles were still present, and investigators meticulously searched for signs of arson. There was no doubt in anyone's mind that the fire had been deliberately set. The two questions I wanted answered were who and why.

An unmarked police car navigated through the street crowded with vehicles and bystanders. It parked in a driveway a few houses away. Detectives Newland and Efird emerged and hurried to us. The shock and concern on their faces preceded their words.

"Are you all right?" Newly asked.

"What happened to your hand, Sam?" Efird stared at the bandage wrapped around my left palm.

"We got torched," I said. "Gasoline on doors and windows. We made it out the back. The doorknob was hot enough to blister my skin."

Newly took a deep breath. "My God, that's more than arson. It's attempted murder."

"The arson investigators have already spoken to us, and they're starting to sort through the areas that have cooled. Nakayla's lost everything. What the fire didn't destroy, the water from the fire hoses did."

"We'll take this on," Efird said. "The arson task force has its job, but we'll expect their full cooperation." He turned to Nakayla. "Any ideas who might have done this?"

"No. We're working the Frank DeMille case, but we're not close to any accusations. At this stage, we're just gathering information through a few interviews."

"And Loretta Johnson?" Newly asked.

"Nothing," I said. "You made it clear we're not to get involved."

Efird and Newly looked at each other, but under the circumstances, they weren't going to challenge what they clearly didn't believe.

"Who have you interviewed?" Newly asked.

"Joseph Gordowski," I said. "He's a computer scientist who worked with Frank and is still involved with PARI. And Loretta, of course. We want to talk with Loretta's ex-husband, Randall Johnson, and Theo Brecht who worked with both Frank and Gordowski." I remembered I'd also set up a meeting with Chuck McNulty, but given the military's guarded reaction, I kept that to myself. And I realized I had to contact McNulty and reschedule.

Newly pulled a notepad from his pocket. "Give me those names again. We have to start somewhere."

I repeated the names and told Newly the contact information

was at the office. I had no cell phone and no keys, but I would get the information to them as soon as I could. Fortunately, Nakayla and I had parked on the street, so our cars weren't destroyed.

"What do you need?" Newly asked Nakayla. "I can generate a police report to get your insurance rolling."

"Thanks. Since I worked as an insurance investigator before joining Sam, I still have contacts, and I've already been in touch with them. I expect someone will be here shortly. Then I'll need to get a new phone and buy some clothes."

Hewitt had been quietly listening on the periphery. "Sam, we've got that key to your office you gave us to take Blue in and out. We'll let you in so Newly and Tuck can have that contact information."

"OK. I'll break away from here as soon as I can."

"Don't wait for my benefit," Nakayla urged. "I'll deal with the insurance people and get a replacement phone. Then I'll call you at the office."

Newly put his hand on her shoulder in a fatherly gesture. "Well, if there's anything we can do, don't hesitate to ask. Now we'd better check in with the fire marshal's crew and make it clear we're involved."

I started for my car when I realized I also had no keys to the CR-V.

"You need a lift, don't you?" Hewitt dangled the keys to his Jaguar. "Take mine. I'll get a ride with Shirley. Cory can stay with Nakayla and drive her wherever she needs to go." He tossed me the keychain. "Between the Jag and the red robe, people will think you're either a prince or a pimp."

I laughed for the first time that morning. "As long as they don't think I'm a lawyer."

I got the building's resident manager to let me into my apartment and managed to shower and dress in time to be at the Verizon store when it opened. Although they tried to sell me the latest and greatest, I was able to use a backup credit card to purchase my same model, keep my number, and restore whatever apps and data were tucked away in various clouds. There seemed to be so many clouds these days that a virtual sun had no chance of shining through.

I also kept a spare set of apartment and car keys at home, so I returned the Jag to Hewitt unscathed. He let me into our office and offered to take me to the CR-V whenever I wanted. I had other priorities, first of which was to reschedule Chuck McNulty.

It was a few minutes past ten when I called his number. Again, it rang and rang. Again, a woman answered. "McNulty residence." A different woman.

"May I speak with Mr. McNulty? Please tell him it's Sam Blackman."

"Mr. McNulty's not here." She sounded hesitant, like she shouldn't be telling me she was alone.

"Do you know when he'll be back?"

"No, sir. I'm the housekeeper. He wasn't here when I came at eight thirty. No breakfast dishes. No note. I let myself in with a key he gave to me."

"Does he have a cell phone?"

"Yes."

"Can you give me the number?"

"Yes. But that's no good."

"Why?"

"His cell phone is sitting on the dining room table."

"Then would you give him a message for me?"

"I need to get something to write with."

A clunk as she set the receiver on a hard surface. I remembered McNulty's daughter telling me the phone wasn't cordless. It could have been rotary for all I knew.

A few minutes later, a rustling and then, "OK. I'm ready."

"Tell him I have to postpone our meeting but to call me as soon as he can." I gave her both the office and cell phone numbers.

"Yes, sir. I'll leave the message right by his favorite coffee mug. He keeps it on the counter."

"Does it look like he used it?"

"No, and there's nothing in the coffeemaker either. Usually a pot lasts him through the morning."

I didn't like the answers I was getting, especially after the fiery attack. "Anything else unusual?"

A pause. "His newspaper was still in front of the door."

"Do you know his daughter's number?"

"Yes, I clean for her sometimes."

I debated whether to call his daughter myself, but that might set off a needless alarm. Better if the housekeeper contacted her. What could I do anyway? If there was a problem, the daughter would take action immediately. I was more than two hours away.

"Speak to his daughter," I said. "Let her know I called but you couldn't tell me when her father might be back. Say I'm anxious to talk with him and reschedule our meeting. If she wants to call me, you can give her my numbers."

The woman assured me she would do just what I requested. I heard a soft tremor in her voice and knew she was concerned.

I ended the call and rose from my desk, uncertain what the next step should be. Nakayla faced a hell of a task reorganizing her life. Fortunately, she was much better than me about backing up her laptop on a drive here at the office, but those things that are part of your personal history—photographs, letters, gifts, heirlooms connecting you to generations of family—those are things that can't be replaced. Although Nakayla was grateful for getting out of the fire alive, a part of her had to have been consumed by those flames. She'd experienced real loss and real heartbreak. I could only do so much, but finding the person responsible was at the top of my list.

I walked to my office window. Below, Pack Square appeared significantly devoid of tourists. Heat waves shimmered over the streets' black asphalt. The haze in the hot air blurred the ridges surrounding the city. What did Nakayla say? We were in a weather inversion? Thermal layers trapped upside down? How appropriate. The fire had turned our lives upside down. Our own personal inversion. Not a weather phenomenon but the consequence of an evil or sick mind. Someone we had provoked into murderous action.

A knock came from the hallway door. A hinge squealed. A man called, "Anyone here?"

The voice was familiar, but I couldn't place it.

"I'm coming." I entered the center room to find Transylvania County Sheriff Hickman just inside the open door.

"Got a minute?" Without waiting for an answer, he reclaimed his spot on the leather sofa.

"Coffee?" I offered and closed the door.

"No, thanks. Can't stay." He glanced at my bandaged hand. "I heard about the fire."

I sat in the chair opposite him. "News travels fast."

"Asheville's arson task force sent out an advisory to neighboring counties. We're pooling information because these fires might be linked."

"You think the fire last night is tied into forest fires?" I couldn't see a connection. Nakayla's house was specifically targeted, whereas the forest fires probably resulted from some psycho wanting to wreak havoc. Then the common denominator hit me.

"PARI. You think this is about PARI."

Hickman remained stone-faced. "Why do you say that?"

"Because your last visit to our office came after we spoke to Loretta and then she confronted you and her brothers. What you've never made clear is why you were at Bobby Case's house in the first place. You had no reason at that time to tie them to Frank DeMille's murder, but you were investigating the fire. You suspect the Cases had something to do with the fire at PARI."

Hickman folded his arms across his chest. "I can't comment on an ongoing investigation."

I nodded. "Then you'll understand I can't comment on an ongoing investigation."

"Your reason?"

"We're working for Hewitt Donaldson. Attorney-client privilege may not apply, but you can bet he'd take the matter to court." I didn't know what rationale might apply, if any, but I was banking that if Hewitt had burned the sheriff in court in the past, Hickman wouldn't relish another encounter.

"Now, sharing information," I added, "that's something else."

The stony expression morphed into someone biting into a lemon.

"Routine," he said. "That fire originated close to the property line between the Cases and PARI. I thought they might have seen something."

"Do you think they would be so careless as to set a fire so close to their own land?"

He shook his head. "I told you it was routine."

His answer didn't square with my instincts, but I had no evidence to challenge him.

"Do you know how the fire started?" I asked.

"We have our suspicions. Given the wind direction and the way it spread, we think we found the source. There's a rock bluff, a bald of granite that would have allowed an unimpeded roll down to the lower pines."

"Roll of what?"

"A tire. You stuff the inside with old rags, soak them in an accelerant, light them, and then send the blazing tire on its way. It throws off flaming pieces and then continues burning when it comes to rest. Rolling it off the bald gives some distance between the arsonist and the tire's location."

"Nobody rolled a tire into Nakayla's house," I said. "They poured gasoline around the exterior. The flames engulfed us in a matter of seconds."

"That's what the fire marshal reported. I just wanted your

firsthand account. Our tire arsonist probably used kerosene-soaked rags. They wouldn't burn off as quickly."

I stared at him. He didn't come to the office to ask me about gasoline.

Hickman smiled. "I hear the Cases think you had something to do with Loretta's death."

"I can't stop them from thinking."

"And I don't have enough evidence to stop them from acting." He stood. "You and your partner watch yourselves. And if you come across something of interest, I'll appreciate a call."

He dropped a business card on the coffee table, gave a two-fingered salute, and went on his way.

During our brief conversation, my cell phone and the office phone had rung. The voicemail on the mobile was from Chuck McNulty.

"Mr. Blackman. Sorry I missed your call. Sometimes I get restless and go on an early morning drive. We can reschedule at your convenience."

I thought the voicemail on the office line would be a duplicate. I was wrong.

"Mr. Blackman. This is Theo Brecht returning your call. I'm free after five today if you want to meet. Give me a time and place. I promise not to hit you with a door. Thanks."

I would get back to both of them, but my first call would be to Detective Tuck Efird. I wanted only one thing from him—the phone number for his ex-wife. It was time to confront the Aliens over Asheville.

# Chapter 15

The Appalachian Mountains are some of the oldest in the world. Geologists claim their height could have topped the Himalayas before eons eroded them to the rounded, tree-covered peaks of today. In fact, the eastern part of North Carolina was created from the debris that time and weather whittled off these ancient ridges and deposited into the ocean. Western North Carolinians cite this as the scientific reason that Western North Carolina barbecue is superior. Who wants vinegar-soaked pork cooked by someone living on debris?

The rivers meandering through the Appalachians are also primeval. The New River, originating near Boone and flowing through Virginia and West Virginia, is new in that it is believed to be the second-oldest river in the world, edged out by the Nile.

Asheville's waterway sporting such a primitive pedigree is the French Broad. It flows as a bisector splitting apart Asheville and West Asheville. The names are more than a compass orientation. They were not once but twice separate towns. In 1917, a final vote in West Asheville for consolidation passed by a whopping 169–161. But the ballot result didn't eradicate West Asheville's distinct identity, and residents take pride in their side of the river. Up until a match ignited gasoline, Nakayla had been one of them.

The east bank of the French Broad had been the site of Asheville's industrial district. Both the river and the railroad offered transportation benefits, and the flatter terrain made construction of factories and warehouses practical. But as the years passed, Asheville wasn't immune to the decline of American industries. Factories closed, warehouses emptied, and jobs evaporated, leaving only the carcasses of abandoned buildings.

Then, in the 1980s, a vision began to take hold: the transformation into a new kind of manufacturing—artists in studios making and selling their creations. Over thirty years later, the River Arts District, RAD for short, housed a variety of artisans whose work ranges from ceramics and glassblowing to sculpture and painting. Rebirth emerging from the floodplain of an ancient river.

So I stood by that river in front of what once had been a cotton mill. The old brick structure matched the address Detective Tuck Efird had given me for his ex-wife. He said she was a gifted and nationally known artist. Bernadette Efird worked in the tedious, slow, and painstaking craft of setting stones, minerals, gems, or tiles to create abstract or realistic images. A master of mosaics.

In contrast, her studio also had an office for her other passion, this one centered around HASTE, the Human-Alien Secret Treaty Exposé. My investigative career had led me into some strange situations and strange interviews. I had the feeling I was about to be propelled into an entirely different level of strangeness.

Nakayla and I had gone on several Studio Strolls as they are called, and I had been through the old cotton mill before. But those events are so popular, I only remembered flowing with a steady stream of people. If I'd seen Bernadette Efird's work, it was lost in the multitude of art that had been on display.

I found the studio labeled "B-Creative" with a honeybee and flower depicted in the door's stained-glass window. B for Bernadette, I assumed. A bell tinkled as I stepped into a showroom filled with mosaics hanging on the walls, mosaics on stands, and mosaics lying flat on counters. Each was tagged with a colored dot that I figured correlated to its price. Many of the designs were abstract, but there were also realistic images of mountain vistas, cats, dogs, even a possum. Bernadette was evidently a gifted artist who used stone, tile, and glass in place of brush, paint, and canvas.

"I'm in the back," a woman called. "Be with you in a moment."

Since I wasn't there to shop, I headed toward the rear door and the sound of the voice. Then a specific mosaic caught my eye. It hung just to the side of the door leading to a back room. The picture was composed of colored stones and glass. Five figures. The iconic alien I'd seen on the banjo player's T-shirt and four human toddlers. They stood side by side and hand in hand with the slender alien in the center. The four children, two boys and two girls, varied in ethnicity. They were dressed in rainbow-colored robes while the alien was yellow, naked, and genderless. The background was a distant ridge with two radio telescopes framing a setting sun.

"May I help you?"

I looked from the mosaic to a middle-aged woman standing in the doorway. She wore a long, heavy apron over a stained, long-sleeved shirt and black jeans. Her round face was framed by short brown hair going gray at the roots. Her smile faded as her hazel eyes widened with recognition.

"Sam Blackman?"

"Yes. Sorry, I didn't remember if we'd met."

"We haven't. I've seen your picture in the newspaper and heard Tuck talk about you. Are you here as a shopper or a detective?"

"I'm afraid for the moment I'm a detective." I swept my left arm toward the display room. "But I'm very impressed. I may need to come back as a shopper."

Her face turned grim. "This is about PARI then. The skeleton up on the ridge?"

"Yes."

"Well, you'd better come in and sit down. I can talk, but I'll have to stop and tend to any customers."

I followed her into a second room, this one unfinished except for several workbenches with mosaics in various stages of completion. In one far corner were stacked boxes and palettes of assorted tiles. Along an exposed brick wall, metal bins held broken pieces as well as stones and glass. I saw a gem cutter and polisher that showed Bernadette refined her own materials.

In another corner, a cage enclosed a desk and two chairs, a laptop and desktop computer, and three standing filing cabinets. Clearly, this lockable space served as the office without the expense of creating actual walls. Hanging on the wire beside the cage's door was the mosaic of colored text reading "Make HASTE." Thanks to Tuck Efird's warning, I knew what it stood for.

"Would you like some tea?" Bernadette asked. "It's herbal."

Her offer reminded me of the awful tea Loretta had served. "No, thanks. I don't want to take any more of your time than necessary."

She pointed for me to take the chair behind the desk. "In case I need to get up," she explained. "Now, how can I help?"

"The niece of Frank DeMille, the man whose remains were discovered last week, is a friend. My partner and I are trying to find out what happened. The Transylvania County sheriff and the FBI have jurisdiction, but we're doing what we can to ensure the investigation is as thorough as possible."

"Tuck's not involved?"

"Not with that one."

She raised an eyebrow. "That one?"

"It's complicated. The woman who was murdered in Rat Alley the night before last. She's Tuck's case. Years ago, she was Frank DeMille's fiancée."

Bernadette made a little O with her lips.

"Yes," I said. "She's also connected to PARI. She worked there during the Apollo days. So I have little pieces of a puzzle stretching out nearly fifty years."

"Not a puzzle, Mr. Blackman. A mosaic."

I had to smile. Of course she'd see it that way. Harder than a puzzle because there was no box top picture for reference or precut puzzle shapes. It was like one of her creations had tumbled into a heap and only she had the vision to put the pieces back into a recognizable image. Had Loretta known the final picture? Was that why she was killed?

"I've read the online material about HASTE," I said. "I know PARI figures strongly into your organization's investigation."

Now she smiled. "Do I look as crazy as people say I am?"

"You don't look crazy to me. I don't know what other people say."

"Come now, Mr. Blackman. Don't patronize me. I'm sure Tuck called me a UFO nutter."

"Something like that," I admitted.

She nodded. "I never could convince him otherwise. Which theory do you think sounds crazier? That we're on the third planet of an insignificant star in a galaxy that's one of countless galaxies and that we're all alone because conditions for life exist nowhere else and God put all his eggs in one basket? Or God wasn't wasteful, and a cosmos filled with suns and planets statistically must produce life because the sheer numbers overwhelmingly demand it?"

"But here? PARI?"

"Why not?" In rapid succession, she ticked off points on her fingers. "One, PARI is isolated. Two, PARI was set up for interspace communications. Those signals weren't just a one-to-one secure-line chat but sent out through the solar system. Three, UFO sightings are concentrated over Western North Carolina. Four, PARI goes dark when the Apollo program ends, and immediately in come the black SUVs, enhanced security, and even poison ivy planted on the perimeter."

"Wasn't that simply eavesdropping by the Department of Defense?"

"Not just the DOD but the NSA—a global operation. Who better to conduct conversations with alien beings?"

"But then they closed it down."

Bernadette rolled her eyes. "They said they closed it down. What better cover for renovations?"

My mind flashed to some HGTV series. *How to Spruce Up Your Intergalactic Spaceport.*

"That's why they expanded the whole tunnel system," she continued. "I'm not saying PARI's not a legitimate educational facility. But what's important is what lies underneath that visitors and most staff don't know exists. We've talked to former employees who confirm there are tunnels. The question is how many and how far down do they go?"

She halted and gave a determined look, daring me to dispute her irrefutable evidence.

"Then what is HASTE's mission?" I asked. "To sound the clarion call?"

"To reveal the truth, Mr. Blackman. We believe contact has been made, technology shared, and some ultimate goal established. Maybe it's a crossbreeding of the species like aliens orchestrated between Cro-Magnons and Neanderthals."

I wanted to shout "Time out" but feared she would only digress into a lecture on Bigfoot.

"I mean, what's spreading faster than the plague?" she asked.

I shrugged, fearful of venturing a guess.

"Ancestry.com. The aliens helped us map the human genome, and now these DNA companies are harvesting the data." She leaned forward and whispered like we were suddenly under surveillance. "Data about our very makeup. And guess who's moving into data storage big time?"

That question did prompt my response. "PARI."

She nodded vigorously. "Exactly."

"So one way or another, you see the aliens as an existential threat."

"Not necessarily. Like our name says, we want to expose that there's already a secret alliance. Our goal is to bring it out into the open. The fact that superior beings haven't eradicated us is reassuring that their intentions are peaceful. But that doesn't mean we ignore what's happening. I might be more afraid of who's representing our species."

"Does everyone in HASTE feel the same way?"

"For the most part. Otherwise, they drop out."

"Do you know the Case family?"

Her body stiffened, and her eyes grew wary. "Those Bobby-Danny Cases?"

"Yes. One of them has an alien on a T-shirt saying, 'I'm coming for you.'"

"That's Danny Number Two, not Junior. He reads our online newsletter and comes to meetings. He's not one of our more enlightened members." She paused. "It's funny you should bring him up. He called me yesterday."

"About what?"

"About tunnels. The ones under Asheville."

"There are tunnels under Asheville?"

"That's the lore. One running from the Masonic Temple to city hall. Another down Patton Avenue. They did find underground bathrooms at Pack Square when they were doing renovations a few years ago."

I saw the connection. "He was asking about Rat Alley, wasn't he?"

"Yes. He wanted to know if it was part of the tunnel network. I told him I didn't know. That was before I heard about the woman being killed."

"He was looking for other ways in and out. Could he believe aliens were involved?"

Bernadette spread her hands. "I believe Danny Number Two could believe anything."

"And act upon it?"

"Like how?"

"Like try to burn down PARI."

She paled. "You think he started that forest fire?"

"It or another." I looked at my left palm, bandage gone but still red from the burn. In my mind, I relived the flames crackling around Nakayla's back door.

"I can't assure you that he wouldn't."

The bell tinkled from the front room. Bernadette stood. "I have to go."

I rose and shook her hand. "Thank you. You've been very helpful."

"I saw you looking at the mosaic by the door. That's my hopeful vision—peace and harmony. But there's another vision on this side of the door. The dark vision. I'm afraid that's the one Danny sees."

I followed her out of the cage. Hanging on the spot on the wall directly behind the first mosaic was a nearly identical one. Five figures. An alien being and four small companions. However, the setting sun was in total eclipse, the rainbow-colored robes were black, and the four children were eyeless, fleshless skeletons.

# Chapter 16

After leaving Bernadette, I spent a few minutes in my parked CR-V thinking through the next steps. Danny the banjo player, a description simpler than Danny second son of Bobby the twin, rose to top priority. But I didn't want to see him or his family alone. Going up Dusty Hollar Road might be a one-way trip.

Normally, Nakayla would have accompanied me, but she had her hands full. Still, she deserved an update, and I was anxious to learn how she was faring.

My call went straight to voicemail without a single ring. Nakayla must not have replaced her phone yet. I called Cory.

"Sam, I'm with Nakayla. Do you want to talk to her?"

"Yes, if I'm not interrupting anything."

Cory laughed. "I think you rank above buying shoes."

There was a momentary pause, and then Nakayla came on the phone. "Where are you?"

"In RAD. Tuck's ex-wife had some interesting information about Danny the banjo player and PARI." I gave her a condensed version of the conversation, leaving out the more fantastic alien theories.

"So we need to see him," Nakayla said.

"Where are you?"

"In Tops. Borrowing clothes is one thing, but shoes are a little more personal. And Cory's feet are smaller."

Tops for Shoes was a huge shoe store in downtown Asheville. Shoe lovers didn't just shop there. They made pilgrimages.

"Should I bring a U-Haul?" I asked.

"Not till I get my insurance check. I'm meeting my agent at two. Also, the dealership is bringing a replacement key for my car. Do you want to see Danny Case after that?"

"I think you should take care of what you need to and not worry about the investigation. I'll meet you at my apartment this evening."

There was a long pause. I knew what she was thinking.

"Sam, there's no way you're going to confront any of the Cases alone. Losing a house is one thing. Losing you is another."

"I wasn't going alone. I thought I'd see if Newly or Tuck can go with me."

"On what pretext?"

"Simple. To ask about tunnels and aliens. Then we'll see if we can bring the questions more down-to-earth."

Another pause followed by a sigh. "All right. But you promise me you'll go with someone."

"I will. And I'll keep you posted."

"Sam, I love you."

"I love you too. Now go shop."

I dropped the new phone on the passenger's seat and started the engine. I planned to return to the office and see if Newly or Tuck would join me in calling on the Cases. Showing up in an unmarked police car promised greater impact than arriving in my Honda.

Under normal procedures, the homicide detectives wouldn't let me tag along, but the attempted murders of Nakayla and me elevated the stakes. I counted on Newly and Tuck to feel some concern for my safety.

The phone rang. I kept the transmission in park and answered. "Hello."

"Is this Sam Blackman?" The voice was old but familiar.

"Yes."

"Theo Brecht here. You left me a message. Sorry to be so late getting back to you."

"That's OK. Let's just say I've had a long morning as well."

"You said you wanted to talk about Frank DeMille. Does this have anything to do with Loretta's death?"

"Possibly. But I'm working for Frank's family. You might be able to help us, and I was hoping we could meet in person."

"Certainly. Today, I'm at the Federal Building. I usually knock off between five and six. We could grab a drink nearby."

I mentally calculated how the afternoon might play out.

"That would work," I said. "Are you OK if I get tied up and have to cancel?"

"No problem. Or if you need to slide it later, I'll just keep working. They're used to my coming and going at odd hours. Call this number when you know your schedule."

Again, I dropped the phone on the seat. Again, it rang. I glanced at the number to see if perhaps Brecht had changed his mind and was calling me back. I didn't recognize it, but the 828 area code suggested it was local.

"Sam Blackman," I answered, ready for sharp words if some telemarketer was spoofing an Asheville identity.

"This is Special Agent Lindsay Boyce. How are you, Sam?"

"Well, I guess you've heard Nakayla and I have had a little upheaval in our lives."

"I did. I'm really glad to hear you're both OK."

Lindsay Boyce was head of the FBI's Resident Agency in Asheville. We'd crossed paths on a few cases. For a fed, she was a straight shooter. She didn't throw her government badge around like it was a royal scepter. But she was no pushover either. Her trim, slim, attractive body housed a spine of pure steel. And although her concern sounded genuine, I knew there was more to this call than checking on our well-being.

"Listen," she said. "I know things must be crazy, but would you and Nakayla have time to meet this afternoon?"

"Nakayla's slammed, but I could. Where and when?"

"My office. Say four thirty?"

The meeting would jam up my afternoon plans, but the FBI was the FBI.

"OK. I'll see you then."

I dropped the phone on the seat and glared at it, daring the device to ring again. It only flashed the time. One o'clock. If I wanted to see the Cases and get to the FBI by four thirty, I needed to head to Dusty Hollar Road as soon as possible. My office would have to wait. I sighed, picked up the phone, and speed-dialed Newly.

He echoed Agent Boyce. "How are you, Sam?"

"Still pissed that someone tried to kill us. Where are you?"

"Physically or with the investigation?"

"Physically."

"At my desk. What's up?"

"How would you and/or Tuck like to ride with me to see Danny Case the banjo player?"

He paused, evidently surprised by the request. "You think that's a good idea?"

"Sheriff Hickman came by the office this morning asking about last night's fire. It became clear to me he suspects one or more of the Case family of setting the PARI fire. He was interested in how ours started."

"And were the methods the same?"

"No."

Another pause. "Well, I don't see how we make a play. True, we're working Loretta's murder, but the Cases have given their statements, and I'm not going to make a move until I get the ME's report."

"In his statement, did Danny the banjo player mention tunnels and aliens?"

Newly laughed. "You caught me. It's the one question I forgot to ask him. Come to the station. We'll take my car."

I rode in the front passenger's seat as Newly drove the unmarked. Efird had remained at the station, waiting on Loretta's autopsy report. I'd briefed Newly on my conversations with Sheriff Hickman and Bernadette, plus the phone calls with FBI Special Agent Boyce and Theo Brecht. I still didn't mention Eddie Gilmore's army buddy, Chuck McNulty, because he appeared to have no connection to Loretta's death or Nakayla's fire, the two crimes falling within Newly's jurisdiction.

"I don't understand how I'm supposed to explain your being with me," Newly said. "Do I mention Bernadette?"

"No. Danny may think she came to us and betrayed him. We should put it all on me and my theory that aliens could be involved. As preposterous as that sounds to you and me, Danny might have a different reaction. Tell him I pitched that idea to you and I said he might know something about it. I saw the T-shirt he was wearing at Jack of the Wood. You say you think I'm nuts, but to humor me and to keep me from bothering him and his family, you agreed to come with me."

Newly shook his head. "You're right about one thing. I think you're nuts. But if you're willing to look foolish, I'll stand on the sidelines and cheer you on."

We were about halfway to our destination when Newly's cell phone rang. He glanced at the number. "It's Tuck." He pressed the Accept icon, then pressed again. "What's up, partner? I've got you on speaker with Sam, if that's all right."

"Sure. He'll weasel the information out of you anyway. Loretta's autopsy just came through. As was obvious, death was caused by strangulation. No sign of a struggle, no skin under her fingernails.

No bruising other than her neck and the subconjunctival hemorrhages in her eyes."

I knew those hemorrhages were ruptures of the small blood vessels in the eye and could be the result of strangulation.

"Whoever killed her knew what he was doing," Newly said. "Fast and lethal. Loretta probably couldn't utter a sound."

"Anything distinctive about the bruises?" I asked.

"There was no cutting through the skin," Efird said. "The ME's pretty confident the killer used a wire but one that would compress the carotids and windpipe, not sever them."

"Like a guitar string," I said. "The thicker wound ones for the lower notes."

Newly shot me an approving glance. "Yeah. A guitar string. Not exactly a scarcity in the Case family."

Nakayla and I had already crossed paths with a killer who garroted his victim with a guitar string when we'd investigated a suspicious death at the Carl Sandburg farm. A guitar string made a beautiful sound when in the hands of a master picker. In the hands of an assassin, a guitar string made no sound at all when pulled tight around a human throat.

We turned onto Dusty Hollar Road, and the conversation stopped. Like me, Newly's thoughts must have turned inward as to how we would handle Danny. My presence would change the dynamics of Newly's earlier interview at the police station. Newly would be looking for inconsistencies. I would be looking for connections to the fires.

We'd just rounded the bend approaching Loretta's house when Newly braked the car to a sudden stop. "What the hell?" he muttered.

A pickup truck was parked next to the front porch. The tailgate was down, and two straight-back chairs were loaded in the bed. No one was visible. Newly eased the car off the road and onto Loretta's driveway. He stopped again, silencing the crunch of gravel before we got too close.

"Have you had forensics go through the house and release it?" I asked.

"Tuck and I came out with a team yesterday afternoon. We didn't find anything that shed any light, but fingerprints needed to be run, her computer drives analyzed, and personal papers reviewed. We sealed the house, and until we know what her will might have stipulated as to heirs, we weren't allowing anyone on the premises. That's clearly posted on the front door." He gave a pat to the left side of his chest where he wore his shoulder holster. "Are you armed?"

"Yes. My Kimber was safely in my car during the fire. Now it's tucked in my back."

"Good. But you don't pull unless I do." He opened his door. "Easy does it. I'd like to get the drop on them."

We walked along the edge of the driveway, keeping our footsteps on the soft earth and not the gravel. When we reached the rear of the pickup, Newly stopped.

"Aren't we going in?" I whispered.

"No. I want us to witness them actually removing something from the house." He leaned against the tailgate and folded his arms.

I did the same.

A few minutes later, the backside of faded blue jeans and a dingy T-shirt filled the doorway. As the figure took slow steps onto the porch, I saw he was carrying one side of a flat-screen TV. His cohort emerged, and I recognized one of Loretta's twin brothers. I didn't know which, although he appeared to be the one with the more prominent beer gut. His mouth popped open like a sinkhole appearing in his gray beard, and for a moment, he nearly lost his grip on the television.

"Taking that to a repair shop, Bobby?" Newly said. "I didn't realize it was broken."

The younger man facing away snapped his head around and froze. Since he wasn't Danny the banjo player, I assumed he was Bobby Junior.

"We were afraid someone would steal it," the old man answered.

"I see. So you're protecting it by stealing it first."

Sweat beaded on Bobby Senior's forehead. "It ain't stealing when it belongs to you."

"Oh, where did you find Loretta's will? We looked for it yesterday."

"Well, who else is it going to belong to than her next of kin?"

"I don't know," Newly said. "That's why we're looking for her will. That's why this house was sealed. That's why I'm inclined to lock you both up for breaking and entering."

"You can't do that," the old man yelled.

"And an additional charge of resisting arrest." Newly pulled back his coat to reveal his pistol in his shoulder holster. He unsnapped the flap.

Bobby Junior's eyes widened. "Pa, me and the boys have got play dates. I can't afford to go to jail."

"Does your twin brother know you're here looting his sister's house?" Newly asked.

Bobby Senior said nothing.

"I didn't think so." Newly moved his hand from his holster to the phone on his hip. "Let's call him so he can bring your bail."

The old man shook his head. "Look, this is a big misunderstanding."

"A big misunderstanding," Newly repeated. "Then we'll sort it out. After you put everything back."

Newly and I followed as the two reversed their steps. If they had any guns, carrying the television made it impossible to get to them. When they'd set the flat-screen back in place, Newly ordered them to unload the chairs. We both accompanied them to the truck and back. Bobby Senior started to slide his chair under the dining room table, but Newly stopped him.

"Set the chairs in the middle of the room back to back."

They did as instructed.

"Now sit down."

Both men glared at Newly. The detective smiled and reached for his phone. They sat. I realized they were more afraid of Newly calling Bobby Senior's twin than the gun. I also understood Newly had them seated back to back so that they couldn't communicate with body language during the questioning.

Newly stepped so close to Bobby Senior that the mountaineer had to crane his neck to look up. "You see, Bobby, when we have a house under seal, we come by frequently to check it."

I figured that was an exaggeration, but at least it explained why we were here.

"Why's he with you?" Bobby Senior asked.

"He's Sam Blackman. He's a private detective and looking into the death of Frank DeMille. You remember Frank, your sister's fiancé. The man you threatened and the man who has now been determined to have been murdered."

"Murdered?" Bobby Junior whispered.

"We had nothing to do with that." Bobby Senior's forceful denial sounded directed more to his son than to Newly and me.

Newly held up his palm to stop the man from saying anything further. "We know you hiked into the tracking station to threaten him when your sister wasn't there."

Gordowski had told us one of the twin brothers did that, but he hadn't known which one. Newly must have figured the odds were fifty-fifty, and if he was wrong, Bobby Senior would probably give up his brother.

"DeMille wasn't there," he said. "And I just wanted to talk to him. Nobody threatened him."

"You expect me to believe if you tried it once and failed, you didn't try again?"

"I ain't expecting nothing of you. I'm telling you I didn't threaten the man."

Newly glanced at me, signaling it was okay to ask a question.

"Then why did Loretta tell me you were there the night Frank DeMille disappeared? That you showed up wearing dirt-coated overalls?" This wasn't true, of course, but I thought I might as well play the odds too.

Bobby Senior leapt from the chair like it had been electrified. He wheeled to face me. "That's a goddamned lie." He hurled the words at me in a spray of spittle.

"I heard her song," I said. "I heard her special verses."

The old man looked down at his son. "Tell him, Junior. We didn't know where that came from. She never told us she was going to sing. She never told us what those verses meant."

"That's right," his son agreed. "We saw her talk to you, then she sings this song, and then she's dead. We thought you killed her. She never told us you were a detective."

That was probably true. I got the distinct impression Loretta didn't want her family nosing into her business.

I looked at Bobby Senior. "So you're calling your sister a liar."

"If she told you I showed up the night DeMille disappeared, then yes. Hell, I don't even know what night that was."

"Then how do you know you didn't show up?"

That stopped him for a moment. "All right," he said. "We didn't like him."

"We?" I prompted.

"My brother, Danny, and me. DeMille was an outsider. We knew he'd break Loretta's heart and break up the band. Yes, we'd talked to him. It was at one of the fiddler conventions while Loretta was backstage. But we didn't touch him. We just told him how things stood. He told us where he stood, and he wasn't backing down. He also said he wouldn't tell Loretta what we'd tried to do. Danny and I had to respect him for that. So we knew he and Loretta had their minds set, and Loretta had the stubbornest head of all of us."

"And you never bothered him after that?" I asked.

"No. Looking back, I wish he hadn't disappeared. At the time, we thought we'd been right. He'd run out on her and broken her heart. Now it turns out Randall Johnson was the only one who hurt her."

"Hurt her how?" Newly asked.

"Cheated on her. With some of the younger women who came to him for flat-pick guitar lessons. He was learning them how to play and play around. Loretta caught him tuning more than their guitars, if you know what I mean."

"And she threw him out?"

"Yep. She would have made him disappear if she could have." He sighed. "Too bad. Randall was a damn fine musician. The band sure missed him."

"And they also met at PARI," Newly said.

"Yep. Loretta met both DeMille and Randall there. She would have been better off if that place never existed."

"Even today?"

Bobby Senior shrugged. "There's stories of strange goings-on. I pay it no never mind."

"Well, somebody tried to burn it down," Newly said. "And somebody tried to burn down the house where Sam was staying. You know, the man you said you thought killed Loretta."

Both men stiffened.

"Hey, man," Junior exclaimed. "I know nothing about that."

"What about your brother, Danny?" I asked the younger man. "He feel the same way?"

"I ain't his keeper. You'll have to talk to him yourself."

Bobby Senior put a hand on his son's shoulder and gave a nearly imperceptible squeeze that silenced him. "Danny was with me," Bobby Senior declared.

Newly and I looked at each other. Neither of us had said when the fire occurred.

# Chapter 17

After giving Bobby Senior and Bobby Junior a severe lecture on the crime of disturbing a police-sealed location, Newly let them off with a warning. He further admonished them that the forensics team had taken numerous photographs of everything, and if so much as a pencil turned up missing, he would come after them. We left after watching them relock the front door. I was anxious to get to Danny the banjo player before his father and brother had time to coach him on a story. The fact that Bobby Senior so quickly proclaimed himself as Danny's alibi had all the veracity of a politician's stump speech.

According to GPS, Danny's house was only a mile farther down Dusty Hollar, and Newly pushed his unmarked Chevy Malibu until the road's washboard surface rattled my teeth. The noise was so loud, I barely heard my phone ring. The screen flashed with Hewitt Donaldson's number.

"Where are you?" the attorney asked.

"With Newly. We're almost to Danny's house. What's up?"

"I've learned something I thought you might find interesting. I'll leave it up to you whether you want to share it with Newly."

I glanced at the detective. He was concentrating on the bumpy road, but I saw he leaned a little closer in an effort to hear me.

"Okay," I said.

"I called around to several lawyers I know who specialize in wills and estate work. Most litigators who've faced me in court wouldn't give me the time of day, but the will and estate shysters are a group I just haven't had the chance to piss off."

Hewitt had never been one to endear himself to his fellow lawyers. "What about attorney-client privilege?" I asked.

Out of the corner of my eye, I saw Newly lean even closer.

"Well, the client's dead. There aren't a whole lot of privileges that come with that status. I made it clear that I'd be happy to return the favor some day. I was looking for the attorney who might have drawn up Loretta's will. Just exploring the old axiom, 'Follow the money,' or, in this case, the property."

"Any luck?"

"Yes. You don't need to know the attorney's name at this stage, but Loretta updated her will a month ago. Her sole heir is her husband, Randall Johnson."

"Really? Even though they're divorced?"

"Evidently, she gave him a mountain divorce," Hewitt said. "Simply chucked him out of the house fifteen years ago. Nothing was ever done officially. She'd made a will leaving everything to her brothers, but her anger cooled, and she worried about Randall in his old age."

"Did her lawyer say whether she'd told her brothers about the change?"

"He didn't know, but he's going to step forward and inform the police that he's in possession of her will."

"Thanks, Hewitt. I'll give Newly a heads-up." We disconnected.

Newly took his eyes off the road a second. "Give me a heads-up about what?"

"Loretta's will." I gave him the details.

"That might explain Bobby and Bobby Junior looting her house," Newly said.

"Yes, but would it explain her murder?"

"If someone in her family got wind she was going to change the will and didn't realize she had already done so."

"Or Randall knew and didn't want to wait around for Loretta to die of old age. Have you spoken to him?"

"Not yet," Newly said. "But he's now at the top of the list."

"I want to talk to him about the night Frank DeMille disappeared."

Newly shook his head. "Wait your turn. I'm doing enough by humoring this UFO escapade of yours."

"Have you gotten Loretta's phone records?"

"We didn't find her phone on her body or in the house. We have to assume her killer took it and probably destroyed it. Maybe he thought that would prevent us from seeing a call number or text message and didn't realize the carrier would have all that information. We found an invoice for her account, and we've made the official request to Verizon. That should give us a way to learn if she'd set up a rendezvous."

"Unless she used something like WhatsApp through Wi-Fi," I said.

Newly grunted. "Is it too much to ask for a little optimism? We're due a break."

He slowed as we neared a battered mailbox. The faded name CASE was hand lettered on its side. It marked a driveway more dirt than gravel. We couldn't see a house.

Newly drove slowly, and soon we were surrounded by trees on both sides. If a vehicle came from the other direction, one of us would have to back up. About a quarter of a mile in, the road opened into a clearing. A small farmhouse sat on a knoll. A barn was off to the left, and a few cows grazed in an adjacent field. Beyond, a slope held Christmas trees in various stages of growth. Guinea hens roamed free in front of the porch. A pen of mismatched boards and chicken wire stood to the right of the house. One half had an open door, evidently the home of the guineas, and the other half contained regular chickens herded in their caged space by a pompous rooster. I recognized the place as the site of the family photograph I saw at Loretta's.

A brown dog of indeterminate pedigree roused himself from under the porch. The only sign of human life was a girl of about ten or eleven who played on a rope swing attached to the overhanging limb of an old oak tree by the chicken coop. She wore tattered blue jeans and a too-large T-shirt knotted at her midriff. Her bare feet were in a loop tied at the end of the rope. She gave us a wave. The dog gave a half-hearted bark to satisfy his minimal effort as a watchdog.

Newly stopped the car before we entered the clearing. "I want to keep the driveway blocked. No sense giving him an escape route if this thing goes south on us."

"You expecting trouble?" I asked.

"Always. I'm a cop."

The girl hopped down from standing in the swing and ran into the barn. Newly and I got out of the car.

"Let's wait for him to come to us," he said. He leaned against the hood. I stayed by the passenger's door.

In a moment, Danny came out of the barn. He wore a greasy yellow jumpsuit like a car mechanic's. He wiped his hands on a soiled rag, and I wondered if he'd been working on farm machinery. As soon as he recognized us, his pace slowed.

"Git on in the house, Louisa." He jerked his head toward the front door for emphasis.

Before the child could react, the screen door opened, and a woman stuck her head out. "Danny, your dad's on your cell phone. It's the second time he's called." Then the woman saw us and opened the door wider. She wore a shapeless brown dress, and even from a distance, I could tell she wore no makeup. She might have been in her midthirties but had aged beyond her years. She turned to the child. "Louisa May, come in right now. You've got chores to do."

Newly raised his hand in a friendly greeting. "Danny, I hate to trouble you, but I've got a few more questions, and you might be the only one who knows the answers."

Danny watched his wife and daughter disappear into the house. Then he started walking toward us. "I've done told you all I know." He stopped about ten feet away and eyed me suspiciously. "What's he doing here?"

From what his wife had said, I knew his father hadn't been able to tell him about the encounter at Loretta's house. That meant we were hitting him cold.

"He's got some cock-and-bull theory about what happened to your sister." Newly managed to screw his face up into a scowl that conveyed he'd rather have an enema than be with me. "He's a private detective, and I didn't want him coming out here alone and bothering you, what with the recent death of your aunt and all."

I didn't know what "and all" referred to, but Newly was letting Danny fill in anything relevant to his own mind.

"A private detective? Who for?"

"The family of Frank DeMille. The man whose bones were found up at PARI."

He nodded slowly. "I heard something about that." He turned to me. "So what's this theory of yours?"

Newly laughed derisively. "Get ready for a whopper."

"The tunnels. That's how they did it."

Danny's eyes widened as he reassessed me. "What tunnels?"

"The ones under PARI. The ones the police either choose to ignore or have been bought off. I saw your shirt Tuesday night. I know you know the truth is out there." I grabbed the tagline from *The X-Files* figuring if Danny watched the show, he'd consider it a documentary.

"What makes you think that?" Danny's question wasn't skeptical. He sounded genuinely curious.

"Why do you think? It's as plain as the nose on your face. Frank DeMille was taken by them in the tunnels. Maybe he saw something he shouldn't have." I gave a quick glance at Newly like I didn't want him overhearing. I looked back at Danny and mouthed the word "Aliens."

"That was a long time ago," Danny said.

"What's time to them? All these years, they might have been studying Frank or kept him in suspended animation until they needed him to reappear. They could pull his skeleton right out of his body and age the bones. If they can travel from another galaxy, they can easily do that."

"But why now?"

"The fire, Danny. The fire. Connect the dots, man. Someone tried to burn them out. You think they're going to let that stand?"

Danny shook his head.

"Of course not. So they issue a warning. Frank's skeleton appears right at the edge of the burn. Hell, they probably made the wind shift. So we have a fire, and then a body appears as if from out of the blue. The message—try that again and you'll wind up like Frank."

Danny nervously licked his lips. "I see that."

I stole a glance at Newly. He gave a barely perceptible nod to keep going.

"Then I step into the picture. I've investigated these paranormal events for years. They've probably got a file on me describing what I had for breakfast." I studied him for a second. "You too I bet."

He said nothing.

"I made the mistake of talking to your aunt. I'm sorry, man. I didn't intend for her to get dragged into this. We inadvertently became two more dots in the pattern. When they saw us connect, alarm bells must have gone off. I'm good at my job, and Loretta must have had information she didn't know was important at the time. We talked at Jack of the Wood. You saw us. And then she tried to tell me something in that song she sang. Something she didn't want them to know. But I didn't understand the message."

"I didn't either," Danny said. "But I knew it was important."

"And they got her, Danny. They got her in Rat Alley. A space that's really a tunnel. I know there must be a link to the other secret tunnels under Asheville. You do too. Aliens and tunnels. At PARI and in Asheville. The evidence is overwhelming. The dots are connected except for one."

"What's that?"

"The man who tried to burn them out. Was that what Loretta was trying to tell me?" I looked at his soiled jumpsuit. "A man with knees earth-covered. Or was it whoever killed Frank DeMille? Either way, she drew their attention. So they killed her. Or was it someone who was afraid she'd give him up to them?"

The color drained from Danny's face. "You think I killed my aunt?"

I looked past him to the rope swing with the single loop at the end. The family photograph from Loretta's home flashed through my mind. The little girl seated in the tire beside her. "Why not, Danny? You set the fire. Who puts up a tire swing for their child and then takes the tire away?"

Danny sucked in air like a drowning man.

I pressed on. "If I figured it out, don't you think the aliens will too? What did your shirt say? 'I'm coming for you.' I believe it. The connected dots are now circled, and you're in the middle."

Newly was right. It was a cock-and-bull story that no one in their right mind would believe. Unless they were paranoid. And guilty.

Danny pivoted and ran to the barn as fast as he could.

"Should we chase him?" I asked.

"Nah. Where's he going to go?"

An engine roared to life, but nothing came out. Then we caught a flash of metal as a jeep looped away from the back side. It became clear that the driveway passed through the barn and out the other side.

"Damn," Newly said. "The barn opens at both ends." He shrugged off the setback. "Let's go talk to the wife."

"You're not going after him?"

He pulled out his cell phone. "I'll call Sheriff Hickman. He can handle it. Besides, he'll understand Danny will be back."

"Because of his wife and child," I said.

"Because he left without his banjo."

# Chapter 18

"He believed a missing tire would convict him?" Special Agent Lindsay Boyce looked at me with unconcealed skepticism.

We were in her office in the Federal Building in Asheville. Newly had dropped me off, and I'd given her the explanation for why I'd arrived thirty minutes late.

"No," I said. "It really was fear that the aliens believed he started the fire. Danny drove out of the barn and within a hundred yards decided he'd be safer in jail. He actually wanted to sit in the back of Detective Newland's unmarked car."

Boyce couldn't restrain a smile. "I might need to have you do some of those alien threats in the Bureau's interrogations. We certainly see our share of weirdos."

"Well, it didn't get me anywhere with last night's fire. Danny swears up and down he had no part of that crime."

Boyce drummed her polished nails on the arm of her chair. We sat at a small conference table in a corner. Her formal welcome had become relaxed conversation as I relayed my adventure. Yet there was no doubt Lindsay Boyce was a consummate FBI professional. From her smartly tailored pinstriped suit to the piercing eyes that seemed to miss nothing, she was someone I'd wouldn't want coming after me.

"Maybe he's just confessing to a case of arson that can't be as easily coupled with attempted murder," she said.

"Maybe. Or maybe it's someone else in the family. Someone who thinks I killed Loretta, or someone who thinks I might be learning too much about Frank DeMille's death."

Agent Boyce straightened in her chair. "What have you learned about Frank DeMille?"

I knew we'd come to the real reason she wanted to see me. For my part, I wanted to make sure I got something in return.

"You've seen everything I have—the letters from Loretta to Frank and her concern about her family's attitude toward him."

"Yes," Boyce agreed. "And no one tried to burn down my house. Whether it's true or not, someone thinks you know something the rest of us don't."

Boyce made a valid point. Nakayla and I had spoken to Loretta at her home. Then she and I had the brief, private conversation before her band played at Jack of the Wood. She'd promised to talk to me afterward. Had the fact that we'd been seen together marked us both as targets?

"Loretta had something to tell me but never got the chance," I said. "I believe she remembered something about the night Frank disappeared. I told her the forensic evidence suggested he'd been killed by a shovel. If I interpreted her body language correctly, that information jolted her. It seemed more than just a reaction to a brutal death."

"She learned Frank hadn't run out on her," Boyce said.

"Yes, but she'd learned that several days earlier with the identification of the bones. Time enough to process the discovery and to compose a song of tribute to her lost love."

The FBI agent cocked her head and arched her eyebrows with intense curiosity. "Song? What song?"

I started to ask "Didn't Detective Newland tell you?" but thought better of throwing Newly under a federal bus. In his defense, Loretta's murder was his case and not an FBI investigation.

"She sang a solo at Jack of the Wood with new verses to the old folk tune, 'Come All You Fair and Tender Ladies.' It was about a woman who thought her lover had abandoned her. Then she learned the truth that he'd been murdered."

"OK. It's not unusual that a singer like Loretta would express her grief in song."

"Yes, but there are two unusual points. Her family didn't know she was going to sing it, and she inserted a new verse referencing the shovel and someone with earth-coated knees. She must have devised it on the spot. My comment about the shovel must have triggered some memory."

"How do you know the verse wasn't already written?"

"Because we found a paper with her lyrics in her fiddle case. The verse wasn't included."

Boyce drew her lips tight and nodded. "So she not only surprised her family but she also might have alerted a killer that she was onto him."

"Including someone in the pub she was about to meet." I explained how her brother said she remarked she was seeing someone that night and her family drew the wrong conclusion it was me. "Her phone was missing, and Newland is getting records from the carrier."

"If it was encrypted text over Wi-Fi, he's going to be out of luck."

I recalled Newly's response when I made the same comment. "He's painfully aware of that."

"Did Newland get the names of everyone present when you discovered the body?"

"Yes. And went through the evening's credit card receipts and food and drink orders for all the tables. The wait staff was thoroughly questioned to identify any patrons who might have left before I found the body. No immediate connections outside the Case family were evident."

"If it's not one of her family members, then someone could have entered the alley without going through the pub."

"Yes. Especially if the meeting was prearranged."

Special Agent Lindsay Boyce sat silently for a few minutes. I did the same.

Then she leaned across the table and folded her hands. "Sam, I asked you to come in because I wanted to know what you might have found that we haven't regarding Frank DeMille's murder. You've gotten ahead of us, and last night's fire makes me wonder if you're too close to an answer for your own good."

I smiled. "That thought has crossed my mind."

"I'm going to talk to Newland, because it's clear to me there very well may be a connection between the two deaths even though nearly fifty years lie between them. I can help him with Loretta's phone records and perhaps some forensic resources. My advice to you, even though I'm wasting my breath, is to back off and let us handle both cases."

"Tell me who you've talked to," I said.

"No one you haven't. Our investigation is just getting geared up. We'll circle back to the family and the former employees of the tracking station. Joseph Gordowski and Theo Brecht said they were at home the nights of Loretta's death and the fire. We're compiling a list of others who worked at the tracking station, although the senior staff members are deceased. Where are you going next?"

"I guess I'm backing off."

"Right. And I'm about to win Powerball."

I raised my hands in surrender. "I'm talking to Theo Brecht, who worked with Frank DeMille and Joseph Gordowski. In fact, he now works in this building for the National Oceanic and Atmospheric Administration's National Centers for Environmental Information. And I'm waiting to hear back from Loretta's estranged husband, Randall Johnson, who worked maintenance at the tracking station. I've learned he's the sole beneficiary of her will."

"Interesting. How'd you get that information?"

"I have my sources."

"Right. Tell Hewitt Donaldson unless he's defending someone, I expect him to play nice and share."

Boyce was no dummy, and I'd have to alert Hewitt she was aware of his machinations.

"Remember your comment about wasted breath?"

She laughed. "Yeah. And I have one more question. You left out an area of your investigation. Why?"

"What's that?"

"A who, not a what. Eddie Gilmore. I'm curious as to what Frank DeMille asked his brother-in-law to do. So I called military records and learned I'm the second person within the last few days inquiring about him. And there is precious little they'll tell me. How did your inquiry go?"

Her question told me that despite being in the FBI, she hadn't been as successful from outside the army as Chief Warrant Officer DeShaun Clark had been from the inside. Giving up my information could put DeShaun in a bind. Time to protect my own. I gave her my most winsome smile. "If they wouldn't play nice and share with you, they wouldn't play nice and share with me." Technically not a lie because I hadn't asked "them." DeShaun had.

Boyce stared at me. I kept smiling, although I had a growing fear she was about to ask me point-blank what I knew about Eddie Gilmore. If I didn't answer truthfully, I'd clearly be in violation of Title 18 United States Code Section 1001 for lying to a federal agent in a federal investigation, and I could be playing nice and sharing space in a federal penitentiary for five years.

She spared me. "Well, if you do find out something, you know where to find me. And, Sam, remember who your friends are. Don't be a hero."

Although I was still in the same building as Brecht, I elected not to show up unannounced at NOAA's NCEI. Acronyms are the bane of government and public organizations, but in this case, the mouthful of words for National Oceanic and Atmospheric Administration and National Centers for Environmental Information definitely deserved their NOAA and NCEI shorthand.

I checked my messages in the hall outside the door to the FBI and saw I had a text from Nakayla and a voicemail from Newly. I checked Nakayla first. Got new phone. Can you make dinner at your apartment at 7? The time on my phone read five thirty. An hour with Brecht should allow me to be home before then. I was anxious to share what I'd learned. I typed, Meeting Brecht but should be there by 7 at the latest.

Then I listened to Newly's message. "Call me." A true cop of few words. I pressed callback.

"Where are you?" he asked.

"Just leaving Agent Boyce. She's offered to help with Loretta's investigation since she thinks it could tie back to DeMille's murder."

"I don't know whether that's good news or bad. At least for a fed, she's got her head screwed on right. I'll contact her. Anything else?"

"You called me."

"Right. Sheriff Hickman sends his undying love. He said a search of Danny's barn found a couple of empty cans that smelled of kerosene. Danny's wife and daughter confirmed he took the tire from the swing a few weeks ago. He said he needed it for something important. Danny admitted taking the tire, rags, and the cans up on the ridge beside PARI. You've convinced him the aliens made the wind shift. A shrink will probably report Danny should be in a mental institution rather than prison."

"He doesn't strike me as violent," I said. "Maybe minimum security with psychiatric attention would be his best outcome."

Newly laughed. "Danny's only concern was can he have his banjo in jail."

"Anything support his story that he didn't firebomb Nakayla's house?"

"That's the other reason I called. The fire marshal's ninety-nine percent sure the accelerant was gasoline. Danny had cans of gasoline in his barn along with the kerosene empties."

"How does he explain that?"

"Farm machinery. Tractor, tiller, mower. The cans were full. He filled them at a Shell station near Rosman on Tuesday."

"The day before the fire," I said.

"Yes. And Hickman said he had the receipt to prove it. Seems as though he always buys his farm gas from the same store, and he's purchased no more gas since Tuesday. The number of gallons on the receipt match the volume in the full cans."

"So it wasn't him."

Newly sighed. "Well, it wasn't his gas. That doesn't mean he didn't help his father and/or his uncle. As far as I'm concerned, those two old men are both good suspects for DeMille's murder and therefore your fire. Hell, one of them could have killed Loretta. Hickman's going to work with us, and maybe we'll uncover something. Mainly I wanted you to know we could have a potential killer on the loose."

"What about Randall Johnson? Have you interviewed him?"

"We've tried to reach him by phone but no answer. Probably screens his calls. Tuck and I are going to run up to his place after I turn in the paperwork on what happened at Danny's. It was Hickman's collar, but he wants my official statement in case some lawyer gets Danny to retract his confession." Newly laughed again. "For God's sake, don't let Donaldson take him as a client. He'll convince a jury there are aliens at PARI."

We disconnected. I checked my phone log and found the number Theo Brecht had used to call me. He answered on the first ring.

"Mr. Blackman?"

"Yes. But Sam, please. Sorry I'm running late. Are you still good to grab a drink?"

"I am. Where are you?"

"At the parking garage on Otis," I lied. I didn't feel comfortable spreading around the fact I was talking to the FBI.

"Then let's meet at the Battery Park Book Exchange. I can be there in five minutes."

The Battery Park Book Exchange & Champagne Bar was across Otis from the Federal Building. I hurried out the nearest door to avoid running into Brecht. The bookstore was fairly crowded with people and dogs, but I found a small table for two that faced the door. The layout of the place was like a warren created by a platoon of librarians who also enjoyed a good bottle of wine. A maze of bookshelves carried volumes ranging from history to religion and from regional topics to global movements. The bar was fully stocked, and appetizers were available. I thought of Nakayla's book club, Reading Between the Wines, that usually met here.

One of the familiar staff behind the bar looked at me and then scanned the area around me. I knew he searched for Nakayla and Blue because I rarely came without them.

"A meeting," I mouthed.

He nodded and went back to pouring a glass of red wine.

The door opened, and Brecht entered wearing a purple-and-orange Hawaiian shirt. The gaudy colors challenged Hewitt Donaldson's most brilliant neon apparel. A broad smile brightened his face, and he hurried to me like I was some long-lost nephew.

"Sam. Good to see you again."

I stood, and he pumped my hand enthusiastically.

"Mr. Brecht, thanks for making the time."

He shook his head. "No, no, it's Theo." He looked at my clothes, a blue sport coat over a yellow golf shirt with khaki pants. "I hope you didn't wear the coat on my account."

I wore the coat to conceal the Kimber semiautomatic in the small of my back, but I didn't tell him that. "No. I had an earlier meeting that ran long."

"Well, you must be hot. How about a drink?"

"Not unless I'm buying. I invited you."

He shrugged. "Who am I to keep you from enjoying a glass of wine? I'll have my usual pinot. Tony knows." He nodded toward the man I knew by sight but not by name. Then he looked at the small table where I'd been waiting. "Why don't we see if we can find a quieter spot up in the stacks?"

"OK," I agreed. I went to the bar, and Tony came over with a bottle of Foris pinot noir.

"Getting a glass for Theo?" he asked.

"Yes. And one for me. Is he in here a lot?"

Tony laughed. "Three or four times a week. He told me if two days go by without seeing him, then I should call the police and the coroner. He's a character all right. Does he want his regular appetizer?"

"He didn't say. What is it?"

"Olives, hummus, and flatbread. Theo's a vegetarian. Must work. The old man's as spry as a twenty-year-old."

"My money's on the wine."

"Amen." Tony poured two glasses. "If you can carry these, I'll be up in a few minutes with the food."

"Up where?"

"Theo usually sits in the art history nook. Just two chairs and a small coffee table. A reserved sign is on it."

"And he sits there any way?"

Tony laughed. "Who do you think it's reserved for?"

I found Theo where Tony had predicted. He slid the reserved sign to one side, and I set the wine in its place.

"I'm sorry we're meeting under such difficult circumstances," he said. "First the awful discovery at PARI, and now Loretta's death. She was a sweet girl. She made the administrative side of the tracking station hum better than our radio telescopes." He took a sip of the pinot and rolled the liquid around his tongue before swallowing. He shook his head. "What a tragedy. They would have made a lovely couple."

"You worked with Frank?"

"Not at first. I primarily backed up Joseph Gordowski fine-tuning signal strength. But I had a knack for computer code, and Frank took me under his wing. I say he took me under his wing, but I was actually a year older. The chief administrator, Dr. Haskford, approved, and the plan became that I would learn from Frank and then take my knowledge and skill to another station." He paused and then shook his head again. "But when Frank disappeared, Haskford decided it made no sense to export me and import someone else. So I headed our computer operations."

Tony arrived with two plates. One held an assortment of olives, and the other, the flatbread and hummus.

Brecht eyed me suspiciously. "Are you two in collusion?"

"Tony knows how to keep his best customer happy," I said.

"Well, Sam paid for everything," Tony said. "I just supplied the data."

Brecht chuckled. "And we all know data is everything."

Tony set the food between our glasses and then stepped back. "You wouldn't need a petabyte to store your dining data. More like a kilobyte. Between us and the Laughing Seed, I doubt if you eat anywhere else."

Thanks to Nakayla's background information, I knew how huge a number a petabyte was and could join in the joke.

"Well, enjoy," Tony said and disappeared around a bookshelf.

"He's a smart kid," Brecht said.

"He seems interested in your work."

"He's active in environmental issues. We've had a few conversations about climate change."

"What's your data show?"

Brecht shrugged. "I just keep the information safe. I don't interpret it. That's for the meteorologists and climatologists."

"What's the difference?"

He dropped a black olive in his mouth, chewed for a second, and then swallowed. He pointed to the plate. "Help yourself."

"No, thanks. I've got dinner plans later tonight. The difference?" I prompted.

"A meteorologist and a climatologist both deal with the weather, but the difference is in the time perspectives. A meteorologist is making predictions over the short term. You know, how's the weather going to be for your vacation at your beach house next week. A climatologist is studying patterns over decades, centuries, even millennia. You know, will the rising seas submerge your beach house in twenty years."

"So then as a citizen, not a scientist, do you believe in climate change?"

He ran his right hand down the front of his Hawaiian shirt. "I'm in what are supposed to be the cool mountains wearing clothing more suitable for the tropics. Outside, the temperature's in the nineties, and the lack of rain has turned the ridges into tinderboxes. As a citizen, I believe we're killing the planet. My work today is not about space exploration, it's about human preservation."

"More important than your work with the NSA?"

His magnified eyes gave me a hard stare. "You know I can't talk about that. Let's just say we may be cooking the planet, but if it's any consolation, we didn't blow it up. The converted tracking station played its role in its time."

"And its new role? You're helping with that?"

The defensive cast of his face softened. "All old things are new again. Our climate and other NOAA data are going into PARI, a secure backup site. Joseph Gordowski and I are working together again."

"He's not full-time I understand."

"No, strictly a volunteer. But he's eager to help. He wants to be involved as much as he can." He raised his glass. "He knows PARI better than I do. It's nice to have one more act with him before the curtain comes down. Nice that we can both be useful."

I decided it was time to focus our conversation on whatever

might have brought the curtain down on Frank DeMille and Loretta Johnson.

"Theo, I'm working for Frank's sister, and you can imagine that even after all these years, the discovery of Frank's remains and the circumstances of his death are hitting her very hard."

"No, I can't imagine. I find it hard to deal with it, and he wasn't my brother."

"Since you heard the news, you must have thought about that night and what happened."

"Yes, I've thought about it, but nothing seemed out of the ordinary. The tracking station had passed the baton, and Frank told me to program the next cycle before we left. He would check it and make sure the radio telescopes would slew to the correct position to begin their tracking again."

"Did he say where he was going?"

"I assumed he was headed to the break room or men's room. Or sometimes he liked to take a walk around the grounds, even at night. He called them his thinking walks."

I remembered Nancy Gilmore said the same thing about her brother's thinking walks. "So he didn't seem agitated or preoccupied?"

"No more than usual. He wasn't the chattiest person in the complex. He kept his personal life to himself. I didn't know he and Loretta were dating."

"Do you think that could have caused any problems?"

Brecht shook his head. "If it did, I didn't notice. They'd been very discreet. I did hear her family wasn't happy about it."

"Who told you that?"

"I think it was Joseph Gordowski. He evidently had a run-in with one of her brothers. Then a week before Frank disappeared, I saw her brother snooping around one of the maintenance sheds."

"What was he looking for?" I asked.

"He said he'd come by to ask Loretta about a family matter. Long way to walk to ask a question."

"How did you know he was Loretta's brother?"

Brecht's jaw tightened as he relived the encounter. "Because I asked him who the hell he was. We were supposed to be a secure site, but the forest made our borders so porous, it wasn't until the Department of Defense took over that we had any meaningful security. They spread the word to stay out and posted signs that threatened long prison terms for trespassing."

"Which brother did you see?"

"Hell, I don't know. I described him to Gordowski, and he said it sounded like the same man who'd come looking for Frank. But then I learned Loretta's brothers were twins, and I never got a first name."

"And the brother you saw, did he ask for Frank?"

"No, claimed he was there to see Loretta."

"Near a maintenance shed."

"Yeah. That didn't feel right, and I asked why he hadn't gone to the office. He said he was curious about what we did. And he swore he wasn't touching anything."

"How did it end?"

"I walked him up to the office and took him to Loretta. I could tell she wasn't glad to see him. I left them because I didn't want to get in the middle of some family squabble."

I thought for a moment about the implications of what Brecht was saying. Either one of Loretta's brothers had made two unauthorized hikes into the tracking station, or the twins had made one hike each. We had no way of determining which scenario was true. Loretta would know, but she was inconveniently dead.

"Just a few more questions, Theo."

"Take as long as you need, as long as my wine holds out."

"Loretta had written a song that we think holds some significance. On the surface, it was a new version of an old folk song, but the verses appear to be both a lament for and a tribute to Frank. She talks about a man who slew the stars."

Brecht nodded. "The Slew Meister. We all called Frank that."

"One of the verses describes a man with a spade and earth-covered knees. We're not sure what that means. Do you?"

"Hmm." Brecht picked up his glass by the stem and swirled the dark red liquid like it could somehow reveal the answer. "Well, off the top of my head, my only theory is maybe she's identifying one of her brothers. Maybe the man I saw had seen a shovel in the shed. Loretta was there that night, and it was late. Frank and she could have gone for a romantic walk and were observed. As soon as they parted company, her enraged brother or brothers could have confronted him. He was killed and buried in the woods. Dirt on the knees could have come from digging the grave." Brecht took another swallow and set down the glass. "Then when she sang the song that night, the murderer or murderers knew she remembered and now associated the dirty clothing with the crime."

"Yes," I agreed. "All that's possible."

He steepled his fingers beneath his chin. "It's only a theory."

"It's a theory that has to be taken seriously," I said.

Brecht sighed. "But someone in her own family? Surely, there's another explanation."

"Can you write a computer program to find it for me?"

"No. But Frank could have."

I left the computer scientist to his thoughts and stopped at the bar and paid Tony to take Brecht another glass of pinot noir. He'd earned it.

I walked through downtown Asheville to the police station where I'd left my car before Newly and I had driven out to the Cases. I'm not a praying man, but as I started the engine, I said a thank you to whomever steers the stars. For Nakayla and me, life would go on. For our investigation, I was afraid we'd hit a dead end.

# Chapter 19

I was halfway down Biltmore Avenue to my apartment when my cell phone rang. I suspected it was Nakayla checking to see if I'd still be there by seven, but the screen displayed the number I recognized as Theo Brecht's.

"Theo?" I answered.

"Yes. Thanks for the second glass of pinot."

"You're welcome. We'll have to do it again sometime."

"Listen, I thought of something after you left. That verse of Loretta's song referencing earth-coated knees. It kept bouncing around in my head, and I think I might have been too quick to tie it to her brothers."

I sensed Brecht was about to tell me something significant, and I didn't want to hear it while trying to navigate the twisting road up to my apartment. I pulled into the parking lot of Lenny's sub shop and put the CR-V in park.

"OK. What's your new thought?"

Brecht cleared his throat and lowered his voice. I pictured him still sitting in his nook at the Battery Park Book Exchange.

"There was someone whose clothes were dirty that night," he said. "Obviously, I didn't think much of it at the time. I had no reason to. I mean who would have thought Frank had just been killed and buried?"

"I understand. So who are we talking about?"

"Now I don't want to get him in trouble with a false charge, but Randall Johnson came in looking for Frank a couple of hours after he left. I was still waiting for Frank to check out the computer program I'd updated."

"And Randall was dirty?"

"Yes. There were stains on the knees of the jumpsuit he always wore. The reason I remember is I fussed at him for coming into the computer room that way. Dust and dirt are the archenemies of electronic equipment, and he should have known better. It was one of the few times I got mad at a colleague, but I guess I was irritated because Frank hadn't returned and I wanted to go home."

"Did you ask him why he was dirty?"

"No. I mean he was a maintenance guy. He could have been working on something in a crawlspace. I just didn't want him around the computers."

"I understand. We'll be discreet. Like you said, he could have been working on something in a crawlspace."

Brecht was silent except for the whispery rasp of his breathing.

When he didn't speak, I said, "I'm glad you called me, Theo. I'll certainly pass it along to the police, and they'll want to speak directly to you."

"But, Sam, there's one other thing. While I was reading Randall the riot act, Loretta came in. She too had stayed to wait for Frank. She heard why I was arguing with Randall. She could have made that connection as well, only right before she sang her song. And if Randall had come to Jack of the Wood to hear his wife perform, well, he would have known exactly what the verse meant."

From what Newly had told me, other than Loretta's brothers and nephews, no one else with any connection to her had turned up in the pub. But that didn't mean Randall and Loretta hadn't planned to meet. He could have walked in from the alley and stood in the shadows, just one more person listening to the music. Or he didn't hear her song at all and she simply confronted him with the scene Brecht had just described. My priority was to get the information to Newly before he started questioning Johnson.

"Thanks, Theo," I said, anxious to terminate the call. "Please don't say anything to anyone until the police contact you."

"Got it."

I speed-dialed Newly.

"What's up?" he answered. "Tuck and I are just leaving to visit Randall Johnson."

"Then I'm glad I caught you. Theo Brecht remembered something very interesting." I briefed him on the details.

When I'd finished, Newly said, "Well, it's circumstantial, but Johnson's got motive, means, and opportunity for both murders. He kills DeMille because he wants Loretta and then kills Loretta because she learned the truth."

In the background, Efird said, "Sounds like a country song."

"And he would now inherit Loretta's house and the music pavilion," I said.

"Definitely another motive," Newly said. "We'll need Brecht to verify his account in an official statement. Tuck and I'll press Johnson as much as we can. Let's compare notes in the morning."

"Good luck."

"Hey, you and Nakayla took the personal hit on this case. Here's to a little good luck flowing your way."

I didn't argue and headed up the ridge to my apartment, hopeful that an investigation that appeared to be dead five minutes ago now had a very promising lead.

The historic Kenilworth Inn dated back to the early 1890s when it had been built as a luxury hotel. That building burned to the ground a few years after the turn of the century and was rebuilt in 1913 as a four-story Tudor that seemed more appropriate for Europe than Western North Carolina. Its incarnations included grand hotel, military hospital for World Wars One and Two, a mental hospital, and now over ninety unique apartments.

I lived in a one bedroom on the fourth floor. There was

something calming in driving up to the inn, like I was perpetually on vacation. I guess the grounds and massive structure dispelled the stress of life outside this fantasy kingdom.

I parked in front and took a moment to savor the scene in the glow of sunset. A tall pole in the middle of the expansive lawn displayed the American flag snapping in the evening breeze. Golden light began to shine from windows as residents returned from work. Behind one of them, Nakayla waited.

Before I could turn the key in the lock, the door opened, and I was greeted with a kiss and a bark. Fortunately, they were not from the same source.

"I'm glad you didn't get tied up." Nakayla gave me a second kiss. Blue sat and cleaned the floor with his sweeping tail.

"Me too." I looked beyond her to the dining area. The small table was set for two, a bottle of red wine breathed in the middle, two candles burned in silver candlesticks, and soft music played through my Bluetooth speakers. "Who did you have lined up in case I did get tied up?"

"Blue. He would have gotten your steak."

I bent down and petted the hound. "Sorry, old fellow. But after your ordeal last night, I'll save you a sliver." I pointed to the candlesticks. "I don't remember owning those."

"Cory and Shirley rallied to make sure we had a decent meal. I asked them to stay, but they insisted we unwind in our own time."

"You must have told them what a romantic guy I am."

"Yeah. That's why they knew they'd have to bring all the romantic stuff."

"Then why don't I pour the wine, and you can romantically tell me about your day."

"All right, but try to control your passion when I reach the part about getting my duplicate driver's license at the DMV."

My stomach turned. I hadn't even started replacing what had been burned up in my wallet.

"I'll do my best," I said. "First, let me get a dry sock for my leg, and I'll be right back."

On a hot day like today, my whole body perspired, and the sock covering my stump became more irritant than cushion. I went to the dresser drawer where I kept a clean supply, retrieved one, and sat on the edge of the bed. Before I could drop my pants, my cell phone rang. I checked the screen. Newly. Not the call you want at the start of a romantic evening.

"Tell me my good luck just got better and Johnson confessed on the spot."

"I don't know about your luck, but Johnson's ran out. He's hanging at the end of a rope." Newly exhaled a deep breath into the phone. "I thought maybe you might coincidentally happen by before I call the feds."

I looked in the mirror over the dresser and saw Nakayla step into the doorway. She saw the expression on my face, and her smile faded.

"Thanks, Newly," I said. "Give me the address. We'll just happen to be there as soon as we can."

We disconnected. I turned to Nakayla. "Randall Johnson's dead. If we're unwinding in our own time, then the clock just stopped."

Randall Johnson's home was on Sandy Hollar Road. He'd gone from Dusty to Sandy in the type of dirt and from Transylvania to Buncombe in his county of residence. The closer address meant Nakayla and I drove up to his small farmhouse a little before eight. Dusk rapidly robbed the daylight, and a deputy sheriff's car sat idling in front of a small barn, headlights on for illumination.

An ambulance was parked behind the patrol car, and the EMTs leaned against its hood. Not a good sign when the first responders weren't responding. Newly's unmarked had been pulled up off the dirt driveway between two poplars. I suspected he'd moved his vehicle to clear access as soon as he and Efird made the discovery. I followed the example and pulled alongside the far tree.

"Looks like the barn's the center of attention," Nakayla said.

"Yes. Let's see how Newly introduces us. The deputy might be exerting the county's jurisdiction and insist we stand clear. I assume Sheriff Browder is on the way."

We approached the scene slowly. The two EMTs looked up, nodded a greeting, but said nothing. As we drew nearer, I could see Newly, Tuck, and a Buncombe County deputy in conversation. They stood spaced like points of a triangle enclosing a figure sprawled on the barn floor. Efird saw us coming. He must have said something to Newly, because the lead detective pivoted to face us and raised one finger, signaling we should hold up.

Nakayla and I sidestepped closer to the house to get out of earshot of the EMTs. Newly left the other two men and joined us.

"I'm going to have to keep you out of the barn," Newly said. "At least until Sheriff Browder has his look. I've offered our mobile crime lab which is better equipped, and I played my best card to keep us in the game."

"Which is?" I asked.

"That I won't call the feds until you've had a look as well. I sort of fudged your role, claiming you were a consultant to the department on a cold case. You had tipped us off to question Johnson in the matter, and you were also in consultation with the FBI. I told Browder I could probably convince you to delay notifying Special Agent Boyce for a few hours."

"Aren't you crawling out on a limb?" Nakayla asked.

"Well, technically Tuck and I are on the Loretta Johnson murder and the firebombing of your house. By the way, there are several cans of gasoline in the back of the barn. One's newer and almost empty. I told Browder you and Sam are on the Frank DeMille murder, and that's the case under the province of the FBI and Sheriff Hickman. Once Browder understood there were multiple intersecting jurisdictions, he focused on protecting his."

"So what can you tell us?" I asked.

"Not much. After I spoke to you, I waited as long as I could before calling Browder. I can delay the FBI but not the sheriff's department, not if we want further cooperation. I informed the sheriff that Tuck and I had arrived to question Randall Johnson and found him hanging from a crossbeam."

Nakayla took in a sharp breath.

Newly glanced toward the barn where Tuck Efird and the deputy were still talking. "Unfortunately, Browder had a man on nearby patrol who was here in less than five minutes. The sheriff instructed him to secure the scene and keep us on the perimeter. Browder also called the EMTs. I guess he didn't trust our assessment that Johnson was dead."

"The deputy's established a pretty small perimeter," I said.

"The deputy's a rookie. I thought he was going to pass out when he saw the body. And I guess Johnson's been dead for twenty-four to thirty-six hours. The ME will make the call, but accuracy might be hard given the heat wave."

"Speeds up decomposition," I clarified for Nakayla's benefit.

"I'm glad we found him when we did," Newly said. "Apparently, Johnson threw the end with the noose over the crossbeam and tied off the other end around the horizontal plank of what used to be a horse or cow stall. Looks like he stood on a small stepladder and kicked it away."

"You cut him down?" I asked.

"No. The deputy did." Newly shrugged. "Shouldn't have, but I don't blame him. It wasn't a pretty sight. And you're not going to get any usable prints off an old hemp rope."

"So should Sam and I leave?" Nakayla asked.

"No. I told Browder you're investigating. And although you can't go into the barn, the deputy said nothing about the house."

Newly looked up at the clear evening sky. "Damned if I didn't feel a drop of rain." He walked away.

Sirens echoed off the ridges. Sheriff Browder and his posse were coming fast.

I grabbed Nakayla's hand. "Let's go in. We might only have a few minutes."

We hustled up the steps of the front porch. A frayed screen door was unlatched, and the solid door behind it stood wide open. Lights were on. I wedged my fingers under the warped edge of the screen door, pulling it open without touching the knob. Browder would want to print anything he could. A good cop considers even the most obvious suicide as a potential homicide.

We walked into a small front room furnished with a La-Z-Boy from the last century and two cane-bottom chairs. An acoustic Martin guitar stood upright beside one of them. I figured that was where Johnson played his instrument and taught his students.

On the other side of the room, a third straight-back chair was placed a few feet from a small dining table. A vintage Remington manual typewriter rested on the edge of the table nearest the chair. I guessed Johnson had no internet service and no computer or printer. It was like looking at a quill and parchment.

A piece of white paper was rolled into the typewriter. The typist had returned the carriage a few times to lift the message higher. Only two words—I'M SORRY.

"That's certainly inconclusive," Nakayla said. "Anybody could have typed that."

Other papers were scattered across the table's surface. The words on the pages appeared to have been typed on the same machine, and most were song lyrics. Some I recognized as classic mountain ballads, but others might have been original lyrics. Directly behind the Remington, I saw an opened package of Martin guitar strings. I wanted to pick it up, but I wasn't gloved.

"Time to introduce ourselves to the sheriff," I said.

Sheriff Browder had recently won a special election when his predecessor resigned for health reasons. I didn't want to get off on the wrong foot with the man, so I decided to play nice. But I also didn't want to embarrass Efird and Newly. They should have checked the house for other possible victims.

We stepped out on the porch and found Newly waiting for us.

"Well, Sherlock," he said.

I knew from his tone that he'd sent us in there knowing full well what we'd find. He hadn't wanted to prejudice us with his observations.

"A typed suicide note isn't worth the paper it's printed on," I said.

"Agreed."

"And the guitar strings. I didn't touch the package, but I'll bet there's a missing sixth string."

"I plan to let Browder make that discovery. Anything else?"

I shrugged. "I'd want a more thorough search, and maybe with someone familiar with the house."

"We have that someone," Newly said. "Sheriff Browder takes guitar lessons. He's out here every week."

"Then he'll know about the lights," Nakayla said.

Newly and I stared at her.

"What lights?" Newly asked.

"The house lights. They're all on unless you and Tuck turned them on."

"No, we didn't touch anything."

"Doesn't it strike you as odd that a man goes out to his barn to hang himself and leaves the lights burning? He's an old man on a fixed income. I think he'd be especially frugal and want to keep his electric bill as low as possible. Even if he was going out to the barn to kill himself, I'd think he'd turn off his lights."

"She's got a point, Newly," I said.

"Well, she certainly has a brain. More than I can say for her partner."

"So what's the significance?" I asked Nakayla.

"That he might not have gone to the barn willingly. And whoever forced him came at night when Johnson would have turned on more lights for a guest."

"Come with me," Newly said. "I've told Browder about the typewriter, but you tell him about the lights." He turned to me. "If you're smart, you'll only nod."

The three of us stopped at the barn door. A couple of deputies were standing guard. Tuck Efird was still inside, but farther from the body. I could make out a lanky man lying on his back. His hair was braided and flowed out from under his head like a snake. He wore green work pants and an untucked, wrinkled shirt that might have been dressier a decade ago. His feet were sockless and shoed with moccasins, not boots. The noose still tightly encompassed his neck.

Newly knocked on the side of the barn door. "A word, Sheriff, when it's convenient."

I recognized Browder from his election posters, a trim man in his late forties. He had been a ten-year veteran of the department, well-liked, and won the job by a wide margin. In other words, he should have been secure in his position and authority.

He looked around from where he was kneeling by Johnson's head. "OK." He stood and rolled off his latex gloves. He came toward us.

Efird, who had been leaning against the stall and watching Browder, followed a few yards behind.

"What's so all-fired important?" the sheriff asked Newly.

The Asheville homicide detective calmly gestured to Nakayla and me. "Sheriff Browder, meet Nakayla Robertson and Sam Blackman. They're investigating the death of Frank DeMille in cooperation with the FBI. As I told you, Randall Johnson was a person of interest, and they came out here to interview him."

"Well, that ain't going to happen now." He turned to Nakayla and me. "I'm not meaning to be a hard-ass, but my department has priority here."

"Of course," I said. "We just wanted to share an observation."

"So what did you see?"

"Lights," Nakayla said. "Detective Newly said he and Detective Efird found the door to the house open and all the lights turned on. That tells me two things—the hanging happened at night, and Johnson had to have walked out of his house leaving the door open and the lights burning."

"Is that consistent with his behavior?" I asked the sheriff.

"Hanging ain't consistent with his behavior. But Newland says there's a note in his typewriter. We'll check it for prints." He looked at Nakayla. "And there might be something to your light observation," he admitted. "Whenever I was here for a lesson, Randall turned on and off lights entering and exiting a room with the efficiency of a motion detector."

Since Browder's tone had softened, I risked pressing for more cooperation. "Sheriff, if Nakayla and I boot up, can we take a look at the crime scene?"

"A look for what?"

"Any indication that we're only seeing what we're supposed to be seeing."

Tuck Efird stepped closer. "I've worked crime scenes with them before. They won't contaminate it, and you'll get two pairs of skilled eyes."

His endorsement spoke not only to Browder but also to me. Efird had been critical and skeptical of Nakayla and me when our paths first crossed. This change of heart meant a lot.

Browder turned to a deputy. "Larry, fetch two sets of gloves and shoe covers."

"Thanks," I said.

"As my mama used to tell me and my brothers in the department store, you can look but don't touch."

When we were properly attired, I went first to the body. Randall Johnson had been a tall man who must have weighed in at over two hundred. He lay on his back, tongue protruding through cracked lips and dried blood caked around his nostrils. It looked like he'd died of strangulation and not the snap of his spinal cord consistent with a proper hanging.

I leaned closer. "Sheriff, would you loosen and lift the rope off the skin?"

Browder grunted as he knelt on the other side. With gloved fingers, he pried the rope an inch or so lower, revealing a bruised area that had a darker band in the middle of two lighter ones. I looked up at Newly and Efird. "See anything familiar?"

"The deeper contact point," Newly said. "It looks identical to the bruise on Loretta's neck."

No one said anything as Sheriff Browder examined the markings. "I see what you mean. Whatever pressed into his skin with the greater force had a smaller circumference."

"Like a guitar string," Efird added.

"Look at this," Nakayla said. She'd moved beyond the body to a section of the rope between Johnson and the stable where the end had been tied off.

Browder didn't even bother to stand but crawled to the spot. I hung back, letting him work without breathing down his neck.

He studied where Nakayla pointed and then stood to look up at the crossbeam. "A good six feet of the rope is freshly frayed. A small length might be explained by Johnson's weight pulling the rope down, but this indicates the rope rubbed across the beam as Johnson's body was being lifted."

Efird flashed me a devilish grin. "Hard for him to do by himself, don't you think, Sheriff?"

Browder ignored the sarcasm. He slowly pivoted in a complete circle, studying everything with a fresh eye. He'd been treating the scene as a possible homicide from the start, but now the protocol was more than just an exercise.

He jerked his head toward the house. "Let's see this so-called suicide note."

We followed him into Johnson's front room. Browder made

no objection. He read the typed words and then regloved before picking up the open package of guitar strings. His tight lips slowly morphed into a smile.

He looked at me. "Good job on those neck bruises." His eyes shifted to Nakayla. "Good job on the frayed rope." He held the strings up. "But this is the clincher for me. They're Martin guitar strings. Randall's favorite guitar was that Martin D-15M." He pointed to the guitar on the stand. "But the only strings he ever used were Elixir PB lights. He took grief from the Martin purists, but he liked the coating on those strings. Claimed he could finger faster."

He counted the strings. "The sixth is missing." He nodded to Nakayla. "If your light theory is correct, then last night, that missing Martin string was jerked around poor Randall's neck."

"Why not Tuesday night after Loretta died?" I asked.

"Because Wednesday morning, he gave me a guitar lesson." Browder searched through the papers on the table and pulled a calendar free. He pointed to the space under Wednesday. "Here's my name. Randall has nothing scheduled for today. That's why no one found his body earlier." He shook his head. "And with four law enforcement agencies and two private detectives involved, we've got more feet stepping on each other than drunks trying to promenade at a square dance."

# Chapter 20

At ten the next morning, the round table in Hewitt's conference room again became headquarters for our team. Armed with hot coffee, croissants, and muffins from City Bakery, Cory, Shirley, Hewitt, Nakayla, and I convened to take stock of the investigation's status. Blue stretched out on his bed that he'd dragged from Hewitt's office.

I'd reported the events of the previous day, concluding with Sheriff Browder's metaphor of the drunken square dance.

Hewitt laughed, spraying muffin crumbs onto the table. "Browder's right about that. It's a jurisdictional tangle. Everybody's pulling at a separate thread, and we don't know whether the mystery's unraveling or becoming more knotted."

"Anybody think it's odd that Sheriff Browder happened to take guitar lessons from Randall Johnson?" I asked. "Very convenient if his prints show up in Johnson's house."

Hewitt shook his head. "You know the old Lovin' Spoonful song, 'Nashville Cats'?"

"Yeah."

"Well, substitute Asheville for Nashville and the lyrics still work. We probably have as many guitar pickers per capita as Nashville. Maybe more. I did a little checking on Randall Johnson. I haven't been just sitting on my butt."

"Really?" Shirley interjected. "What else could you do with your butt? Rent it out as shade?"

Hewitt ignored her. "Johnson didn't teach beginners. He only worked with skilled musicians who wanted to elevate their playing. And Sheriff Browder's a good guitarist. I saw him perform at a charity function to raise money for the Diana Wortham Theatre. With that personal connection, Browder won't slough off Johnson's death as a suicide, and he won't take kindly to anyone who he thinks is horning in on his case. No matter if they're the FBI, Sheriff Hickman, or the Asheville Police Department."

"But he's the last one to the square dance," Cory said.

"Doesn't matter. The U.S. Army, Navy, and Air Force could all move in, and Browder wouldn't cede his ground without a fight."

"Don't forget the new space force," Shirley said.

Hewitt grimaced. "Space farce. I'd like to put the politicians who dreamed that up on the first saucer out of PARI. Let them go set up a base on Mars where they'll do less damage to the rest of us here."

Cory was seated beside Hewitt. She grabbed his wrist and blinked back tears. "But what can we do? I don't want my uncle to be reburied by bureaucratic squabbling."

"We have to focus," Nakayla said.

"How can we focus when we don't have a clear motive?" Cory asked. "Was my uncle killed because of his work? Was he killed because of his relationship with Loretta? And what about Randall Johnson? Was he killed because he knew who murdered Loretta, or was he killed because someone like one of her brothers or nephews thought he killed Loretta himself?"

Hewitt tapped his legal pad. "Don't forget with Johnson dead, Loretta's estate will go to her brothers. Cory's right. It's damned hard to focus on a clear motive."

"I know," Nakayla said. "But barring that the perpetrator is some random homicidal psycho lurking in Rat Alley, the most likely motive for Loretta's murder was to silence her. That pulls us back to the summer of 1971 with her brothers or tracking station colleagues as suspects."

"But not a colleague who could be dead now or living far away," I added. "The investigation into Frank DeMille's death compelled someone to take extreme actions. That could be the senior twins, Danny and Bobby, or Joseph Gordowski and Theo Brecht from PARI."

Hewitt shook his head. "Or someone still in the area who goes back that far and we just haven't discovered them yet."

Something nagged the back of my brain. "Do we know if either Sheriff Hickman or Special Agent Boyce have cross-referenced all the staff members working at the tracking station in 1971?"

"Don't look at me," Hewitt said. "Neither of them has me on speed dial."

Nakayla jotted a note on her pad. "We need to follow up with Boyce. She told you they were checking the 1971 personnel. The FBI has the fastest access to those records."

"And what's your leverage?" Shirley asked. "The FBI doesn't hand out information like Wikipedia."

"No, but I might have something to trade," I said.

Everyone looked at me. I was still running the possibility through my head and didn't elaborate.

Hewitt held a final bite of a muffin poised in front of his mouth. "Well, are you going to tell us or make us guess?"

"We have a thread we haven't pulled yet. Cory's uncle, Eddie Gilmore. Lindsay Boyce suspects we've been inquiring about him, but I didn't tell her we'd tracked down a veteran in Charlotte who shared Eddie's covert missions in Vietnam. Then Nakayla's house was firebombed, and I haven't had the chance to interview the guy. Whether I get any useful information from him or not, I can dangle that prospect in front of Boyce and maybe entice her to share where the Bureau stands on running down the former tracking station staff."

"Is this vet ready to talk?" Hewitt asked.

"I think so. He didn't seem reluctant or secretive. But then I really didn't ask him anything substantial. I told him we'd have to reschedule and I'd get back to him."

I recalled the phone call, the one that Chuck McNulty finally answered later that morning. He claimed he'd been driving because he couldn't sleep. Had my bringing Eddie Gilmore back into his life been the reason? I now wondered how long he'd been driving? Long enough to get to Asheville and back? Long enough to have set a house ablaze?

"Has Newland or Efird shared any information?" Cory asked.

Nakayla flipped through her notepad. "Some. No one that they've talked to at Jack of the Wood had any connection to Loretta other than her family. No one appeared to act suspiciously or leave without paying their bill. The pink bicycle found on the body belonged to one of the waitresses. It wasn't involved in the actual attack. The marks on Loretta's neck are consistent with a heavier gauge guitar string. Sam and I saw the marks on Johnson's neck. Despite the rope, the darker bruising looks identical."

"The significance is the strings weren't so thin that they sliced the flesh," I added. "They compressed arteries, veins, and windpipe to knock each victim unconscious within a matter of seconds. Neither Loretta nor Randall Johnson would have had the chance to cry out or struggle. There was no skin under their fingernails, not even their own. Often the victims will claw at their necks in a desperate effort to loosen the garrote."

With an audible swallow, Hewitt washed down a large bite of a fresh croissant with a gulp of coffee and then set the half-eaten pastry aside. The talk of strangulations had stifled his appetite. "How much strength would a person need in order to successfully use a garrote?"

"A trained assassin utilizes technique as well as strength. A small stick at each end of the wire could be used as handholds to draw the noose tighter. That device could slip into a jacket pocket. Strength definitely helps, but in my military training, a quick, small soldier could take out a larger opponent, especially if he half turned and pulled the victim over his back."

"Could a woman have done it?" Shirley asked.

Shirley was the last person whom I wanted to tell she wasn't capable of garroting someone. She'd strangle me just to prove me wrong.

"It's not inconceivable," I said. "But hoisting Randall Johnson's body up off the ground would be more difficult. So I think our killer is a man."

"And not a particularly smart one," Hewitt said. "Any half-competent ME would have noticed the inconsistent neck markings."

Shirley nodded in agreement. "A smart man. The original oxymoron."

*No,* I thought. *Not a smart man. An extremely smart man whose strategy was to keep us running in circles.*

The meeting broke up around eleven. Hewitt and his team offered to research the Cases and Randall Johnson further. Although Nakayla had already made one pass through their history, the law firm could go deeper and broader with an eye to any connection between them and the tracking station. Their scope included any public records, debts, police reports, internet references, or news articles that could give insights into the family dynamics, especially in the twins' early days.

All of us encouraged Nakayla to step back and concentrate on dealing with the aftermath of the fire. I planned to reschedule my meeting with Chuck McNulty for tomorrow morning. Although it would be Saturday, I doubted that made much difference to a full-time retiree when a weekday and weekend became indistinguishable.

The rest of my Friday would be spent rebuilding my life— replacing my identity as defined by a driver's license, ATM card, and whatever else a twenty-first-century man needs to prove he exists. Fortunately, my passport had been tucked safely away in my apartment, because the sad truth is you need proof of identity to reconstruct your identity.

Blue, Nakayla, and I walked down the hall to our office. As I reached for the doorknob, Blue gave a low growl.

"Blue?" Nakayla asked softly.

He growled again.

"Did you lock the door?" I whispered.

"No. You were the last one out."

"Oh, right. Then I'll be the first one in." I swung open the door and stepped across the threshold, Blue at my side. Five startled faces looked at me from the sofa and chairs.

"It was unlocked," one of the Case twins said.

All five heads nodded in unison.

"It wasn't breaking and entering," said the other twin. "We just entered." He dropped his gaze to Blue. "That's a fine-lookin' coonhound. You should have told us you have a dog."

"Yeah," I said. "His name's Blue. And yours would be?"

"I'm Danny. Danny Case Senior. This here's my son, Danny Case Junior."

A man in one of the chairs waved.

"And my other son, Bobby Case Number Two."

The man in the second chair waved. It was like an introduction of quiz show contestants.

"He ain't a junior, but he was named after my brother, just like my brother named his second son after me."

Bobby Case Senior sat in the middle of the sofa next to his twin. He nodded, "That's me. We met at Loretta's house."

*Yeah,* I thought. *When you were trying to loot it.*

"And you remember my son, Bobby Case Junior. My second son, Danny Number Two, is in lockup."

So if anyone was keeping score, we had three Bobbys and two Dannys. If they'd been a poker hand, we'd have a full house. In fact, we did have a full house. We were out of chairs.

"How can we help you?" I asked.

"We just came to talk," Danny Senior said. He stood and gestured for his two sons to get out of the chairs. "Let the lady and gentleman have seats. It's their place."

Nakayla moved toward her office door. "That's all right. Sam and I can roll in our desk chairs."

We wheeled them to each end of the coffee table so that we were flanked on either side by Cases. I wasn't keen on having Danny's two sons between me and the hall, but I figured if they wanted to start something, they would have done so as soon as we entered.

I took a moment to study them. The five sat stiffly, dressed not in jeans or overalls but ill-fitting suits with wrinkled shirts and ties. The two fathers looked like they couldn't stretch their suit coats around their bellies if Nakayla and I held guns to their heads. In their minds, they were on some important mission.

Blue went to his bed in the corner and plopped down. The meeting could begin.

Bobby Senior stroked his gray beard and then cleared his throat. "First of all, as the oldest—"

"By eight minutes," muttered Danny Senior.

"As the oldest," Bobby repeated, "I want to apologize on behalf of the family. We shouldn't have jumped to conclusions that you were putting pressure on our sister. That night at Jack of the Wood, she seemed so distraught after talking to you, and then you found her body in the alley. Well, you can see how it looked."

Nakayla and I said nothing.

"Then you come talking to my son, Danny Number Two. It was like you was pickin' on our family."

His voice rose, signaling he still harbored animosity under the veneer of politeness.

"But I heard from Danny's lips to my ears that he set that fire. The one at the space place as we call it." He looked at Nakayla. "Not the one at your house."

"We'll talk about that later," I said.

"Fair enough. But we want you to know Danny Number Two wasn't in his right mind. Those UFO people filled his brain with all sorts of crazy thoughts. The boy just fell in the deep end of the pond."

I frowned. "And you're telling us this because?"

He tugged his beard again. "Because we now know you're helping the family of that DeMille fellow. We figure Loretta was going to help you set things straight. You had no reason to harm her."

"She said she was going to meet someone?" I asked.

"Yeah. We thought it was you. But from where we were on the stage, that looked like a spur-of-the-moment thing. She was surprised to see you."

"What can you tell me about the solo she sang?"

Bobby Senior swept his eyes across his kinfolk. "We have no idea where that came from."

Again, the heads bobbed in unison, only faster this time.

"You know it was a song about Frank DeMille," Nakayla said.

"So we gathered," Danny Senior said. "Loretta had to be both happy and hurtin' to learn her boyfriend hadn't run out on her."

"What did you have against him?" I asked.

"I already told you. We didn't trust him or any of those people up there. All those men isolated in the forest. Like bucks in rut. So there's our pretty little sister in a house of the horny. Of course we worried about her."

"They planned to marry," I said. "There wasn't anything sordid going on."

The five men sat quietly for a few seconds.

Then Bobby Senior spoke. "She told us after he disappeared. We felt bad because she thought we'd run him off. If we'd known he was making an honest woman out of her, then we'd have thought differently. But we sure as hell didn't kill him."

"And how did you feel about Randall Johnson?" I asked. "He could have been one of your bucks in rut."

"Randall was different. He was born here. He played guitar."

Played guitar. And probably had a coonhound, I thought. In their eyes, Randall was a top-notch matrimonial prospect.

"Which one of you plays guitar?" I asked.

Five hands shot up.

"All of you weren't playing guitars last Tuesday."

"Everybody picks some guitar," Bobby Senior said. "When all of us are playing, then Danny Senior and I are on guitar. When it's just the four boys, then Bobby Junior plays guitar, Danny Junior plays fiddle, Bobby Number Two plays mandolin, and Danny Number Two plays banjo."

"Not any more, Pa," Bobby Junior said.

"Yep. We're goin' to have to do some thinkin' about that."

"What's your favorite guitar strings?" I asked.

The men studied me a moment.

"You play?" Danny Senior asked skeptically.

"Play at it," I lied.

"What's your guitar?"

I racked my brain for a make but all I could think of was Martin. I was afraid that was too fine an instrument for a novice. Then I remembered a guy in basic training who played a guitar. He was nicknamed for it.

"Washburn," I said. "Picked it up in a pawn shop." I forced a laugh. "All I know is it has six strings that need changing. Somebody told me I should try Martins."

"They're OK," Bobby Senior said. "We used to play them. Now we only play Elixirs. Randall recommended them, and we've never looked back."

So much for my effort to narrow the suspect pool by brand of guitar strings.

"Poor Randall," Danny Senior muttered and stared at his shoes. "If he'd kept it in his pants, Loretta would have kept him in the house." He looked up, saw Nakayla, and turned red. "Sorry, ma'am."

"Well," she said, "you were good to come clear the air. We're sorry about the loss of your sister. I met her only twice, but she seemed to be a remarkable woman."

They nodded.

Bobby Senior cleared his throat again. "We wondered if you could do us a couple of favors."

I shot a glance at Nakayla. Evidently, our peace powwow wasn't over.

"What are they?" she asked.

"We thought maybe you could put in a good word for my son Danny Number Two. We know he did wrong, but if he hadn't started that fire, then we'd never have learned what happened to Mr. DeMille. That's got to be helpful to his family. And he's got his own family to consider."

I didn't know what to say. Turning their logic around, we could argue if Frank DeMille's bones had not been uncovered, then both Loretta and Randall would still be alive.

"I'm afraid we can't help you there," Nakayla said. "We won't be called to testify, because the arson case is a matter for the FBI and Sheriff Hickman. We're only involved with the death of Frank DeMille."

Tears glistened in the twins' eyes.

"Well, ma'am," Danny Senior said, "would you and your partner consider taking on an investigation into who killed our sister? Our family's not in good graces with the law, what with my nephew Danny Number Two's screwup. They ain't about to tell us anything. And there's got to be some overlap with DeMille's death." He reached inside his coat pocket and retrieved a worn wallet. "We pooled our money together. Cash money. Six hundred dollars. We can pay more later." He looked at me. "I'll throw in guitar lessons."

"We can't take your money, Mr. Case. It wouldn't be right, since we're already working for another client. But among us, I agree that the murders are connected. When we find the guilty party for one of them, then I believe we'll have found the guilty party for all of them. And we'll gather here and give you a full report."

"We'd be much obliged, sir." He stood. "Well, boys, I think we're done here."

Nakayla and I headed for the door to bid them goodbye. Each of the men first stopped to pet Blue and then shook our hands.

When we heard the elevator descend with the Case clan, Nakayla said, "That was interesting. Either their visit was a genuine effort to find justice for their sister or a calculated maneuver to remove themselves as suspects. What do you think we should do next?"

I picked up my car keys for my dreaded trip to the DMV. "Why don't you fill Newly in on what just happened."

"Where are you going?"

"I guess I need to buy a Washburn guitar. What song would you like me to learn first?"

"'The Sound of Silence'—literally."

# Chapter 21

I left for Charlotte a little after eight on Saturday morning. Traffic was light, and I used the two hours to mull over all that had happened since DeMille's bones had been unearthed.

Dots were plentiful, but connecting them to support a coherent theory proved elusive. The dot named Chuck McNulty could be a total outlier with no connection whatsoever to our case. But McNulty's revelation that Eddie Gilmore had also been murdered linked the two deaths in a totally unexpected way. As each mile brought me closer to Charlotte, my excitement for meeting McNulty intensified.

Charlotte, the Queen City, prided itself on being one of the jewels of the New South. What once had been the intersection of two Indian trading trails was now the intersection of I-77 and I-85. Ranked either the second or third largest financial center in the country, clearly behind New York City but dancing back and forth with San Francisco, Charlotte proclaimed its success through a shining skyline of office towers and high-rise residences. But Chuck McNulty wouldn't be found there.

When I'd spoken with him the night before, he'd said he'd be in his rose garden, pruning and weeding before the heat drove him inside. I'd looked up his address on Google Maps and learned his house was in a neighborhood called Dilworth, one of the city's first suburbs, now almost within the shadows of the skyscrapers.

As I followed my GPS for the final mile, I was struck not by the variety of old yet well-maintained homes but rather the proliferation of tall trees lining the streets and gracing yards. The neighborhood was an arborist's dream.

My journey ended at a two-story brick house that I guessed had been constructed in the 1920s. I parked on a shady street in front. McNulty's home stood on a corner lot that appeared to be twice the size of those around it. What I'd envisioned as a couple of rose bushes in a backyard turned out to be a large garden adjacent to the house and encompassed by a decorative black wrought-iron fence. A separate cement sidewalk branched off from the one to the front porch and ended at the garden's gate.

Inside the perimeter, rose bushes grew in raised beds bordered by railroad ties. Red roses, pink roses, yellow roses, white roses, and varying shades of these major hues. Well-worn pathways crisscrossed among the beds. A breeze carried nature's sweet perfume. Here and there, a few benches created the feel of a bucolic park. Maybe Mr. McNulty would let me hang out the rest of the day away from fires, murders, and mysteries. *Sam,* I thought, *if ever there was a time to stop and smell the roses.*

A metal plaque attached to the gate read:

## A Gardener's Prayer

Thank you, God, for sun and shower,
Thank you for each stately tree;
Thank you for each lovely flower—
Through all these, you speak to me.

The poem sounded like something my grandmother would have cross-stitched.

A second plaque was mounted beneath the first.

Welcome all!
This gardener supposes
You can pick your noses
But not my roses.

That sounded like something I would have said—in middle school.

The gate had no lock. I opened it and entered.

I didn't see anyone along the side of the house, but I heard water running behind it. I followed the path and rounded the corner to find the garden continued across the back of the lot.

An older man in brown Bermuda shorts and a khaki safari shirt held a hose spraying water across a rose bush laden with blossoms. He wore a wide-brimmed hat for sun protection and gloves to guard against the thorns. But what caught my eye wasn't his head or hands. Extending below his left knee was a prosthetic device, perhaps a generation or two before mine. You didn't need to be a detective to understand why Chief Warrant Officer DeShaun Clark was able to locate Chuck McNulty through his disability checks.

"Mr. McNulty!" I called his name loud enough to be heard over the water.

He relaxed his grip on the sprayer, and the stream ceased. He turned to me. His wrinkled, tan face broke into a welcoming grin. He was about my height, five nine or five ten, and trim and fit.

He laid down the hose. "Damn aphids. Tricky to wash them off without destroying the blooms." He took off his gloves and offered his right hand. "Chief Warrant Officer Blackman. It's a pleasure to meet you."

His hand was calloused, and I wondered if he even needed the gloves.

"Sam's fine. My military days are over."

He looked down at my left pant leg. "Are they? I took the liberty of doing a little background check on you. These computers are something these days, and I still have a few contacts. If I heard correctly, we're not only brothers-in-arms, we're brothers-in-legs."

I laughed because he expected me to. It was a corny joke, obviously from the same mind that penned picking noses, not roses.

"Well, you can call me Chuck." He reached in the bush behind him and retrieved a walking stick. "My leg's pretty good. It's my balance that's a little shaky. Something for you to look forward to."

I surveyed the garden. "It's amazing what you've done here."

"Thanks. I get my exercise without straying too far from home. The leg bothers me a little more. Guess my skin's getting thinner. My daughter keeps pushing me to go back to the VA and get something that might be a little more comfortable. But what I've got now is adequate for what I do. I'd rather see the military spend the money on the men and women coming home wounded who have a whole life ahead of them."

The tough set of his jaw told me he firmly believed what he was telling me. In only a few moments and few words, the man had won me over.

I pulled up my left pant leg so he could see the articulating metal ankle. "This is what I got. I call it my Cadillac."

"Your Cadillac?"

"Yeah. The 'ride' is smoother. I have a second leg I dubbed my Land Rover. It's for more rigorous activity. I can run on it pretty well, but it's a little stiff for day-to-day use. The Cadillac might be right for you."

McNulty laughed. "Maybe. Or maybe I'll ask for a Buick. Seems to be the car for folks my age. You know I just turned eighty."

"You don't look a day over seventy-nine."

He laughed harder and then slapped me on the back. "Just what I'd expect from a chief warrant officer. No bullshit." He headed for the back door. "Come on in. My daughter was by earlier and made up some fresh lemonade and pimento cheese sandwiches. No sense eating out when we can have more time to talk here." He paused a beat. "In private."

I followed him into the kitchen.

"It's only a little after ten," he said. "If it's OK with you, how about a cup of coffee, and we'll have lunch after a while."

"Fine. Black, please."

We took our mugs into a small den. The room was more of a library with bookshelves on three walls, a couple of armchairs with strong lights beside them, and a velvet love seat. A feminine touch to a masculine decor. Light classical music came from somewhere.

"Alexa, stop," he shouted.

Immediate silence.

"Thank you." He smiled. "Isn't that amazing? And I can't help but say thank you when she does something for me. I read an article that kids today aren't learning manners because they order people around like they order their devices."

He gestured for me to take one of the armchairs. "Well, you didn't drive all the way here to listen to me complain about the younger generation. You're here about Eddie."

"Yes. Specifically as he might tie into his brother-in-law, Frank DeMille. But why don't you start with what you'd want me to know about Eddie?"

McNulty nodded and took a long sip of coffee. Then he sighed and set the mug on the floor beside his prosthetic leg. "Well, he was a helluva guy. That's what I want you to know. And smart as a whip, although he had a great gift for a man so blessed."

"What was that?"

"He listened. I mean he really listened. Not only to what was being said but the context and the consequences. And he didn't just see, he observed, as the Sherlock Holmes saying goes."

"Listening and observing. A good combination for an intelligence officer."

McNulty smiled. "A good combination for a chief warrant

officer. Eddie was a couple of years younger than me. He could have had a desk job in the Pentagon as an analyst, but he wanted to be on the ground. And he was prepared. He had learned some Vietnamese and some of the Montagnard languages."

"Those are the mountain people, right?"

"Yes. Indigenous people before the Vietnamese migrated there. They were loyal allies and saved many a shot-down pilot from enemy capture." McNulty shook his head. "It's a crying shame the way our government abandoned them. But then look at the way we treat our own veterans." He gave a quick glance at my prosthetic leg.

I wondered if he'd researched me enough to discover my testimony before a congressional committee deploring the conditions at Walter Reed Hospital. It was the event that got me shipped off to the VA hospital in Asheville and away from the media lights.

"Can you tell me what you and Eddie were listening and observing for?"

"I don't see any harm after all these years. We were tied to the Kit Carsons."

I gave him a blank stare. Obviously, I'd missed something about his war in my military history studies.

"The Kit Carson Scouts," he explained.

"The only Kit Carson scout I know is the guy from the Old West."

"Right. He was a scout and a tracker. Our Kit Carson Scouts were NVA and VC deserters."

I knew NVA stood for North Vietnamese Army and VC abbreviated Viet Cong, those who lived in the South but rebelled against the South Vietnamese government.

"The Marine Corps first used them in the 1960s. The Marines are foolhardy enough to try anything. In exchange for amnesty, the deserters actively joined our side. They knew the hidden trails, the VC hidden among the innocent villagers, the signs of booby traps like trip wires and pressure plates, and the locations and movements of advisors."

"Advisors?"

"Yes. Chinese and Soviet. They not only supplied arms but their own intelligence. Of course, there was always the possibility that a deserter was still working for North Vietnam. The new Kit Carson Scouts were heavily monitored, but the percentage of those still in the enemy's camp was small. Many of the scouts made great contributions and suffered casualties working for our side. Many more Americans were saved, and the Marine program was so successful, it expanded into U.S. Army operations."

"That's what you were doing in 1971?"

"Yes. Specifically, we were charged with seeking out Chinese and Soviet advisors on the ground—and that ground wasn't always Vietnam."

I did know enough history to understand McNulty meant secret incursions into Cambodia and Laos, incursions our government vehemently denied. No wonder Chuck McNulty's and Eddie Gilmore's missions were highly classified. Embedded with Kit Carson Scouts and army platoons, had they taken out—the euphemistic word would be *neutralized*—some of these Chinese and Soviet advisors?

These operations, especially outside of Vietnam, would be highly sensitive. The Soviets would deny their presence, and we would deny eliminating them. No wonder the file was still classified after all these years. Now that I understood the background, I was ready for the war story.

"So what happened?"

"We were up country. Eddie and I were embedded with a platoon of seasoned combat veterans still within the borders of the Vietnams. Three Kit Carson Scouts were with us. The lead scout, Nguyen Van Bao, a former NVA officer, had heard through the villages' network that two Soviet advisors had been seen with a party of NVA regulars. Bao spoke excellent English. He said he could lead us to the most likely spot to intercept. Bao had proven himself in previous operations, although we'd never confronted either Soviet or Chinese personnel.

"We were moving quickly and had made camp for the night. The platoon leader, a Lieutenant Norris, had told his men he would set an extra watch, given our location. As dusk deepened, I realized I hadn't seen Eddie since Norris issued his orders. We had a twelve-man platoon plus three scouts and Eddie and me. Seventeen total. I thought maybe Eddie had stepped off a few yards into the underbrush for a whiz. But no one should move outside our camp perimeter. I asked Norris for an escort to accompany me in looking for Eddie.

"We saw his body lying off the side of the path. He had evidently backtracked, maybe to piss, maybe to check for any overt sign that we had passed this way. Eddie was always careful.

"And I made a stupid mistake. I ran to him."

I winced, anticipating what his mistake had been. "Booby-trapped," I whispered.

McNulty nodded. "Yes. But not the body. A trip wire to a grenade on the path about fifteen feet in front of it. Simple, but highly effective." For a moment, he stared down at the metal device in place of flesh, bone, and blood. "At least Eddie's body wasn't mutilated by the blast. My comrades carried me to a spot where a chopper could evacuate us. I lost consciousness somewhere along the way."

McNulty picked up his cup and had another swallow of coffee. I held my tongue, letting him tell the story in his own time.

"I came in and out and wasn't in a fully conscious state until they were prepping me for transfer to a hospital ship. No one would tell me anything." He smiled. "That is until a chief warrant officer named Len Axelrod showed up. He asked me what happened. What did I know about Nyugen Van Bao? Had I ever heard Eddie speak about a doctor named Jean Louis Caron? I refused to answer his questions until he told me what happened to Eddie." His smile broadened. "I guess I don't have to tell you how tight-lipped a chief warrant officer can be. But I held to my advantage. He told me Eddie had been garroted."

Garroted. The word jarred my ears like a clanging gong. Garroted. A silent assassination in a war zone where you expected the enemy from the outside, not within.

"The Kit Carson Scout Bao," I said.

"The one Eddie trusted the most. He'd been a rat all along. And he murdered Eddie and disappeared. Over the years, I've thought about how we were taken in. The Kit Carson Scouts were a real asset for our troops. More than two hundred died in service. Eddie just happened to connect with the wrong one." McNulty paused and shook his head. "No, I don't think it was coincidental. Bao knew we were intelligence officers. He ingratiated himself. In Saigon, he would run errands for Eddie. In hindsight, I should have noticed that he kept himself aloof from the other scouts. And I'd found him in Eddie's quarters several times, but he'd claim to be getting something Eddie needed or taking something to post. As for that last mission, I believe he led us to a place where he could kill Eddie and then safely cross into the protection of the NVA."

"But why? Why then?"

"Maybe Eddie was onto him. Suspicious about something he didn't share with me. Chief Warrant Officer Axelrod told me Bao had been seen visiting this French doctor in Saigon, Jean Louis Caron. He was later proven to be a spy."

"For the North Vietnamese?"

"No. For the Soviets. He'd been working for them since Vietnam was a French colony."

I began to see the implications. "Bao could inform him where your next patrol would focus. They could be clear. But why not have the NVA attack you?"

"Bao had cultivated his relationship with Eddie. It was more valuable to keep that going. And there was the very real danger that Bao could be killed in a firefight."

"Something drastically changed the priorities. Did Eddie say anything about his brother-in-law?"

"No. But Chief Warrant Officer Axelrod did. Eddie had requested a meeting with him. They'd spoken briefly by radio phone as Axelrod was investigating alleged civilian casualties caused by our troops in another province. Eddie said he would send him a summary of his request."

"That summary was probably his report on whatever his brother-in-law Frank DeMille brought to his attention. Passing the information to someone who was an investigator would have been the logical move. That person could evaluate the situation and then inform the FBI if appropriate." I thought about McNulty's statement that Bao was often in Eddie's quarters and ran errands for the officer. "Bao could have seen the letter Frank DeMille wrote to Eddie."

McNulty nodded. "If Eddie asked Bao to take his summary to Axelrod's quarters, Bao very well could have gone to Caron instead. Axelrod claimed he never received Eddie's report."

"What network of spies could coordinate murders half a globe away?" I asked. "Not the North Vietnamese."

"No," McNulty agreed. "And I don't think Eddie was killed to protect Bao. I think he was killed because DeMille's letter set off alarm bells for Eddie, and he'd find out that Chief Warrant Officer Axelrod never received his report. From what you've told me, I believe the key to the whole thing is the link from Bao to Caron to the Soviets to DeMille."

McNulty's assessment sounded far-fetched, but Eddie Gilmore had been murdered, and his report hadn't reached the intended recipient. So the scenario he sketched wasn't impossible. What it did mean was that if the Soviets had directed Frank DeMille's elimination, they surely wouldn't have used Bobby or Danny Case as their agents. It also meant whatever was worth protecting in 1971 was still worth protecting today, long after the Apollo missions and Soviet Union were history.

I voiced my skepticism. "How do you know that whoever killed Eddie didn't take Bao captive? They could have wanted to make a public spectacle in front of their own troops of what happens to someone who deserts and joins the Kit Carson Scouts."

McNulty leaned forward in his chair, and his eyes narrowed. "Because I've seen the bastard."

"You've seen him? Here in the States?"

"No. A couple of years ago, when the trade policy of our country went haywire, Vladimir Putin made a trip to Vietnam in an effort to increase commerce between Vietnam and the Russian Federation. CNBC carried a news story as Putin met for photo ops in Hanoi. And there he was. Nyugen Van Bao, now the defense minister. Of course, he'd aged, but you don't forget the face of the man who blew off your leg."

"No, you don't." I flashed back to that moment I learned my wound had come at the hands of corrupt U.S. soldiers and not an ambush by Sunni insurgents.

McNulty gave me a strange look, hearing in the tone of my voice that he'd struck a nerve.

"Clearly, the embrace Putin gave Bao wasn't a formal nod or handshake," McNulty said. "The former KGB agent and the traitorous Kit Carson Scout had a history, and maybe that history involved shared knowledge of Dr. Jean Louis Caron and the assassination of Eddie Gilmore. I saw that scene and wrote a letter to my congressman, but now that Vietnam is a trading partner, no one is interested in opening old wounds." McNulty threw up his hands. "I'm afraid I'm not much help."

I sat quietly for a moment, my mind whirling as I tried to put the pieces together. There was no proof of anything, just this man's story that provided no concrete connection to Frank DeMille. I was left with conjectures. This was dangerous territory where you were tempted to adopt a theory and then interpret the facts to support it. Build a case that was a house of cards and see one wrong assumption bring it crashing down.

"This Frank DeMille," McNulty said. "He must have worked with classified information."

"Computer code and programming as it related to the Apollo project. If you can't track your astronauts, you have no space program. Evidently, DeMille was a computer genius."

"So you think someone was copying and stealing the work?"

"If we rule out a domestic angle, then yes. And if the connection was Soviet intelligence, then a threat that they learned about in Vietnam must have triggered an assassination in North Carolina."

McNulty nodded. "They had a mole—a mole in the Kit Carson Scouts and a mole in the tracking station. Even though the Soviet Union is no more, the Russian Federation is still run by thugs. And computer data is more valuable than ever. My guess is they still have an agent in place and the motive isn't to cover up a crime in the past but rather an ongoing crime in the present. Where's the FBI in all this?"

The former intelligence officer had crystalized the events into a workable hypothesis. Moving from the Case family as perpetrators to an international spy ring certainly moved the investigation from Sheriff Hickman, Sheriff Browder, and Newly and Efird into the highest priority for the FBI. There was no question about sharing information with Special Agent Lindsay Boyce. And the three persons who spanned the decades were Joseph Gordowski, Theo Brecht, and Randall Johnson. Was Johnson silenced because he had been bought by the Soviets? He wasn't a scientist himself, but as a maintenance man, he could have probably gone anywhere. Now, no longer needed, he was a liability. He could be guilty and still have been murdered by person or persons unknown because he transformed from being an asset to being expendable.

Joseph Gordowski and Theo Brecht were both scientists with not only physical access to the work areas but with the knowledge of which of DeMille's computer programs would be the most innovative and therefore valuable. Brecht had moved on from PARI, but Gordowski was still there. He was the one who had supposedly left early the night DeMille disappeared. He had no alibi. Like Brecht, he had stayed with the high-tech complex after it was taken over by the Department of Defense and its highly classified eavesdropping operations run by the NSA. What a plum of a position for a spy.

And then Brecht's career mirrored Gordowski's, although he had stayed that night reprogramming the radio telescopes to slew to the eastern horizon for the next pass of the moon. Brecht's current job sounded pretty mundane, and he seemed to use his occasional work at PARI as a break from the NCEI. Brecht had said the PARI secure data storage project was the final act for Gordowski and him. But that act was more than PARI. I remembered Brecht saying Gordowski had asked to help with the NCEI work as well. Was the desire to expand his volunteer role more than simply keeping busy?

McNulty cleared his throat, bringing me back to his den.

"Son, I don't know where your thoughts might be leading you, but here's a bit of advice from one wounded vet to another. It's the Russians' playbook for the twenty-first century. Disinformation creates doubt, chaos breeds confusion, and a doubting, confused adversary is a weakened adversary. Look what happened to our democratic election process. Doubt and confusion. Whether that applies to your situation, I don't know." He leaned forward and pointed his blunt forefinger toward me. "But if I were you, I'd tell myself that the first thing every morning. Disinformation creates doubt, chaos breeds confusion. It might keep you on track. It might keep you alive."

# Chapter 22

McNulty and I ate pimento cheese sandwiches and drank lemonade at his kitchen table. When we'd finished, he asked me to keep him informed regarding my progress.

"It's about justice for Eddie," he said. "I know we can't touch that bastard Bao, but we can find out what happened and make a stink about it."

We walked out into his rose garden, and he retrieved a pair of pruning shears from a small shed.

"Have you got a little missus at home or a sweetheart?" He laughed. "Or both?"

"Just one. My partner Nakayla."

"Then let me send you back to Asheville with a bouquet."

So I drove home immersed in a rose-perfumed environment more powerful than any air freshener.

On the way, I phoned Nakayla and asked if she could gather Hewitt and company for a Saturday afternoon conference. I had new information, and I preferred to share it sooner rather than later. Since Nakayla and I were technically working for Hewitt, I wanted to report to him before contacting the FBI or other law enforcement agencies including Newly and Efird at the Asheville Police Department.

At three o'clock, Nakayla, Hewitt, Cory, Shirley, and I took our customary places around the table in Hewitt's conference room. Blue slept on his cushion. I relayed the story of my visit to Chuck McNulty and the murder of Eddie Gilmore, which changed the whole scope of our investigation.

Cory struggled to comprehend the implications. "You're saying both my uncles were murdered by Russian spies?"

"I know it sounds preposterous, but your uncle Eddie's letters clearly indicate your uncle Frank was concerned about something at the tracking station and Eddie tried to help him. Chief Warrant Officer Len Axelrod never got Eddie's report other than a brief phone call. At this point, all we can do is speculate and share our findings with the FBI. Espionage is in their wheelhouse."

Shirley shook her head. "And then we'd need our own spies if we ever want to learn what they discovered."

Hewitt nodded in agreement. "That is a concern." He turned to Cory. "If the military kept Eddie's murder quiet in 1971, then I see no reason for them to open up now, even if the FBI comes knocking on their door. But at least your aunt will know what happened to her husband."

Cory's eyes teared. "And what comfort is that if she doesn't know why? What comfort is that if she doesn't know who killed her brother?"

The room was silent. Glances shot back and forth, but no one could answer her questions.

I took a deep breath and looked at Nakayla. "Then we delay sharing information. At least for a few more days. It's Saturday afternoon. I seriously doubt that Lindsay Boyce is in the FBI office. And tomorrow's Sunday. Nakayla and I can make a run at finding this Len Axelrod. If he's still alive, he might be willing to fill in more of Chuck McNulty's story. As for a killer at PARI, I figure we have three suspects. Joseph Gordowski and Theo Brecht, with Gordowski having no alibi, and Randall Johnson, who might have been paid to make computer code copies without really needing to know what the code meant."

"But all the evidence points to his being murdered," Shirley said.

"Yes," I agreed, "but if the Case brothers thought Randall was the one who strangled Loretta, they might have killed him despite their unsolicited visit to us professing their innocence."

"Or someone unknown," Nakayla said. "Someone who needed to keep Randall quiet. Putin's not shy about his agents eliminating potential problems in any country."

"I think that's a stretch," I said. "I keep coming back to the fact that since the bones were uncovered, two people have been murdered. Someone's trying to protect something here and now. And this person or persons acted very quickly once Frank DeMille's remains were discovered. So what's happening that merits extreme action? PARI is putting in a new, high-capacity, secure digitized data storage system. The encryption must be the cyber equivalent of Fort Knox. What better time to create a back door or work-around for later access."

"Access to what?" Hewitt asked.

"Access to whatever is stored there." I looked around the table, trying to sell my case to everyone. "Data that would go into such a secure site is obviously valuable to someone. We know that NOAA is creating a backup for its historic and ever-growing weather data. Who's to say how extensive the impact would be if that data was corrupted?" I turned to Hewitt. "A weapon to be used by the naysayers of climate change. The industrialists and fossil fuel producers who will deny climate change to their last polluted breath."

Hewitt nodded slowly. "The computer scientist who designs the lock—"

"Knows how to pick it. That brings us to Gordowski and Brecht. And Brecht said Gordowski had asked to help him with his work for NOAA."

"And he was the first to be interviewed," Nakayla added. "The first to know we were investigating. And then my house was firebombed."

"So how do you call him out?" Hewitt asked.

"We don't," I said. "I don't want to get tunnel vision on this thing and force Gordowski into the role of chief suspect when we've got other sources of information yet to mine. We need to get Len Axelrod's Vietnam story, and I want to learn more about the potential value of this weather data, data that's being migrated to PARI as backup for all these petabytes housed in NOAA's facility."

"Then aren't you going to have to talk to Brecht again?" Nakayla asked.

"Maybe. If I can't find another way to get the information."

Hewitt pushed back his chair and got to his feet. "Maybe I have a way." He walked around the table to Shirley.

She looked up at him. "What are we playing? Duck, Duck, Goose?"

"We're playing Can You Remember Owen Sharp?"

"I can. Good idea." She smiled. "Let me write down the day and time you had it."

"Who's Owen Sharp?" I asked.

Hewitt gestured to Shirley. "You tell him, almost former employee."

"Owen Sharp is the executive officer for the NOAA headquarters here in Asheville, including the NCEI. There have been times when we've needed certified weather information entered into evidence in court."

"I get it," I said. "How it might have affected a crime scene."

"Or time of death based upon body temperature and air temperature," Hewitt said. "I've had three acquittals thanks to Owen Sharp's records."

I repeated aloud the words ringing in my head. "Disinformation creates doubt, chaos breeds confusion."

"What's that?" Hewitt asked.

"Something Chuck McNulty said to me. What would happen if the security of the weather data was breached? If the records could have been tampered with?"

"Which ones?"

"Would it matter? If the data hurt your case rather than helped, what would you do?"

"Scream bloody hell that the data was tainted and inadmissible. Wouldn't matter whether it had been altered or not, I'd claim the whole trove was suspect."

"See," I said. "Even your own realm of the courtroom would be affected. I want to talk to your Mr. Sharp. How soon do you think you could arrange it?"

"Are we done here?" Hewitt asked.

No one said anything.

"Then I'll track him down now. Shirley, pull his number from the file. We must have his home and cell. We'll find him even if we have to use Ol' Blue to sniff him out."

I looked at the coonhound lying stretched out on his cushion. He opened one eye, fixed it on Hewitt a few seconds, and then fell back asleep.

Nakayla and I walked down the hall to our office, and I immediately called Chief Warrant Officer DeShaun Clark.

"Sam, my man, if I knew you were going to be so chummy, I'd have invited you down for the weekend." Clark spoke above the clinking of glasses and a multivoiced buzz of conversations.

"Sorry to bother you. I can tell that you're on duty."

Clark laughed. "Yeah, trying to solve the case of why the Carolina Panthers are losing what should be a cakewalk exhibition game."

"You in At Ease?" I named one of the longtime off-base bars frequented by Fort Bragg soldiers.

"Sitting right next to your favorite stool. So is this a thank you call or another favor request?"

"Both. Your McNulty contact unearthed that the officer I was checking on had been murdered."

Clark gave a soft, low whistle. "My, my, what have you stepped in this time?"

"We both know what it is. Now I need to know how far it spread, and that might be into my backyard."

"Vietnam to Asheville. That's no coincidence, my friend."

"So I'm trying to stay one step ahead of the feds without facing an obstruction of justice charge. They and the military could clamp this thing down so tight, a Freedom of Information request would go into bureaucratic limbo until we're all dead."

"I hear you. What do you need that won't have my fingerprints on it?"

"McNulty gave me the name of the chief warrant officer who looked into the murder in 1971. If he's still alive, I want to talk to him."

Clark let out a long sigh. "OK. Give me the name and the other particulars."

"Chief Warrant Officer Len Axelrod. He was based in Saigon in the summer and probably early fall of 1971. The murdered man, Eddie Gilmore, set up a meeting to talk to him about his brother-in-law's concerns regarding the Apollo tracking station's security. I only know what McNulty told me. Axelrod interviewed him as he was headed to a hospital ship. McNulty lost the lower part of his left leg when the murderer booby-trapped the path to Gilmore's body."

"So you want to know if this Axelrod solved the case?"

"No. McNulty told me who did it, and the man's now the defense minister of Vietnam and close to a guy named Vladimir Putin."

For a few seconds, all I heard was the sound of a televised football game.

Then Clark laughed. "OK, Sam. I'll admit you had me going there."

"DeShaun, I'm not kidding. Unless McNulty's lying to me, this case has gone from cold to white-hot. Two people have been murdered within the last week, and my partner's house was fire-bombed. I really need to track down Axelrod."

"Okay. You got it, pal. And if you need me up there, just say the word."

"Thanks. I owe you big time."

"You do. So be careful. You can't repay me if you're dead."

# Chapter 23

I'd just finished briefing Nakayla on my conversation with DeShaun Clark when Hewitt entered our office.

He gave a thumbs-up. "You're meeting Owen Sharp at noon tomorrow."

"Great," I said. "What did you tell him?"

"That you were working on a case for me that involves weather data and that I'd appreciate if he spoke with you directly and as soon as possible. Once you're talking, you can shift the conversation to how protected their data is and the potential consequences if security is breached."

"So will I have any problem gaining access to his office on a Sunday?"

"No, because you're not going to his office. I told him you were basically clueless and not to assume you knew anything about NOAA. That's when he said it would be better to meet at the Grove Arcade."

The Grove Arcade was a historical building that occupied an entire city block. E. W. Grove, the same millionaire visionary who created the Grove Park Inn, had wanted to construct a unique and impressive building that would elevate his beloved Asheville to the status of a city many times its size. Today,

Grove Arcade was a favorite destination for locals and tourists alike who were drawn to its mixture of shops, restaurants, and apartments. It was right across the street from the Federal Building and housed the Battery Park Book Exchange where I'd met Theo Brecht.

"Did he say exactly where at the arcade he wanted to meet?" I asked Hewitt.

"At the corner of Battery Park and Page where the street vendors congregate. He said the covered booths will provide some shade for what's going to be a particularly hot day. I guess these guys live and breathe the weather."

"Maybe Mr. Sharp is in his office on a Sunday to get the jump on hurricane season," I said.

"Another reason their work is so important," Nakayla said. "Do you want me to come with you?"

"No. There might be other threads that need to be worked, especially if we can find Axelrod and learn more about his investigation into Eddie Gilmore's murder."

"Let me know if there's anything more we can do," Hewitt said. He turned to Nakayla. "Or if you need us to light a fire under your insurance company."

"Thanks. So far, they've been very responsive. We're meeting Monday morning to discuss whether I rebuild or sell the lot and relocate."

Hewitt eyed me for a second, and I knew he was trying to discern whether Nakayla and I were thinking about setting up house together. That prospect also ran through my mind.

"Well," Hewitt said, "don't hesitate to ask for anything. And let me know if Sharp or this Axelrod have something to contribute." He reached for the doorknob. "Oh, do you want me to take Blue? I'm just hanging out at home."

"Sure," I said. "You'll be better company this weekend. Just don't go sharing your scotch with him."

Hewitt left all smiles.

Nakayla rose from the sofa and headed for her computer. "You know if Blue ever goes missing, Hewitt's the prime suspect."

"Yeah. I wish this case were as easy to solve." My cell rang. "It's DeShaun."

Nakayla grabbed a legal pad and pencil from her desk. "Put him on speakerphone. I'll take notes. At least I can read my own handwriting."

We settled back on the sofa. I accepted the call and laid the phone on the coffee table. "Hey, DeShaun, a word of warning. My partner, Nakayla, is on the line."

"No warning necessary. You know I'm always a perfect gentleman. Nakayla, I hope I don't tarnish your opinion of Sam after you hear how a real detective operates."

"I'd love to hear how a real detective operates. Do you know any?"

Clark's deep laugh vibrated the phone against the table's surface. "Serves me right," he said. "But I do have some information. Chief Warrant Officer Len Axelrod is alive and retired in Raleigh. He left the army after putting in his twenty years and became a Raleigh police officer and then homicide detective. He's one of us, and he'd love to talk to you."

Nakayla and I looked at each other. Clark not only had found Axelrod but he'd also spoken with the man.

"What did you tell him?" I asked.

"A limited version of the truth. I said I'd been asked for help by a friend who claimed he had reason to believe a lieutenant named Eddie Gilmore had been murdered in Vietnam. I told my friend I wasn't in a position to investigate, but I'd try to put him in touch with someone who might have been involved at the time."

"What did he say?"

"One word. 'Bullshit.' He said he doubted I'd found any Gilmore file with his name attached. His words, 'That file was sealed tighter than a deep-diving submarine. Tell me the truth or this call is over.'"

"Sounds like a chief warrant officer," I said.

"I told you he was one of us. So I said you were a former chief warrant officer helping Gilmore's widow and you had found Chuck McNulty, who led you to him."

Clark had actually found McNulty, but I understood his desire to keep a low profile. He was the one still subject to military discipline.

"Do you think he'll talk straight?" I asked.

"You'll have to judge for yourself, but he said to call him. If he wanted to evade questions, why agree to talk?"

"Why indeed?" And then I thought, *unless he hopes to spin me a tale that brings the investigation to an erroneous conclusion.*

"Thanks," I said. "What's his number?"

Nakayla jotted down the ten digits.

I picked up the phone. "I'm keeping you out of this, DeShaun."

"Appreciate it, brother. But if a fellow officer was murdered, you do what you need to do to get justice for all of us." He disconnected.

Nakayla handed me her notepad with Axelrod's number. "You going to drive to Raleigh?"

"No. It's twice as far as Charlotte, and I've got the meeting with Owen Sharp tomorrow. If I don't like Axelrod's answers, then I'll show up on his doorstep Monday morning. Let's call him on the office phone so we can record it."

Our landline consoles had been modified to permit the call to be recorded on a small SD card. North Carolina law required only one party of a conversation to have knowledge of a recording, not both. Of course, this assumed both parties were in North Carolina at the time of the call. Raleigh, the state capital, certainly qualified.

"Hello?" The man's voice was strong without a trace of an old-age warble.

"Is this Len Axelrod?"

"Yes. Is this who I think it is?"

"I hope so. Chief Warrant Officer DeShaun Clark gave me your number. My name's Sam Blackman."

"Is it true you found me through Chuck McNulty?"

"Yes, sir. I'm hoping you can shed some light on what happened to Eddie Gilmore."

"What happened to him was he got murdered. Didn't McNulty tell you?"

"Yes, sir. But we don't know why. McNulty said Eddie Gilmore wanted to talk to you about his brother-in-law Frank DeMille. That ties back to the Apollo tracking station and our area. You might not have known, but the remains of Frank DeMille were discovered at the station the week before last."

Silence. I waited him out.

"Cause of death?" The flat tone of his voice was suddenly infused with curiosity.

"Indications he was struck in the head with something like a shovel blade. He was buried on a wooded ridge above, and the skeleton was unearthed during an attempt to contain a recent forest fire. We're working on behalf of Eddie's widow, who is Frank DeMille's sister. Our progress to date is that we suspect the investigation has generated two murders and an attempt on our lives."

More silence. I let Axelrod's cop brain assess the information and possible consequences.

"I understand you were a chief warrant officer in Iraq and now are a private detective."

"That's correct, sir."

"So you know when we undertake an investigation, no one is immune from our questions, whether they're a private or a general."

"I've interviewed my share of both," I said.

"So I have this radio phone conversation with Gilmore while I'm in a village outside of Saigon. He wants to know if I'd run a concern up the investigative chain regarding a potential leak at a NASA facility. Now NASA isn't a military agency, but rocket development and support systems clearly overlap with the priorities of the Department of Defense. He said his brother-in-law was hesitant to raise the issue internally if there was the better option for someone from the outside to review the matter."

"Did Eddie say what proof his brother-in-law might have had?" I asked.

"He'd created some kind of gateway that didn't block access to his files but counted whenever the program was copied. Sort of a cyber turnstile. The problem was he didn't have a way to know who had tapped the data. However, since the system was closed, it had to be someone on-site. He didn't want to accuse his colleagues, but a duplication had to be internal. There was no reason to do that unless you were taking the data external. I guess back then, it could have been some sort of floppy disk."

"Did you initiate any action after talking to Gilmore?"

"No. We were to meet in Saigon. Then he was murdered. I made sure I was assigned to the investigation, and when the Kit Carson Scout became the main suspect, I was encouraged to close the case."

I thought I knew why. "Because of the embarrassment of a traitorous Kit Carson Scout. It tainted the whole program."

"No. It wasn't about the scout. It was about Dr. Jean Louis Caron. The Soviet agent had been on counterespionage's watch list, and a public investigation into Nguyen Van Bao's movements would have alerted Caron. The murder was folded into the espionage case, and I was taken off. I got to interrogate neither a private nor a general. I was shut out."

"And no one followed up on Frank DeMille?"

"I tried, but by then, he'd vanished. I suspected the disappearance tied into the Soviets, and I passed that along. But Caron was their main target, and NASA wasn't on their radar. It was all about the war." He sighed. "The irony was computer hacks and cyber thefts have become the war."

"And Dr. Caron?"

"They closed in on him. He put a bullet through his brain, blowing out all his secrets. No telling how much damage he'd done or how many spies he ran in addition to Nguyen Van Bao."

"You know Bao's defense minister of Vietnam."

Axelrod's intake of breath was audible. "That son of a bitch. Are you sure?"

"McNulty claims he saw him in some news footage a few years back. And he appeared to be best friends with one Vladimir Putin. I realize Putin would have been too young in 1971 to be involved. He didn't join the KGB until 1975. But that sly fox probably knows all operatives and operations before, during, and after his intelligence days."

"Blackman, do you still have cases that are crawling under your skin?"

"Yeah. Ones I couldn't prove but knew the guilty party. Ones I couldn't solve but I'm haunted by the victims. I'm afraid this case might fall into one of those two categories."

"And you've brought Eddie Gilmore and Chuck McNulty back to me. I can still see McNulty in that hospital bed, the stump of his amputated leg wrapped in bloody bandages. His only concern was that I get who killed his friend. That's one of the cases under my skin, so if I can do anything at all to help, you call on me."

"Yes, sir."

"And a favor, if you would be so kind. Let me know how I can get in touch with McNulty."

"He's in Charlotte. I'm sure he'd love to hear from you."

Nakayla scribbled out the phone number and address. I relayed the information.

"Thanks, Blackman. Good hunting."

He hung up.

"What do you think?" Nakayla asked.

"I think we learned the military screwed up and left a potential mole at the tracking station. And he's not only a spy, he's a killer."

# Chapter 24

The noon sun beat down from a cloudless sky. Asheville tourists crammed underneath the awnings covering the sidewalk vendors as much to escape the direct rays as to peruse the handcrafted wares. I'd arrived at the designated rendezvous fifteen minutes early and stood on the corner of Page and Battery Park Avenues until the heat drove me to a nearby bench partially shaded by an anemic tree.

At precisely twelve o'clock, a tall man with curly black hair walked to the corner and waited beneath the street sign. He was neatly dressed in navy slacks and an open-neck white dress shirt, but the real clue that he was NOAA executive Owen Sharp hung around his neck. The photo ID badge proclaimed he could access some restricted area the rest of us could not.

He saw me as I approached and offered his hand. "Mr. Blackman. I'm Owen."

"Then I'm Sam. Thanks for taking the time on a Sunday to meet with me."

He smiled. "Better Sunday than trying to squeeze in time during the week. Not that my job is so important. It's just there's never a day without weather."

I laughed. "I can't argue with that. And you were right about today. It's a scorcher."

His smiling face turned grim. "Better get used to it. Now, Hewitt said you had some questions. Is it about a case? Hewitt usually sends us a written request."

"Not a specific case. Primarily some background questions. I thought Hewitt told you I'm pretty ignorant about how your operation works."

"He did. That's why I thought we'd meet here. Where things began." He gestured toward the huge, five-story Grove Arcade. "Do you know much about the building?"

"Only that it was built by the same Grove who constructed the Grove Park Inn. And I think it was supposed to be bigger."

Owen Sharp started walking toward one of the entrances. "That's correct. It was supposed to be a five-story base and fourteen-story tower. Retail and residential. A visionary concept for the early 1920s. But Grove died in 1927. Only the base was finished when it opened in 1929. Then the market crash eliminated any chance that the original design would be completed."

We stepped into the cavernous interior with shops flanking either side. "It was the center of commerce for thirteen years. Then in 1942, it was taken over by the federal government."

"Why?"

"The war effort. The shops were vacated, the ground floor exterior windows were bricked up, and important records were housed, including weather data. The Western North Carolina mountains were considered to be unlikely bombing targets should the Nazis have gotten so far. The same way city hall and the Biltmore House were utilized."

"City hall? I know the National Gallery sent priceless paintings for safekeeping at Biltmore, but why city hall?"

"During World War II, the entire Asheville city hall was leased to the U.S. Army. It was made the headquarters for its Weather Wing and Communications Services branch, the forerunner of the AF-Triple-C of today."

I looked at him blankly.

"The Air Force Combat Climatology Center. No military operation happens without weather and climate assessment. A short history lesson. Back in the 1930s, a WPA project had collected weather data on paper punch cards that had been developed for the 1890 census. The cards were adapted to record the weather data, and in 1934, the project punched two million weather and climate observations from 1880 to 1933. Others followed, bringing the database constantly up to date. That data was made available to the military and became critical information during World War II. Military operations factored in climatological input. The forecasts for missions, landings, including D-Day itself depended upon this data. Even how runways were laid out or where bases were located." He stopped walking. "I hope I'm not boring you."

"Not at all."

He gestured to a coffee shop beside us. "Good. Why don't we sit down, or else I'll have us lapping the building."

We paused the discussion long enough for me to treat him to an iced tea while I ordered iced coffee. We found a small corner table separate from the other patrons.

"So to make a long story shorter, the collected data needed to be consolidated and stored somewhere. The government already owned Grove Arcade, so moving the records here would be an internal operation, drawing little external attention. In 1951, the National Weather Records Center was established here. Then it was known as the National Climatic Data Center and is now the part of NOAA called the National Centers for Environmental Information. Asheville's still the headquarters, and all the information is digitized."

Fortunately, I'd become familiar with these more recent incarnations and could act like I threw those titles around every day. But Owen Sharp's mini lecture had revealed a new aspect that rose above the plethora of names and acronyms.

"Are you still providing military information?" I asked.

"The army and navy now have their own data centers, but the air force, through AF-Triple-C, shares our data stream." Sharp took a sip of tea and set the glass on the table. "We're a civilian agency, not a military one, but AF-Triple-C has a presence in the Federal Building with us."

"How secure is that data?"

Sharp began to rotate the glass as he thought about my question. "Is this what Hewitt's going for? Is he concerned someone could impeach our data if used in court?"

I shrugged. "Hacking has been the weapon of assault in the twenty-first century."

Sharp nodded. "I don't disagree. But we call our core data our golden data. It's highly, highly secured."

"How can people access it then?"

He laughed. "Like everything else. Go to our website. Specifically, our Climate Data Online page."

"Anybody?" I couldn't keep the incredulity out of my voice.

"It's historical data. It's free unless there are retrieval costs like certified hard copies to be sealed for court."

"And you're confident that this data couldn't be altered or manipulated?"

Sharp threw up his hands. "We can't control what happens to the data after a customer receives it. But for our part, it's as secure as possible, backed up in case of catastrophic failure and matched up against other data through publications like the *State of the Climate* report put out by the *Bulletin of the American Meteorological Society* that can be verified by other groups."

"And you've never been hacked?"

"There are attempts daily, but so far so good."

"And the data accessed by the air force?"

"They have their own encrypted pathway."

I kept pressing for what I sensed was just a question or two away. "And the data can't be altered, but if you're inside the firewall, would you know what data was being requested?"

"Yes. Though the searches would give us that information up front."

"Not if the request came from the military."

My statement seemed to startle him. "You're asking if we could monitor what data was mined through the military channel?"

"Yes. You said it was the same data stream."

He took the last swallow of tea and wiped his lips with the back of his hand. "That's not specifically built into the protocols, but I guess it could be reported out. It's shared data."

"And is it possible that the data could be secure but a false trail created to make it look like the protective firewall had been breached?"

Sharp shook his head. "I don't know. That's a question for our computer techs. What would be the purpose?"

"To throw suspicion on the integrity of the data. In the climate change debate, for example. The breach wouldn't actually have had to occur, only the suspicion of a breach."

Sharp smiled. "You certainly ask some thought-provoking questions, Sam. I'd like the answers myself."

"Before you ask them, would a day or two delay matter? I'm handling a sensitive case for Hewitt, and I don't want to raise any doubts about what is probably only my hypothetical musings."

"Fair enough. But I might do some preliminary digging without mentioning your name. Say later in the week?"

"Agreed."

We stood and walked back through the center of the arcade. I wondered what it was like when it was filled with punch cards.

"You're constantly backing up your data, I trust."

"Yes," Sharp confirmed. "On- and off-site."

"I was out at PARI the other day. Looks like they're planning to be a repository of secure data themselves."

Sharp eyed me curiously. "We're using them. But I have an idea you knew that already."

We stepped out into the blazing sunlight and walked toward Otis Street and his building. "A day for the record books," I said. Sharp shook my hand. "Yes. And the records are only going to be broken more frequently." He reached in his breast pocket and handed me a business card. "If you have any more questions, feel free to call any time."

I waited, watching him cross to return to his office. Again, the sentence ran through my mind. Disinformation creates doubt, chaos breeds confusion. From what I'd learned from Sharp, we weren't just talking about disrupting and corrupting data supporting climate change, we were talking about the accuracy of data used by the United States military. The air force still depended upon that data.

A new thought flashed through my mind. Not only would climate data serve to inform long-term military strategies like where to build bases and how to lay out runways, but the very act of drawing upon that data was information unto itself. If someone could learn where and when the air force was retrieving critical weather data, was that not a tip-off as to where an operation might be targeted? Where drones might be deployed? Where air support might be planned for troop advancements? From Hewitt's courtroom to strategic and tactical global warfare, weather data played a critical role in ways I'd never imagined.

I turned to cross to the Otis parking deck where I'd left my car. I saw them before they saw me. Joseph Gordowski and Theo Brecht strolled down the other side of Otis, apparently engaged in deep conversation. Had either of them seen me with Sharp? If so, they gave no indication.

I let them get half a block ahead before I followed. They turned onto Wall Street, the short, narrow lane that ran parallel to Patton Avenue and provided street side entrances for the lower street's second-story buildings. As I trailed them, I realized Rat Alley lay directly beneath me.

The two men stopped at the Laughing Seed Café. I remembered the barman at the Battery Park Book Exchange saying

Theo Brecht usually ate there because he was a vegetarian. The two friends disappeared into the restaurant for what I assumed would be Sunday brunch.

I pulled out my cell phone and called Nakayla.

"How did it go?" she asked.

"Very interesting. I'll fill you in later. But I need you to get me the home addresses for Gordowski and Brecht."

"Are you going to see them?"

"No. I just saw them enter the Laughing Seed. I want to check out where they live while I know they're away."

"What if they're just picking up takeout?"

"Then I'll see if one of them invites me in for lunch. But the sooner you get me the information, the less likely that will happen."

"Back in five." She rang off.

True to her word, Nakayla called with the addresses and descriptions within the promised time. "Both men have houses, not condos or apartments, and both men live alone. Gordowski has a small house in Brevard. Brecht lives in East Asheville."

The addresses were about forty-five minutes apart.

"I'd better start with Gordowski," I said. "Get out there and back. Maybe they're both working today and Brecht will leave late enough I can swing by his place."

"Too risky," Nakayla said. "I have a better idea. You go to Brevard, and I'll check out Brecht's house. What are we looking for?"

"Whatever it is we need to find."

"Wow, Chief Warrant Officer Blackman, brilliant doesn't begin to describe you."

I waited for her punchline. Silence. Too late, I realized that was it. Brilliant doesn't begin to describe me. She disconnected midlaugh.

# Chapter 25

Brevard, North Carolina, is the small mountain town that's the county seat of Transylvania. Once named as one of the top ten places to retire, Brevard now has a heavy population of retirees and second-home owners. But it is a vibrant cultural community, home to the renowned Brevard Music Center and Brevard College.

As I drove past the entrance to the four-year school, I spotted another unique trait of Brevard—white squirrels cavorting on the campus lawn. These creatures aren't albinos but rather the alleged descendants of escapees from a traveling menagerie of many decades ago. Every year, Brevard holds its White Squirrel Festival to honor these unusual animals and to encourage an influx of tourist dollars into the local economy.

I crested the hill on which the intersection of Main and Broad Streets claimed the high point of the neighboring topography. Seeing the Transylvania County Courthouse reminded me I'd entered Sheriff Hickman's jurisdiction. I wondered if arsonist Danny Number Two awaited trial in the county jail or had managed bail. I doubted he was free on bond unless he'd passed a thorough psychiatric evaluation.

GPS led me to a small brick ranch on a corner lot within

walking distance of the town center. The house faced one street while the driveway connected to the side road. I decided my CR-V would be less likely to draw attention if I pulled into the driveway. The double-wide concrete strip ended at a detached two-car garage. The closed door blocked a view of the inside.

I reached under the passenger's seat and pulled out my investigative prop—a clipboard. Holding a clipboard gave one purpose and an air of official business. I could be a meter reader, contractor, or inspector.

Stepping out into the sunlight, I heard a dog challenge my arrival with a series of sharp barks. The furry sentinel jumped up against a bordering, chain-link fence, but his stubby tail wagged so vigorously that he was more Welcome Wagon than Neighborhood Watch.

I ignored the pooch and walked to the garage door. Grabbing the handle, I tried to lift it, but whether it was locked or controlled by an automatic opener, the door didn't budge.

A screened porch was attached to the left side of the garage. A covered walkway provided shelter from the porch to the back door of the house. I tried the doorknob. Also locked. Peering through the mullioned window panes, I saw a tidy kitchen.

I carefully stepped into a weedy flowerbed and looked through an adjacent window. The slats of the blind were open, and I saw a dining table with four chairs. Beyond, a sofa and armchair suggested one end of the front living room. A guitar leaned against the cushion of the sofa. Had Joseph Gordowski taken lessons from Randall Johnson? The men knew each other from work. Could the strings be Martins?

I took out my phone and zoomed the image tighter for a closer shot of the instrument. I could examine the photograph more closely when I returned to the office.

Turning back to the screened porch, I noticed a side entrance to the garage. The porch door was unlocked, and I moved through the outdoor furniture in hopes I could gain entry.

There was a time when folks in a small town didn't lock their garages. That time had passed. But not for Joseph Gordowski. The door opened, and as I crossed the threshold, a motion detector turned on the lights.

The double garage had a vacant spot were a car had been parked. A few aged oil stains indicated a vehicle with a leaky seal once had been housed there. On the other side, a small lawn mower with a grass clippings bag had been rolled against the wall. A five-gallon metal can sat beside it.

I lifted the can. The hollow slosh of liquid told me it was nearly empty. I unscrewed the top lid and smelled the distinctive odor of gasoline. Five gallons would have been more than enough to engulf Nakayla's home in flames.

The back wall of the garage held a surprise. A workbench at standing height and a desk with an expensive leather chair demonstrated Gordowski spent a lot of time there. The workbench didn't have a vise or saws or other tools for woodworking. The pieces scattered on its surface were electronic in nature. Circuit boards, chips, diagnostic equipment, screwdrivers, and soldering irons.

On the desk sat a shortwave transceiver. The gear appeared to be old school with a headset and microphone and a telegraph key. In an age of Facebook and encrypted email accounts, Gordowski stayed within the era of Marconi. Was it low-tech under the radar of a high-tech world?

I noticed a black, shielded cable coming out of the rear of the transceiver and disappearing through a matching diameter hole in the wall near the upper rafters. Outside, I circled behind the garage to where the cable came through the wall and ran up to the roof. An antenna rose from a bracket mounted on the eave. The pitch of the roof hid it from the driveway and from the house.

Again, I used my phone to photograph the antenna, the electronic equipment, and the gas can. Since I'd had no search warrant, they'd be shared only with Nakayla so that together we could formulate a plan to bring Gordowski to the attention of the FBI.

Before backing out of the driveway, I emailed the photos to Nakayla and asked her to call me after she had the chance to review them. Then my mind went into overdrive as I imagined how the history behind this case must have played out.

Frank DeMille became suspicious that his sophisticated software codes were being duplicated and shared beyond the Apollo tracking station. He was hesitant to make an accusation without proof, so he asked his brother-in-law, Eddie Gilmore, for advice. Evidently, Eddie planned to discuss the matter with Chief Warrant Officer Len Axelrod in Saigon. Eddie didn't realize one of the Kit Carson Scouts close to him, Nguyen Van Bao, had intercepted the information and delivered it to his Soviet handler, Dr. Jean Louis Caron. Once Moscow got wind of the potential investigation, word must have gone out to Bao and Gordowski, half a world apart, to eliminate the threat.

But why kill DeMille at the tracking station? Maybe he caught Gordowski copying his computer program that night? Maybe he spooked Gordowski with his suspicions. Either way, DeMille was murdered, Gordowski remained untouched, and the Soviets must have been delighted when the tracking facility was taken over by the NSA and their mole stayed in place.

The discovery of Frank DeMille's remains nearly fifty years later shouldn't have been a concern, especially since the NSA no longer controlled the site. PARI was a public science lab and museum. But Gordowski's friend, Theo Brecht, had landed a computer job at NOAA, and Gordowski had wormed his way into helping him. Furthermore, backup data storage was tying NOAA and PARI together, and Gordowski was now positioned to work in both. If Gordowski fell under suspicion, his activities would be greatly curtailed.

Although the Soviet Union no longer existed, I felt certain the link still went back to Russia. Inside and outside coordinated hacks might penetrate NOAA's safeguards, not to mention the value of knowing the air force's weather and climate priorities.

Yes, the danger of their spy's unmasking brought out the same response—kill anyone who could be a threat. Nakayla and I for spearheading a more tenacious investigation into Frank DeMille, Loretta for what she remembered the night Frank disappeared, and Randall Johnson to be a ready-made fall guy. The pattern seemed clear, but we still needed hard evidence. Evidence like catching old-school Gordowski transmitting some coded message in the middle of the night. I found myself anxious to be a part of any raid.

My cell rang as I merged onto I-26 for Asheville. It was Nakayla.

"How did you do?" I asked.

"Not so good. The blinds were drawn on all the windows. Brecht has a single garage with rudimentary tools hanging on a pegboard wall."

"You got inside the garage?"

"Yes. An unlocked side door. Everything in there was very tidy."

"Any gas cans?"

"No. Just a small lawn mower. Looks like you unearthed more."

"Gas, guitar, shortwave radio, and no alibi for the night Frank DeMille died. Or the night your house was firebombed."

"All circumstantial," Nakayla cautioned. "I'm at the office, and I blew up the photo you took of the guitar. It's classical. Not the style Randall Johnson taught. And a classical guitar has gut or nylon strings, not the wound steel suspected in Loretta's murder."

"But he obviously knows strings," I countered. "Buy a steel set since Randall played steel."

"Maybe that's the question. Ask Gordowski what brand of strings did Randall play. If they both played guitar and worked together for years, they must have talked music."

"And if he say's Elixir, why would he use Martins to fake a suicide?"

"Exactly. So if he says Elixir, then it's more likely he's innocent."

"Kind of an odd question for me to ask him out of the blue."

"Yes, but Newly could, or Sheriff Browder. You might pass it along."

Nakayla was right. Cops were always questioning a suspect from a multitude of angles and non sequiturs. Or maybe I'd hold that question for the FBI. They had the ultimate say if Gordowski turned out to be a Russian spy.

"OK. You staying at the office?" I asked.

"No. I'm going to pick up some more things I need to replace from the fire. And I thought I'd run by Hewitt's and get Blue before returning to your apartment. You?"

"I'll stop by the office and download these photos from my phone. And I'd like to think about how I'm going to approach Lindsay Boyce. I think we need to see her first thing in the morning. Maybe I should call Newly and bring him up to speed before meeting Boyce."

"What about dinner?"

I glanced at my watch. Five after three. "Where would you like to go?"

"How about the Laughing Seed Café? We shouldn't have to worry about running into Joseph Gordowski."

"OK," I agreed. "Say six? I'll be the macho carnivore amid all your artsy vegetarians."

Nakayla laughed. "Yeah, Macho Man. The thing you eat most is crow. But maybe you can sneak down to Jack of the Wood and smuggle up a few sliders." She hung up.

I stared straight ahead, not really seeing the traffic in front of me or hearing the eighteen-wheeler beside me. "Maybe you can sneak down to Jack of the Wood and smuggle up a few sliders." Jack of the Wood was on Patton Avenue, the Laughing Seed Café on Wall Street, but it was the same building. A staircase connected the two restaurants. Had the police checked who was in the upper restaurant? Someone who could have come down at any time and seen Loretta? Possibly even heard her song?

I phoned Newly.

He growled at me. "For God's sake, it's Sunday afternoon. Don't you know God wants me to have an uninterrupted nap?"

"Just one question. When you followed up on the diners and drinkers in Jack of the Wood the night Loretta was killed, did you also check the clientele at the Laughing Seed Café?"

Silence. I suspected Newly was embarrassed to say the police had overlooked the physical link between the two restaurants.

"You woke me up for that question? What kind of rube department do you think we are? Yes, we talked to the wait staff the next day and went through the credit card receipts. No tie to what went on in the pub. Why is this question now so urgent?"

I'd planned to wait till the next morning to get into our suspicions about Joseph Gordowski, but Newly asked a legitimate question.

"I think Gordowski might have been a Russian spy all these years." I quickly summarized the computer programming codes of DeMille, the years inside the NSA, and now the climate data and potential link to the air force.

"When we interviewed Gordowski, he said he was home that evening. No one claimed to have seen him at the pub. Other leads within the Case family or Randall Johnson were stronger."

"Well, you might want to question him again. At his home. You'll notice he has a guitar, so it wouldn't be inappropriate to ask if he knows what kind of strings Johnson played. And you might see if he'll let you in his garage to check his gas cans. You'll then notice a shortwave transceiver."

"Should I ask how you know all this?"

"No."

"And this can wait till tomorrow?"

"Your call. He was working with Theo Brecht today, but he might be home this evening. That's after you've enjoyed your nap."

"And what are you going to do?" Newly asked.

"What I do best. Think."

Newly laughed. "Then, Sam, I'd hate to know what you do the worst."

# Chapter 26

Despite Newly's teasing me about my little gray cells, as Hercule Poirot would say, I did need time to concentrate on what I'd learned and develop a theory of how the crimes could have occurred. The goal was to create a cogent argument I could lay out for Special Agent Lindsay Boyce and her FBI team.

Arriving at the office, I first brewed a fresh pot of coffee and then took a steaming mug along with a pencil and legal pad to the sofa. I listed the names of all the people who had been caught up in the investigation of the four murder victims—Frank DeMille, Eddie Gilmore, Loretta Case Johnson, and Randall Johnson. I even included intelligence officer Chuck McNulty and Chief Warrant Officer Len Axelrod because of their Vietnam War connection.

In sort of a makeshift Venn diagram, I described how relationships entwined, what alibis existed, and what might be motives.

*Joseph Gordowski—worked for Apollo, NSA. Volunteers for PARI, and NOAA. Has no alibi for night of DeMille's disappearance. Close to DeMille, knew his work. Also has no alibi for night of Loretta's death or the firebombing. Asked Brecht to bring him onto NOAA-PARI data backup project. Operates shortwave radio and has gas can.*

*Theo Brecht—came later to Apollo as assistant to DeMille but also worked NSA and now NOAA. Has an alibi for night of DeMille's death as both Loretta and Randall saw him. Was learning from DeMille and replaced him. No alibi for night of Loretta's death or firebombing. Agreed to Gordowski's request for part-time work with NOAA data project. No visible gasoline cans at his house.*

*Randall Johnson—on-site the night of DeMille's disappearance. Brecht says Johnson's overalls were muddy but only remembers that because of potential damage to the equipment. Johnson had a crush on Loretta and would have seen DeMille as a rival. Possibly had enough knowledge to copy files and could have been paid by Soviets. No alibi for night of Loretta's murder or firebombing. A faked suicide didn't mean he couldn't have killed DeMille or Loretta. His death could have been from someone who believed he killed Loretta. The Case brothers most likely. The Martin guitar strings could have been used by them for another reason.*

*The Case brothers and their sons all heard Loretta's song, but only her twin brothers were alive at the time of Frank DeMille's murder. Least likely suspects to have been involved in any espionage connection if that was the underlying motive.*

I stopped writing and went to my computer. A quick search showed the Martin strings to be half the price of the Elixirs. Could the Martins have been nothing more than a cheaper option for a murder weapon? I'd witnessed stranger things in my career. I returned to my legal pad and added the sentence, *Martin strings don't necessarily exonerate Case family*. It was then I noticed one name wasn't on the list. Loretta Case Johnson herself. The least suspected person. The one who had written letters to Frank. The one who had written to Frank's sister. Could all of that have been to cover her tracks? Was she what the spy game calls a honey trap? Seduced Frank and then learned enough about what he did to copy the codings and then send them on to someone who could deconstruct and understand Frank's genius?

No. On her front porch, her grief had been too real, too raw, too spontaneous when Nakayla and I had told her of the discovery and identification of Frank's remains. And she'd provided alibis for others. Why do that if you're the guilty party? Why not sow suspicion elsewhere?

That thought stopped me. Gordowski hadn't said anything that incriminated anyone else. Just that he had left when the tracking station's role had ended for that cycle. Brecht had said he'd then waited for Frank DeMille to return to check his programming for slewing the radio telescopes to the next quadrant of the heavens.

My grandmother always told me I had two ears and one mouth for a reason. I should listen twice as much as I speak. I'd learned that was a cardinal rule in investigative work. Something that Chuck McNulty said Eddie Gilmore had mastered. Interviews may be conversational, but they aren't conversations. You are listening for what's said and what's not said. What had Brecht told me that could be verified? Had we attributed more to his statements than was warranted? I closed my eyes and tried to reconstruct our encounters.

Brecht had told me Randall Johnson had dirty overalls, but Randall died before that statement could be checked. Brecht had told me Loretta had come looking for Frank and seen Johnson's dirty overalls. But no one else could corroborate his claim. What if it was Brecht who had the earth-covered knees? At the time, Loretta wouldn't have made much of it, since no one knew Frank's body lay in a freshly dug grave. But when I'd told her about the shovel, the memory must have come flooding back. Johnson having dirt on his clothes wouldn't have been unusual. But Brecht? And who was the person she was planning to meet that night after their gig? Not me, but surely someone involved in the case. That would have been Randall, Gordowski, or Brecht.

Then a more damning thought emerged. Brecht and I'd been talking, and I'd mentioned Loretta's song lyrics. He'd commented how it must have alarmed someone when she sang it. Thinking back, I was pretty sure I'd never said she'd sung it that night. I'd just shared the lyrics. Brecht could have been on the stairs between the vegetarian restaurant and the pub, heard her, and realized the implications of what she might do. Had she contacted him to discuss their memories of the night Frank disappeared? Or had he contacted her to see what she remembered? Had the planned rendezvous become an opportunity to silence her?

The firebombing had occurred before I'd spoken to Brecht. But Janet at PARI said she told Gordowski and Brecht that the famous detective, Sam Blackman, was investigating. Had my reputation created such an extreme response that he'd turned to arson? When that failed, did he feel compelled to return my call? And the gas cans? Nakayla said Brecht had a small mower but no can. Who hauls a mower to the gas station? The fact that he had no gas can was more significant than the nearly empty one in Gordowski's garage. Randall Johnson had multiple ones including a new one. Was Brecht's can planted among them?

I opened my eyes and saw Gordowski was no longer my main suspect. I'd attributed guilt to things that had other explanations. Gordowski had no alibi for that Apollo mission night because he had gone home just like he said. He specialized in maximizing the communications between the astronauts and mission control. Why couldn't his hobby be ham radio? And he was helping with the NOAA computer system and PARI backup because Brecht worked there. Who had asked whom? We'd only heard Brecht's version.

I felt an icy shiver. If Gordowski was out of the picture, there was no one left on my list of suspects who could challenge whatever Brecht said.

I looked at my watch. Ten minutes after four. Brecht and Gordowski would have left the restaurant hours ago. Had they gone back to work? I fished through my pockets for Owen Sharp's business card. There was a direct number and a cell number. I punched in the cell.

"Owen Sharp."

"Owen, it's Sam Blackman."

He laughed. "That was quick. More questions?"

"Are you in your office?"

"No. I just arrived home. What's up?"

"Do you know if Theo Brecht and Joseph Gordowski are still in the building?"

He paused. "What's this about?"

I gave him an off-the-top-of-my-head answer. "It's a question about PARI, not NOAA. I'm aiding the police on a cold case, and they might be able to help me."

"That skeleton they found?"

"Yes. Both men knew the victim. We're trying to help the family."

"I see," he said sympathetically. "Well, they were in the building this morning. I overheard them tell someone they were going to PARI tonight after it closed. When I returned from meeting you, they were at lunch. I don't know if they came back."

"Do you have a cell number for either one?"

"Not with me. Their numbers would be at the office. I'll see if I can raise anybody there. Maybe they're still working."

"Thanks. Oh, one other thing. How did Joseph come to be part of the computer team?"

"Theo suggested it. Like you said, they've worked together for years. Their security clearances were above mine, so I said go ahead. But Joseph's not full-time."

"I understand. So Joseph didn't come to you for the job?"

"No," Sharp said. "I knew we needed some extra help for this secure data project, and Theo said he had the perfect person.

I told him to pursue him." The edge of uncertainty crept back into his voice. "Is there something about Joseph I should know?"

"No. I just hope I'll have his and Theo's energy when I'm their age."

"They're scientists," Sharp said. "A scientist never retires as long as he's got his curiosity."

*Or someone's paying or blackmailing him for classified data,* I thought.

"Thanks," I said. "If I can reach them today, it will be a big help."

I hung up, untucked my shirt, and slid my Kimber .45 into a holster that fit against the small of my back.

Hurrying down the sidewalk of Biltmore Avenue to my parking garage, I noticed a change in the weather. The hot, humid air began to move in short, strong gusts. Maybe the inversion was breaking up. Maybe somewhere behind the ridges, a storm was brewing.

I phoned Nakayla and half shouted, "It's Brecht."

"Are you sure?"

"Hell, no. But things he's said don't add up. Get to the Laughing Seed and ask if anyone remembers Brecht eating there last Tuesday night. Someone should know him, and he and Gordowski ate lunch there today if that helps jog a memory."

"Where are you headed?"

"Wherever I can find Gordowski. I'm expecting a call from Owen Sharp with Gordowski's cell phone number. Sharp said Brecht and Gordowski are working at PARI tonight. I'm hoping Gordowski has gone home in the meantime."

"You think he's in danger?"

I entered the parking garage and pressed the remote key to unlock the CR-V. "Brecht's made claims that Gordowski can refute. If Gordowski's gone, there's no one left to contradict him. For all I know, Brecht might be setting Gordowski up to be the final fall guy."

"Are you going back to Brevard?"

"Yes, assuming Gordowski's headed home. If I can make sure he's safe, then we can focus on Brecht."

"We?"

"Newly, Boyce, Hickman, Browder. Whoever's closest and willing to question him again. That's why discovering if he was near Rat Alley when Loretta died is so important."

"Then I'm on it," Nakayla said.

I started the engine. "Thanks, my love."

"You can thank me by not being a hero. If things start to break bad, promise you'll call for help."

"Trust me. I have no intention of putting myself in danger."

"Intentions aren't promises, Sam." She rang off.

I headed for the interstate with every intention of keeping my promise. Five minutes later, Owen Sharp called.

"I've got the cell numbers for Theo and Joseph."

"Do you know when they left?"

"The person I spoke with said about fifteen minutes ago."

"Together?"

"I didn't ask. Does it matter?"

"No. No. I just thought if I caught them together, it would save a phone call. Thanks, Owen. I'm driving, so it would be better if you could text me the numbers."

"You got it."

A few minutes later, I heard the ding and took a quick glance at the phone's screen. Two 828 area codes and no indication of which number belonged to which man. My phone highlighted them so that all I had to do was touch to activate the call. I tried the second one first, thinking full-time staffer Brecht would be alphabetized first.

"Hello." Brecht's voice.

"Sorry. Wrong number." I disengaged and realized my mistake. I should have come up with some nonthreatening reason for the call. Like Cory DeMille wanted to learn more about what her uncle was like. I'd created a problem, because Brecht knew my cell number.

I called Gordowski.

One ring and then, "This is Joseph. Leave a message."

"Joseph. Sam Blackman. Please return my call." I didn't want to say any more. The fact that I went straight to voicemail suggested he was on the phone, in a dead zone, or had a dead battery. My next option was to wait at his house and hope to intercept him.

I turned onto highway 280 and passed the Asheville airport. Windsocks snapped as gusts intensified. Thunderheads towered over the ridges to the west, blocking the late afternoon sun and casting the world into unnatural twilight. Perhaps the storm would dissuade Brecht and Gordowski from even traveling those narrow, curving roads to PARI. Or perhaps the storm would isolate the two, creating an opportunity for some accident to be arranged that would leave Brecht the sole survivor of the Apollo tracking team.

Ingenuity put a man on the moon. What ingenuity would be devised to put another man in the earth?

# Chapter 27

I drove past Gordowski's driveway. The white concrete was becoming blotched with dark, wet splotches created by raindrops the size of small water balloons. I saw no sign of lights in the house or garage, but I couldn't be sure that Gordowski's car wasn't behind the closed door.

I turned around and parked in the driveway. A mad dash from my vehicle to the screened porch semisoaked me. I vigorously shook off the water in a manner that would have made Blue proud. Then I opened the garage's side door. No car. Gordowski wasn't home yet.

A quick look at my watch confirmed it was only forty minutes till PARI's scheduled Sunday closing time of six o'clock. Gordowski must have elected to go straight there.

My cell rang. Nakayla.

"Are you at the Laughing Seed?" I asked.

"Yes. Both Gordowski and Brecht were well known by the manager on duty. In fact, sometimes Brecht ordered takeout and then went downstairs to Jack of the Wood so that Gordowski could have a burger."

"And were either one there last Tuesday night?"

"The manager took a quick poll of his wait staff. One of them remembered serving Brecht."

"He claimed he was home," I said. "And Newly checked the patron receipts."

"Brecht never asked for his check," Nakayla said. "He left more than enough cash. No card swiped, no restaurant record with a name. And the waiter was off when the police did their follow-up the next day. Get this. Brecht's table was next to the stairs. He could have heard Loretta singing from where he sat."

"And then slipped down to the pub," I added.

"All he had to do was catch Loretta's eye and suggest they step into Rat Alley."

I could see it happening, because now we had confirmation of Brecht at the scene. "Loretta probably confronted him and then turned away. The garrote would be around her neck in less than a second."

"He came prepared to kill," Nakayla said.

"Yes. And then he tried to use Loretta's song to throw suspicion on Randall Johnson. He probably saw Randall's guitar at some point over the years and bought Martin strings because he thought he was matching the brand."

"Where are you now?"

"I'm at Gordowski's house in the middle of a thunderstorm. I think he's gone straight to PARI."

"Sam, you're not going out there alone." It wasn't a question.

"I'll call Hickman. He and his deputies can at least provide protection if Brecht means Gordowski harm. You brief Newly on what you've learned at the Laughing Seed. He'll want to bring Brecht in for questioning."

I ended the call. The Transylvania County Sheriff's Department was in the 911 system, and the operator quickly routed me. A Deputy Hanes answered.

"This is Sam Blackman. I'm reporting trouble at PARI. Please alert Sheriff Hickman that he needs to send deputies for what might be a hostile situation involving a possible hostage. Have him call this number if he has any questions."

Deputy Hanes assured me he would handle it. I dashed back through the torrent, climbed into the driver's seat, and drove into the heart of the storm.

There was a good reason I joined the army rather than the navy—I preferred being on land rather than sea. But the excruciating drive from Brevard to PARI had to be more of an underwater submarine experience. The wipers slapped across the windshield in a futile attempt to clear the glass. Thunder boomed like artillery, and the bursts of lightning could have been muzzle flashes.

My hands cramped from gripping the steering wheel, and the twisting, narrow road kept my speed to a crawl. I hoped Sheriff Hickman had responded quickly, although I was concerned he'd neither called nor had a patrol car overtake me. Maybe the storm hampered the deputies as much as it did me. After thirty minutes, I risked a quick glance at my phone. No service. Hickman might have tried to reach me only to be thwarted by my dead-zone location.

A few minutes before seven, I glimpsed the PARI sign with barely enough reaction time to make the left turn. At least from this point on, the road wouldn't be as winding.

I crested a small hill and made out the shadowless gray shapes of the radio telescopes standing like impervious sentinels, neither aware of nor alarmed by the antagonistic wind and rain.

I leaned over the steering wheel, searching for any sign of law enforcement. As I neared the parking lot of the main building, I saw only two cars, parked side by side, head-on against a wall. I couldn't be sure, but odds were they belonged to Gordowski and Brecht.

I circled and brought my vehicle broadside as close to the rear bumpers as I could, effectively barricading the cars in place.

The wind had slackened, but the rain still fell in a steady stream. The sun dropped behind the ridge, and the heavy, black clouds created an eerie darkness as night came prematurely. I could either sit in my car and wait for the cavalry or confront what might be occurring inside. I made my choice, had made my choice when I took on the case. I adjusted the pistol under my shirt and ran for the door of the Visitors Center. It opened with a barely audible squeal.

Voices sounded somewhere farther into the building. I remembered from Gordowski's tour that a room was being converted into a multiterminal space that would link to the servers planned for a new building to house the stored data. Hardware and software needed to be upgraded and designed.

I looked at the floor. Wet spots indicated the men had come in during the rain. Perhaps they'd only been here a little longer than me. They could have sat in their cars until the worst of the storm passed. Although there must be a staff entrance, the visitors' door was closest to their parking spots, and I was lucky they'd left it unlocked. From their perspective, who in his right mind would come to PARI in a tempest?

I crept along the wall into the room that controls the telescopes. Careful to avoid stumbling against chairs or display tables, I followed the hum of voices until the words became intelligible.

"It must be the power supply, Joseph. It was working fine on Friday, but you can see the circuit breaker's been tripped."

Joseph Gordowski muttered something and then spoke louder. "The power wire might have been stripped or loosened. Heat could have caused expansion that displaced it enough to short it out."

I edged around a corner and saw the two men through a door left ajar. Both wore damp rain slickers. Gordowski was bending in front of a black metal rack of equipment that sat on a raised floor. Several panels of the floor had been removed to reveal cabling running underneath. One of them must have been to the faulty power supply.

Brecht stood beside a breaker box built into the wall. He watched Gordowski with his head cocked at an angle as if considering Gordowski's conclusion. "Maybe," he said. "It was Friday evening, and I was anxious to get back to Asheville. I hope it isn't damaged beyond repair."

"Let me take a look." Gordowski picked up a screwdriver from a toolbox beside him and began to work on a piece of equipment on the bottom of the rack.

Brecht's hand jerked up to the breaker box.

"No!" I shouted.

Gordowski turned his head toward me. Lightning flashed in his hands as the storm seemed to have exploded through the floor. Gordowski's face contorted into a rigid mask of pain. His body twitched in a macabre dance. A loud pop released him, and he fell into one of the open floor panels.

I drew my pistol as Brecht charged me, slamming his shoulder into the half-open door. I fired, but the door's impact knocked the shot wide to the left. I staggered backward, trying to keep my balance. My prosthetic leg buckled, and I fell to one knee. The hand holding the gun braced me against the wall.

Brecht saw his avenue of escape and darted past me. He disappeared around the corner before I could fire a second shot.

I scrambled to Gordowski. The sharp odor of ozone hung in the air around him. I pressed two fingers against his carotid artery. At first, I felt nothing, and then the faintest trace of a pulse. But he wasn't out of danger yet, not if Brecht came back for us both.

Holding the gun in front of me, I retraced my steps to the lobby. Outside, a renewed onslaught of wind and rain beat against the building. Lightning streaked the black sky, briefly displaying the world in strobing, frozen images. Above the howl of wind and crack of thunder, I heard the crunch of metal and glass. Brecht was in his car, ramming the side of my SUV in a desperate effort to flee. I bolted through the door and down the steps. Gordowski's vehicle blocked a clear shot, but I could get an angle on Brecht's rear tire as it spun in an effort to shove back my CR-V. I fired two rounds into the side wall. Then I saw enough of the rear window to send a .45-caliber slug through it. The glass exploded as lightning turned the shards into sparkling diamonds.

A quick count. The Kimber's magazine had held seven cartridges including one in the chamber. I was down to three, and I didn't know if Brecht now had access to a gun.

My firepower must have foiled his escape plan, because the car ceased moving. Although visibility between lightning flashes was nil, there was no way to anticipate when the landscape might suddenly be illuminated. I hesitated to approach from the front and be caught in the open at point-blank range. I chose to loop around my SUV so that it would provide some cover until I could assess the situation.

A bolt of lightning struck so close that the thunder boomed simultaneously. I saw that Brecht's door hung open and the driver's seat was empty. Had he circled around me? Another sequence of flashes revealed the jerky motion of a man running up the hill toward one of the towering radio telescopes. Brecht was trying to escape on foot.

A man in his midthirties should have no trouble outrunning a man in his late seventies. But a man with a prosthetic leg, and not the one he'd wear for rigorous exercise, found his youthful advantage diminished. Yet I was determined not to let this killer disappear into the forest and possibly be extricated through some preset plan that would take him beyond the reach of American justice.

I hurried up the hill, using the dim outline of the giant steel telescope as my guide.

Lightning flashed, and I saw I'd cut the distance in half. In those few seconds, Brecht turned, and I knew he'd seen me pursuing him. He stumbled, regained his footing, and pressed on.

I felt a burning in my stump as the soaked sleeve rubbed against my flesh. The slope put even more pressure on my leg, but if I could get close enough to fire a warning shot, I hoped Brecht would think I wouldn't hesitate to put the next one in his back.

The intervals between the lightning grew longer. I knew I neared the telescope's base and that the forest lay another fifty yards beyond. Better to take him in the open ground than try to track him in the even darker woods where trees would be impeding obstacles.

Another flash and I saw I was beside the girders supporting the giant upturned dish. Brecht had disappeared.

A rustle of fabric came from behind me and then a choking pressure as a wire looped around my neck. Brecht had circled the telescope with his deadly garrote ready to strike.

I felt him shift his weight as he tried to lift me onto his back, effectively becoming a human gallows. Sparks flared behind my eyes. My grip on the gun loosened, and it fell to the grass. Fear welled up. Seconds were all I had. And then my army survival training kicked in. I didn't clutch at the wire but turned into him, ducking my head into his shoulder to halt his turn.

Now my body was between him and his hands pulling the noose. I head-butted him and heard the crunch of breaking cartilage. He took a step backward, pulling me with him. I punched him in the solar plexus, but I couldn't put enough power behind it. He wheezed and then tried to step around me, still holding the garrote. I swung my left leg up between his two, catching him in the groin with the shank of my metal prosthesis. He snapped forward in a reflex of pain. His violent motion pitched me backward onto the ground, but the wire loosened, halting my descent into unconsciousness.

The lightning flashed. I saw Brecht struggle to stay standing. He looked down at me through his thick, rain-splattered glasses as his hand pulled something from the pocket of his slicker. A short stick. A flick of his thumb turned the stick into a knife. A switchblade. He staggered toward me, his silver disheveled hair swirling in the wind, his face twisted into a grotesque embodiment of rage.

He shouted something, but the roar of blood pumping through my head drowned his words.

I pushed my hands into the ground in an effort to get to my feet. My left palm felt the butt of the Kimber.

The stormy world was dark again, but I knew he was coming. I fired left-handed into the space where he'd been. The muzzle flash showed blood flying from his shoulder. The second flash captured the crimson spurt as the bullet ripped through his chest. He tumbled across my legs.

I rolled him off me, keeping the pistol with its one remaining cartridge aimed in his direction. Each subsequent lightning flash revealed rain washing more blood into the sodden ground. Brecht's ragged breaths exhaled in gurgled whispers. I slid closer, putting my ear to his lips.

"They didn't want me," he rasped. "They threw me away. Had to show them I was useful. Never failed, never failed the cause."

"What happened to Frank DeMille?"

A long pause as Brecht fought for breath.

"He suspected me. No other choice. Loretta came back. Saw my clothes. She remembered. No other choice. My mission, too important. They would want me back."

"Who are they?"

A choking cough. He was drowning in his own blood.

"Who threw you away?" I shouted.

My question went unheard and unanswered. Theo Brecht was beyond time and space, beyond even the reach of the massive radio telescope towering above me.

I stood up, my whole body trembling. Slowly, I made my way down the hill. Somewhere, a siren wailed.

# Chapter 28

At nine o'clock on Tuesday morning, two weeks and one day after learning about the skeleton at PARI and two days since my nearly fatal encounter with Theo Brecht, Nakayla and I sat in a conference room in the FBI offices in Asheville's Federal Building.

We weren't alone. At the table were Homicide Detectives Newland and Efird, Transylvania County Sheriff Hickman, Buncombe County Sheriff Browder, and Special Agent Lindsay Boyce. She'd requested the meeting, and one didn't say no to a resident agent of the FBI. Coffee had been served. Note pads, file folders, and forensic reports were in front of everyone except Nakayla and me. Our presence carried no official status.

Boyce rose to her feet, signaling the meeting would begin. "Thank you for coming. I thought it would be a good idea to gather all of us who have a stake in this investigation so that we can come to a unified understanding regarding the events that transpired, the jurisdictions involved, and the procedure going forward."

The rest of us exchanged glances, knowing "procedure going forward" was Boyce's code that an investigation was ongoing and she didn't want it compromised.

She sat, opened a folder, and then turned to Hickman. "Sheriff, your department had initial involvement with the discovery of DeMille's remains. But as things developed, your jurisdictional case became last Sunday night's attack on Joseph Gordowski and Sam Blackman. What can you tell us?"

Hickman had scribbled some notes on a pad. He studied them a few seconds before speaking. "With the help of your tech team, Special Agent Boyce, we've determined that the power supply that nearly killed Gordowski had been tampered with. Our speculation is that if Mr. Blackman hadn't intervened, Theo Brecht would have made sure Gordowski died. We also found that the damaged vehicles, garrote, switchblade, and injuries sustained by Gordowski, Brecht, and Mr. Blackman support Mr. Blackman's and Mr. Gordowski's accounts."

I dropped my hand from my neck where I'd unconsciously brushed it across the dark bruise displaying the savagery with which Brecht had attacked me.

"As for the case of Frank DeMille," Hickman said, "we've ceded that to the FBI."

Boyce nodded. "Thank you, Sheriff Hickman."

The sheriff held up a hand to signal that he wasn't finished. "One more thing, please." He let his gaze sweep the room. "I've already spoken to Mr. Blackman and Detective Newland, but everyone should know the facts. I and my department owe Mr. Blackman an apology. He had called alerting us that a dangerous situation was unfolding at PARI. We didn't take him seriously, and it wasn't until Detective Newland called my private number that we took action."

Nakayla had reached Newly to tell him about Brecht's dinner at the Laughing Seed Café. He'd immediately headed for PARI and reached Hickman along the way. By the time Hickman checked with his department, twenty precious minutes had elapsed.

"But I'm not one to throw my own team under the bus," Hickman continued. "PARI is the subject of numerous crank calls to the department, namely that alien ships are landing and we need to do something about it. Consequently, I'd set up the procedure that we immediately call PARI to speak with someone we have on an authorized list. There's a code word they use if there's an emergency. Janet Ingram, the receptionist, was just leaving. She assured my deputy that other than the storm, nothing was happening. Neither Brecht nor Gordowski had yet arrived. So my deputy ignored Mr. Blackman's warning. I took action the minute I learned it was he who had made the call. Unfortunately, my deputy wasn't aware Mr. Blackman had been working with us."

He leaned across the table to better see me. "I'm sorry we weren't there when you needed us. I'm grateful you did what you did and also for the contributions you and Ms. Robertson made in identifying the arsonist who started the forest fire." He looked down at his pad and then back at Boyce. "I've said my piece."

"We completely understand," I said. I'd made my own mistakes, like seeing Gordowski's licensed ham radio operation and immediately assuming he was tapping out crucial secrets in Morse code.

Hickman gave me a nod of thanks.

Boyce flipped a few pages down into the file folder.

"Sheriff Browder, you're involved in the investigation into the death of Randall Johnson."

"Yes. Evidence found at the scene of Johnson's death contradicts the initial impression of suicide. The guitar strings meant to suggest Randall Johnson had strangled Loretta are not his brand. An interview in the hospital with Gordowski established that Johnson often brought his guitar to work to play at lunch or on breaks. Gordowski and Brecht both knew it was a Martin. Gordowski said he would have assumed the strings would be the same as the guitar.

"We also did a search of Brecht's garage and found gasoline stains indicative that a can had been stored there. Some of the stains had been created by gasoline on the bottom which gave us the diameter of the can. We've matched it to a newer can in

Johnson's barn. Your team is analyzing the gasoline left in that can and the gasoline in Brecht's mower to see if both grade and chemical composition can be matched. Looking at Johnson's death through the lens of the larger picture, we feel confident Theo Brecht was the killer."

Browder turned to Nakayla. "And he's the person who fire-bombed your house. We don't know if that was before or after he killed Johnson. Brecht thought he was playing it safe bringing the can to Johnson's just in case some trace elements could tie it to the arson scene."

Boyce made a note on her pad. "All right. We'll let your department know the results of the analysis." She flipped a few more pages. "Detectives Newland and Efird, that leaves you with the murder of Loretta Case Johnson."

Tuck Efird nodded for his senior partner to take the lead.

Newly passed several typed sheets down to Boyce. "We took the liberty of bringing a written report. At your discretion, you can have them photocopied and shared. But with your permission, I'd like to yield the narrative of this most remarkable case to Sam, because none of us, in our own jurisdictional realms, would have closed our cases without the work of Sam and Nakayla." He stopped and smiled at me.

I didn't smile back. Newly had caught me off guard. He'd not warned me because he knew I'd have protested that it was not my place to make an official report. But he had created the written report. He simply wanted me to share the story that had nearly cost me my life.

So I walked them through the familiar ground and the new ground. The link to Vietnam, Eddie Gilmore, Chuck McNulty, Len Axelrod, Soviet spies, the mole buried first within NASA, then the NSA, and finally NOAA and its treasure trove of climate data. "From what Brecht told me as he was dying, I can infer he was an ardent supporter of the communist cause of the old school. A dedicated recruit who was probably a product of the radical, turbulent 1960s. Placement in NASA and then the NSA must have been extremely valuable to the Soviets. I'll leave that to the FBI to determine.

"But then time and the Soviet collapse left Brecht without a cause. What happens to an aging, discarded spy? He tried to make himself relevant again. When Nakayla and I first met him, he told us he wanted to be useful. Now we have a fuller understanding of what that meant. And just when he thought he'd found a way back into the espionage fold, Frank DeMille's skeleton was unearthed, and everything he'd worked for was threatened. Brecht killed to protect his past. He killed to safeguard what he hoped would be his future. I can't help but wonder if his actions wouldn't have been in vain. From the desperation of his final words, I have the feeling he was a spy who'd been left out in the cold and hoped the weather data was his way back in." I looked to Agent Boyce. "Was he a mole, or was he reduced to nothing more than a rat who murdered in Rat Alley?"

I finished, and the room fell silent. I felt a lump in my throat as if the very telling had been cathartic in releasing the pent-up anxiety I'd suffered since escaping through the flames with Blue.

Special Agent Lindsay Boyce took a deep breath. "Thank you, Sam, Nakayla. For all of us." She closed her file folder and clenched her hands on top of it. "Now I'm requesting everyone's cooperation. As you can guess, there's much more we want to learn about Theo Brecht, like how and when he might have been recruited. I'm not disputing Sam's conjecture that Brecht had been discarded, but we have to determine if there's a handler and if Brecht was indeed an active Russian asset. What damage did he cause, and more importantly, what has he done recently or prepared to initiate?

"There's no question his infiltration into NASA and the NSA had grave consequences at the time. DeMille's stolen computer programs and algorithms would not only have helped the Soviet space program but also could have been adapted for antimissile defenses, offensive missile guidance systems, and any weapons system relying on computer programming. Then Brecht's work for the NSA put him in position to know what information was being intercepted, and perhaps more importantly, he knew what disinformation was having the greatest effect. What lies were being believed and acted upon and what lies were ignored.

"We're taking Brecht's home apart, board by board, nail by nail. We've discovered three burner phones, two unused and one used to communicate with Loretta. Her carrier's records show calls to and from that phone the afternoon before her murder." Boyce looked at Nakayla and me. "Probably soon after the receptionist at PARI told Gordowski and Brecht you were investigators. I'm confident we'll find something else—a code book, a dark web internet site, a buried email account."

She looked around the table. "For each of you, your case is closed. Theo Brecht is the guilty party. But I'm asking you to keep the motive vague. Brecht could have snapped and first killed Loretta, then Randall Johnson, and finally turned on his colleague Gordowski. Our nation is awash in crimes of indiscriminate rage. But references to Frank DeMille's death and the trail of espionage are to be left to the Bureau. And we don't want the word 'espionage' floating around out there during an ongoing investigation. I hope that can be agreed to and understood before we leave this room."

She paused, giving her words time to sink in. "Is there any objection?"

Nakayla and I looked at each other.

We spoke in unison. "Yes."

# Chapter 29

The heat wave finally broke, and a hint of fall crept into the air. Over a month had passed since my ordeal at PARI, and the media had moved on from the unhinged Theo Brecht to other grist for their news cycles.

Lindsay Boyce had acquiesced to our request that her veil of secrecy surrounding the extent of Brecht's espionage be lifted for those most impacted by it. So Cory had brought her aunt to Asheville, and we used Hewitt's conference room for a limited briefing in which Boyce outlined how Eddie Gilmore and Frank DeMille died. We spared Nancy Gilmore the details that her husband's murderer was now a high-ranking official in Vietnam and beyond our reach.

Subsequent updates from Boyce indicated the FBI investigation was finding no evidence that Brecht was being run as an active spy. He had been discarded, and that could have been a terrible error by the Russians. According to Boyce, Brecht had correctly assessed the value of creating a back door into a secure data repository, not only of NOAA's records but other private and government data as well. A team of forensic computer analysts was meticulously going through everything Brecht touched. But that was the FBI's case, and Nakayla and I would probably never know the final outcome.

On a cool, clear Sunday in late September, Nakayla and I walked in a procession behind a simple wooden casket as pallbearers carried it across the hillside of a cemetery adjacent to a small Presbyterian church. The mountain ridges around us began to show early fall colors. The scene could have been near Asheville, but we were in Roanoke, Virginia, where Frank DeMille was being laid to rest in the home soil of his native state.

Hewitt and Shirley were behind us. They'd driven with Special Agent Lindsay Boyce. She had made sure the remains had been released and properly transported.

Directly in front of us, Boyce walked between two older men, one with a slight limp and an armful of roses. Chuck McNulty and Len Axelrod had made the trip together because this final chapter was as much about their comrade Eddie Gilmore as Frank DeMille.

A few folding chairs were placed graveside under a green funeral tent. Nancy and Cory sat with a few of Nancy's friends, men and women who might have known her husband and brother so many decades ago.

The rest of us stood. I grasped Nakayla's hand.

The interment ceremony was brief. A few words. The twenty-third psalm and the Lord's Prayer, then the commitment of DeMille's earthly remains.

I don't know about an afterlife. Sometimes I think this must be all we'll experience. Other times, when I consider the miracle that life exists at all, I accept that there's so much we don't understand. Like solving a mystery, you journey into the unknown, leaving yourself open to all possibilities.

When I was convalescing in Walter Reed before being moved to the VA hospital in Asheville, I'd had a conversation with a fellow wounded vet who'd been clinically dead for five minutes on the battlefield. He claimed to have left his body and experienced the light and love of a powerful presence common to other near-death accounts. Then he shared the pragmatic argument he made to his atheist friends. "I'm betting on an afterlife," he said. "You're betting there's nothing beyond this world. If I'm right, I'll know it. If you're right, you won't know it. I'll always take the choice to be proven right."

Cory and her aunt stood and laid their hands on the casket one final time. As they moved away, others came forward. Chuck McNulty started distributing his roses to our little group, two to each. Then he and Axelrod put one rose on the casket. Boyce followed, then Nakayla, me, Hewitt, and Shirley. We moved on to a second grave, this one with a weathered headstone and well-established grass. Edward James Gilmore. Born March 26, 1945. Died August 19, 1971. McNulty and Axelrod nodded for us to lay our roses first. We did, and then some unspoken force kept us standing there, gathered around the rectangular grave. The two Vietnam veterans leaned their roses against the headstone, not content to have them flat against the ground. I took Nakayla's hand. Hewitt grasped my other one. I looked around and saw we had all joined hands with McNulty and Axelrod each placing their free one upon the headstone, bringing Edward James Gilmore into our connected humanity.

Maybe there isn't an afterlife. But I sensed the power of love might not know the limits of time and space. Love like Loretta held for Frank DeMille, love that Nancy felt for Eddie, love that bound us together in that moment as we honored two murdered men.

We broke away in silence. Nakayla and I lagged behind.

"I'm glad we came," she said.

"So am I. I thought I was doing it for Cory, but after all we went through, I admit I was doing it for me. I wanted to see Frank come home."

"You're a good man, Sam Blackman."

"You're a good woman. I think I'll keep you."

"I think you'd better rethink that comment or I'm going to use the insurance money to buy a new sofa that you can sleep on."

I wrapped my arm around her waist. "Keep you close to my heart. You didn't let me finish."

"Nice save."

"From the sofa?"

"From walking back to Asheville."

# AUTHOR'S NOTE

Although this story is a work of fiction, many of its elements are factual. The Pisgah Astronomical Research Institute (PARI) exists in Rosman, North Carolina. It was constructed in Pisgah National Forest as an Apollo tracking station and then ceded to the Department of Defense for classified operations. An exchange of land enabled the facility to become a scientific learning center. The museum's exhibits and interactive programs are open to the public and well-worth visiting. PARI has also moved into secure computer data storage. Information about the institute is available at pari.edu.

The belief that PARI is an interstellar UFO hub also has its adherents. A quick internet search of *Pisgah Astronomical Research Institute UFOs* provides articles on the alleged alien connections.

The Kit Carson Scouts were a special program in Vietnam using defecting NVA and Viet Cong fighters. It was so successful that it expanded from the Marines to all infantry units.

NOAA's National Centers for Environmental Information is headquartered in Asheville, North Carolina, and houses vital weather data. Its history as depicted in the story is factual; the link to PARI's secure data storage is fictional.

All characters and their events are the author's creation.

# ACKNOWLEDGMENTS

A novel doesn't happen without the help of others. Special thanks to Timothy Owen, executive officer with NOAA's National Centers for Environmental Information, for sharing the history and mission of the more than seventeen petabytes of vital weather data housed in Asheville. Any errors or variations from fact are my responsibility.

I'm grateful to Poisoned Pen Press, Robert Rosenwald, Barbara Peters, and the staff for making this adventure of Sam and Nakayla possible. Also to my family members Linda, Melissa, Pete, Charlie, Lindsay, Jordan, and Sawyer for being the best-loved characters in my life.

## ABOUT THE AUTHOR

Mark de Castrique grew up in the mountains of western North Carolina where many of his novels are set. He's a veteran of the television and film production industry, has served as an adjunct professor at the University of North Carolina at Charlotte teaching The American Mystery, and he's a frequent speaker and workshop leader. He and his wife, Linda, live in Charlotte, North Carolina.

Contact him at markdecastrique.com.

by Linda de Castrique